Hard as Stone

Beatrice B. Morgan

AUTHORS 4 AUTHORS PUBLISHING
Marysville, WA, USA

Published by Authors 4 Authors Publishing
1214 6th St
Marysville, WA 98270
www.authors4authorspublishing.com

Library of Congress Control Number: 2019956031

E-book ISBN: 978-1-64477-132-7
Paperback ISBN: 978-1-64477-133-4

Edited by Rebecca Mikkelson
Copyedited by Brandi Spencer

Cover design ©2022 Practically Perfect Covers. All rights reserved.
Interior design by Brandi Spencer

Authors 4 Authors branding is set in Bavire. Headings are set in IM FELL English Pro. All other text is set in Garamond.

Hard

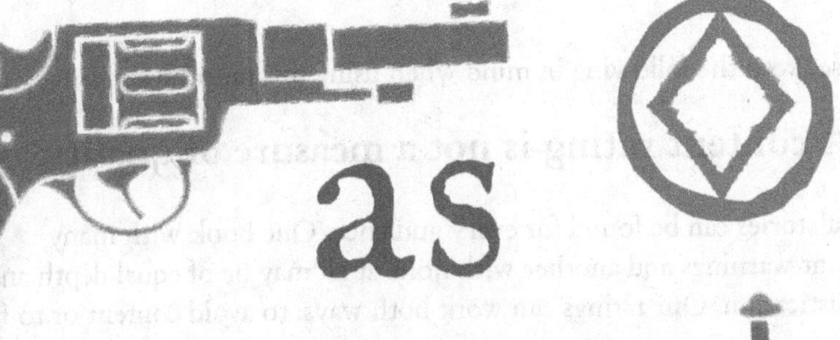

as

Stone

Beatrice B. Morgan

Authors 4 Authors Content Rating

This title has been rated 14+, appropriate for teens, and contains:

- moderate language
- intense violence
- moderate implied sex
- negative moderate fantasy drug use
- negative mild illicit drug use
- moderate alcohol use

Please, keep the following in mind when using our rating system:

1. A content rating is not a measure of quality.

Great stories can be found for every audience. One book with many content warnings and another with none at all may be of equal depth and sophistication. Our ratings can work both ways: to avoid content or to find it.

2. Ratings are merely a tool.

For our young adult (YA) and children's titles, age ratings are generalized suggestions. For parents, our descriptive ratings can help you make informed decisions, but at the end of the day, only you know what kinds of content are appropriate for your individual child. This is why we provide details in addition to the general age rating.

For more information on our rating system, please, visit our Content Guide at: www.authors4authorspublishing.com/books/ratings

Dedication

To Stephanie, for being there and listening to my complaints,
no matter how weird or silly or unchangeable. Having someone
who understands is an unimaginable relief, and you have no
idea how glad I am that I have a friend like you.

Works by Beatrice B. Morgan

Stars and Bones:
Thief in the Castle
Mage in the Undercity
Dreams in the Snow
Nightmares in the Ice (Spring 2023)

Hard as Stone:
Hard as Stone
Thick as Blood
Strong as Steel (October 2022)

N
W E
S
Silver Glen
Rhynwier
Dwellers' Treehouse
Oun
Newalt
Hammel Forest
Himata River
Lenhala
Sorrow Hills
Gilini
Tinatun
Wayward Point

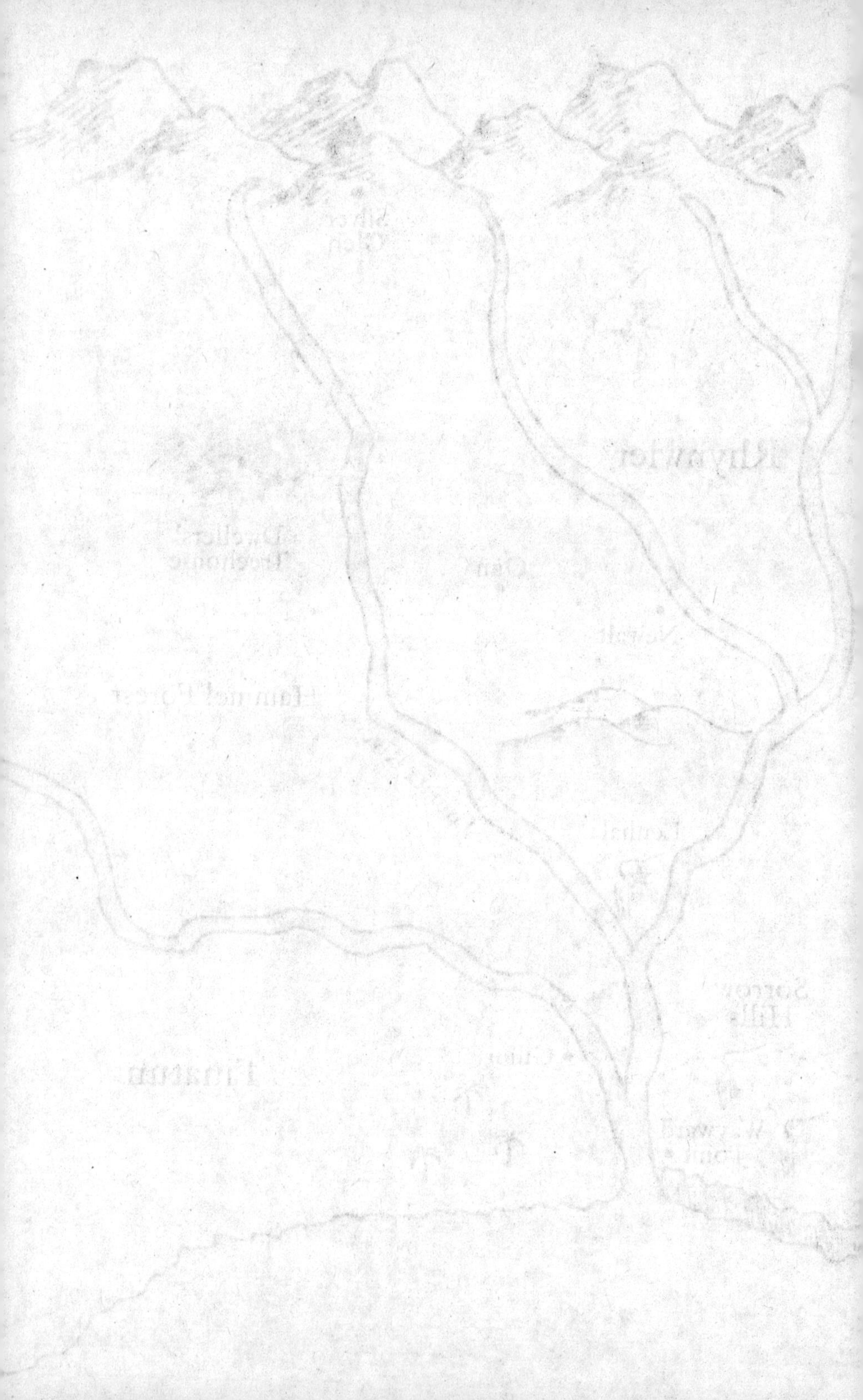

Table of Contents

Table of Contents

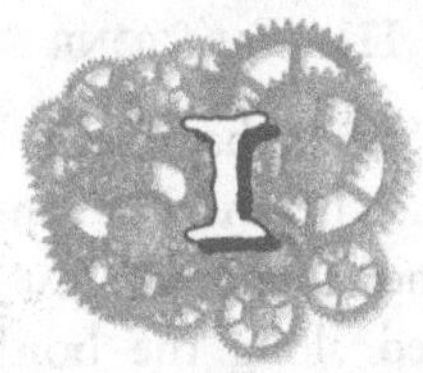

Raven Thane spotted a glint of metal among the shifting greens of Hammel Forest, and her entire body stilled in reflex. Her heart stilled and then skipped a beat. On the other side of the oaks, the sunlight glinted off metal.

Metal. An automaton.

Raven flattened herself against the trunk of an oak. Had it seen her?

The dappling sunlight shifted as the wind rustled the leaves; the metal itself did not move. After her heartbeat returned to normal and her nerves had hardened, she stepped away from the tree. She picked up the few blackberries that had fallen out of her basket in her rush to hide and set the basket on the ground.

She knew she should turn around and head back home, but her curiosity won out. She dusted off her skirt and slowly made her way through the summer's thick foliage toward the glint. She squeezed between two ageless oaks and into a clearing.

A soft gasp escaped her lips at the sight; within the clearing, tree roots, saplings, and weeds had ruptured what had once been a white stone structure. The walls and ceilings had long since fallen, leaving sun-bleached chunks of stone tangled and half-swallowed in the weeds. The glint of metal came from the far side of the ruin, amid a pile of crumbled white stone.

Raven shuddered, despite the warm air—she had stumbled upon a forgotten temple of Wilyn, Goddess of the Forest and Keeper of the Stars. Wilyn's temples had been made of white stone, Raven recalled. Marble.

A prickle started at the base of Raven's neck and worked its way down her spine. She had never seen one of Wilyn's temples; she had only heard about them, and she had the strangest feeling that she had invaded something private.

A hundred years ago, Wilyn's temples and shrines had dotted the northern forests of the kingdom of Rhynwier, just as her sisters' temples had: Minerva, Goddess of the Sea and Wind, prevailed in the south and along the coasts; Solen, Goddess of Stone and Steel, prevailed to the west and the mountains. According to folklore, the Sisters had gifted magic to the ancient people of Rhynwier, who worshipped them. The Sisters did not show such favor to the ancient people of their neighboring kingdom of Gracita, where they favored machinery over magic.

The followers of the Sisters had been the first slaughtered when Gracita invaded and the war began. For one hundred years, Gracita's automatons and war machines fought against Rhynwier's magic, leaving villages and towns devastated along the border. Entire cities had been reduced to rubble and ash. Legends told of a river turned black with the ashes of a port city.

Then, fifteen years ago, Gracita ended the war with the assassination of Rhynwier's king and queen. The Gray Elite—Gracita's military—took control. Their automatons scoured the countryside for remnants of the magic they fought to stomp out; magic became illegal and punishable by death.

After three years of Gray Elite rule, magic had vanished.

Raven didn't remember magic; she had been barely two years old when the war ended. What she knew of her kingdom's history came from word of mouth, passed down stories, and books bought from the rare trader.

Even those were becoming fewer.

Raven took a steadying breath and tiptoed to the edge of the crumbling foundation. Would Wilyn be angry that Raven disturbed her temple?

She scoffed silently at herself for such a thought. Of course not. Wilyn didn't exist, or she would have saved her people from their slaughter.

She climbed onto a wide piece of marble. She kept her eyes open for movement in the surrounding forest and her ears alert for any sound that shouldn't be there—be it man, beast, or automaton.

She ran a finger along the ebony hilt of her favorite dagger, tucked safely into the buckles of her leather boot. Just in case.

As she listened to the sounds of the forest, the sounds that she knew by heart, one became apparent. No birds chirped from within the clearing. No birds perched in the young trees. Her feeling of invasion became something sickeningly like sacrilege.

No threat from the forest made itself known. She straightened, tore her eyes off the empty trees, and carefully made her way across the uneven foundation. Tree roots and vines threatened to trip her, and the sun's reflection off the stone threatened to blind her. She kept her eyes pinned on the glint of metal.

The glint came from what had once been the sanctum, where offerings and prayers were sent to Wilyn. Now, it was a ruin. As Raven approached the sanctum, the glint became weathered brass.

Not an automaton—a piece of one. An arm.

The body of the automaton had been crushed by the fallen sanctum, and the left arm had been bent at the shoulder, jutting upward in a grasp of survival. The brass panels and steel plates had rusted and dulled, and the smallest finger on the four-pronged hand had rusted entirely off, leaving a skeletal three-bolt mechanical bone behind.

Raven listened harder to the forest for the crunch of gears or the hiss of steam, but it never came. She had never been this close to an automaton, dead as it was, and her heart rattled with every tiny step closer she took. She had read that automatons had the strength of one hundred men, could withstand magic and bullets, and understood only logic; they were incapable of compassion or emotion. The Gray Elite had programmed them with their laws, and automatons understood those laws and only those laws.

She imagined the automaton bursting from the rubble, its red-gleam eyes focusing on her, its gears churning, its engine whirring, steam hissing from the joints.

A bird darted overhead at such speed that Raven ducked; the bird vanished in the trees. She scanned the sky but saw nothing. Her stepmother often said that birds carried the first warnings of disaster, but Raven had stopped believing those silly stories years ago.

Raven closed her hands around the automaton's wrist and gave it a hard yank. Metal creaked and whined, and with a few more strong tugs, rusted bolts gave, connecting wires snapped, and the arm came free of the crushed shoulder. A few pieces of scrap metal fell out of the arm's shoulder joint, and Raven scooped them into her pocket.

With no small amount of triumph, Raven started home with the automaton arm slung over her shoulders and her basket of blackberries hanging from her elbow. She stayed within the thick shade and kept alert for any stray automaton that happened to have wandered this far north. Rare but not impossible.

Maybe it would come looking for revenge for its fallen comrade, if automatons could understand such a thing as revenge.

She jumped over a fallen tree, jostling the arm and the berries. What a find! She couldn't wait to see the look on Brent's face. All she had to do was get the arm past her father first.

Raven had lived her entire life in Silver Glen, a small village nestled into the shadow of the mountains. A century ago, it had been a booming mining village, but with the war, the silver depleted. Most of the village had fallen into ruin. What remained of Silver Glen consisted of a few lopsided houses, a trading post, an inn that rarely got used, a few farms, livestock, a tannery, the mill—the things simple people needed to survive. The woods reclaimed everything else—old homes and buildings. Tree roots grew through stone foundations and timber walls, slowly returning the minerals to the earth.

On the surface, Silver Glen looked small and rundown, sparsely populated. The majority of the village couldn't be seen from above ground; it had been built into the mine.

Raven walked through the old streets—now grassy paths—and down the alley between the trading post and the inn. The narrow path led underneath a thick canopy of oak and pine and led into the mine's main entrance. An old wooden sign leaned against the pale gray stone of the mountainside and warned of dangerous caves, loose rock, and instability. Another warned of a cave-in. Raven walked past the signs and straight into the mine. The sunlight illuminated the entrance enough to see by, though it diminished with each step. Rather than go straight, to where a cave-in had blocked the main shaft, she turned right, into an old room.

"It's me," Raven announced to the dark room. Her voice echoed. "Open up!"

"I'm going to need your password," came a female voice from the speaking tube hidden in the shadowed corner.

"Oh, come on, Sweets! It's me, Raven."

"Password," repeated Sweets.

"Sweets!" Raven pleaded.

"For all I know, you could be the Revenant," said Sweets. "I've heard he can steal voices."

Raven scoffed; the Revenant was a ghost story they told to small children to scare them into good behavior. It was a ghost of a monster that swooped from the darkness to snatch its victims without witness, without prejudice.

"Password," Sweets chimed.

Raven groaned and began to tap her foot. Sweets had told her the password just that morning. Sisters, why couldn't she think of it? "'Gooseberries,'" she guessed.

"That's the old password, Rae."

"I know it is!" She huffed. The arm over her shoulder rattled. "Just let me in. You know it's me."

Sweets sighed. "Fine. I'll let you in this time. By the way, your password was 'jackrabbit.'"

Raven cursed under her breath. She remembered it now. "Thanks, Sweets."

A thunk resounded from within the stone wall. Locks released, and with a powerful hiss of steam, gears began to revolve—the stone wall opened to reveal a spiraling metal staircase. Bioluminescent fungi grew along the ceiling, lighting the space in a pale yellow-green glow. Raven started down the stairs, and the door closed behind her with the same thunks and clanks.

Down, down, down into the mines of Silver Glen she went. At the bottom of the stairs, she came to an iron door. She kicked it twice.

"Open up; my arms are full," she said.

The door opened with a vicious creak. Sweets stood in the doorway so that Raven could not pass. She wore her dark blonde hair in a bun on the top of her head; a crossbow hung across her shoulders, and a pistol hung at her side in an old leather holster.

"Not the Revenant," Raven motioned to herself. She tried to step past Sweets, but the other girl stepped in the way. Her eyes fell on the automaton arm, and her straight-line mouth fell into a frown.

"What is *that*?" Sweets asked.

"I thought Brent would enjoy it," Raven said with a smile.

Sweets knew better than to argue. Rolling her eyes, she stepped aside. "Password."

"'Gooseberries,' right?"

"Raven," Sweets sighed and put a hand to her temple.

"Right, right, it's 'jackrabbit.'" Raven skirted through the doorway. "Thanks again, Sweets!"

Raven quickly left the entry hall and whatever lecture Sweets had been preparing. Despite being only a few years older than Raven, Sweets often acted more like a mother than a friend.

Raven made her way through the old mine's tunnels, which had been reinforced with steel and wood to accommodate its inhabitants. The bioluminescent fungi grew along the ceiling in every hall and most of the rooms, lending its sickly light. Raven made her way to the cannery and stepped through the door basket-first. No one paid her mind. The girls were working furiously, washing, mashing, spooning, and canning berries into preserves for winter. Steam from the canners vanished into vents, pulled upward by humming fans. Raven set the basket on the front counter and cleared her throat.

"I've brought you blackberries," she said.

Raven took a step backward toward the door when her half-sister, Lena, appeared from the kitchens. Both girls shared their father's brown-blonde hair, but Lena had her mother's vibrant green eyes, whereas Raven had her mother's brown eyes. Or so her father said. Raven had never met her mother. She had died when Raven was small.

Lena's green eyes fell onto the basket of blackberries, and she smiled. She had a beautiful smile, one that spread like a plague. Raven found herself smiling back. Even at fifteen years old, Lena would become a beautiful woman, and everyone knew it. She would grow into a beauty, while Raven would remain plain.

But that was how their lives had been: Lena excelled; Raven sufficed. Despite that, Raven loved Lena. Her insides were as beautiful as her outside.

Lena picked one of the berries and rolled it between her fingers. "Nice and ripe. Great for canning or eating." She popped the berry into her mouth and hummed her delight.

Raven took another step backward, toward the door. "Well, if that's all you need..."

Lena frowned. "Oh, come on, stay a while. You need to learn how to can."

Raven jostled the arm. "I'll think about it. I've got to drop this treasure off with Brent first."

Lena's eyes wandered the length of the arm, and her frown deepened. In that moment, she looked so much like her mother.

Raven left the cannery before her sister could start lecturing her about the importance of food preservation and roles within society or whatever else she thought Raven needed to hear. She'd heard it all before, and she doubted it would stick any better this time.

Raven made her way to the other side of the mine, to the workshops and smiths. She kept her eyes open for any sign of her father—she didn't feel like a lecture from him either. Luckily, she didn't see him, and she made to the Corridor of Smiths—as she had always called it. They had built the tinker shops and metalsmiths on the far edge of the mine for safety, as they were prone to mess and destruction, and for the noise. The banging of hammers and saws against metal and wood clattered from the dozen workshops. The Corridor of Smiths had a strong stench of molten iron and grease.

Brent's tinker shop was on the far end. Unlike some of the others, his iron door was propped open. Mechanical innards and scrap metal cluttered the narrow entrance to his shop and formed a single-file path to the workshop itself. Brent had stationed Alarms—tiny metal birds that tweeted at detected movement—about the clutter.

Only Raven knew the secret to the Alarms. If one moved slow enough, they would not tweet. Feeling up to a challenge, Raven crept into the room one tiny step at a time. She held the arm and herself still as possible. The birds did not sing. After what felt like ages, she made it to the other side. Once through, she relaxed, glanced over her shoulder at the silent Alarms, and walked straight into something large and metal.

She stumbled backward with a yelp—she'd walked into the Scrapper, a machine that Brent had built from salvaged parts to grind other salvaged parts—those he couldn't use—into easy-to-smelt pieces. Glad no one had seen her stumble, she pushed herself back to her feet, rubbing the bruise forming on her backside.

Brent stood hunched over at his worktable. The thick leather strap of his goggles stretched across the back of his head, further messing up his brown hair. Like the entrance, the workroom was cluttered and piled with salvaged machine parts, steel, brass, copper, and metals she didn't recognize. Though the bioluminescent fungi grew along the ceiling, a lantern on the worktable lit the workspace in bright yellows and whites.

"Hello, Brent," Raven announced.

"Hello," he said absently in the same calm, distant tone he used when he worked. "I've told you about sneaking past my birds. You're giving the children bad ideas."

"I'm helping you improve them." She navigated through the scrap metal maze to the middle of the room, where Brent kept the space around his worktable clear. "I've brought you a present." She jostled the automaton arm. It clicked and rattled.

Brent straightened; his magnified eyes settled on the arm and widened. Dropping his tools with a clatter, he fumbled to pull his goggles off his eyes. He blinked at the arm a dozen times, then took it from her.

"Where did you get this?" he asked, awestruck.

"I stumbled across it while picking blackberries," she said innocently.

He slowly moved his gaze from the arm to her. His stare became suspicious. "Picking blackberries? This arm is old. It wouldn't have been by the bushes. Unless you went farther than the bushes." When she didn't deny it, he sighed. "Raven, we've talked about this. Scavenging is dangerous beyond the borders. What if an automaton had caught you? Samuel would be furious if he knew where you'd gone."

Raven heaved a sigh and tried to look as though Brent's mild threat of her father's reprimand didn't frighten her. If her father had his way, she'd be off scavenging duty and canning fruit and making soap with her sister.

"But..." Brent started, gazing longingly at the arm. His fingers twitched with excitement. "The parts this arm contains may well have been worth the trip. But, please, promise me you won't go looking for treasure beyond the safety of the borders."

She didn't answer. Instead, she pretended to find his cabinet of bolts, nuts, and screws fascinating. He knew as well as she did that there wasn't any treasure left within the borders.

"Raven," Brent warned.

"I'm not a child anymore," she said, setting her hands on her hips. "I'm nearly eighteen. Practically an adult. I can hold my own."

"Against one of these?" He held up the arm. "And this is an old model too. The automatons now are twice the size. If you met one of these out in the woods, there'd be no helping you. You'd either be killed on the spot or hauled to the capital."

She rolled her eyes. She knew the risks.

"And you're not 'nearly eighteen.' You just turned seventeen." Brent heaved a sigh and brought the arm to one of the few clean spots on his worktable. He grabbed for tools without looking and began to uncover the insides of the arm. "These parts are old but look to be in decent shape. Oh, there are some miniature parts in here, too small to make with the tools I've got. Oooh...this looks like silver."

Her pride swelled. She knew Brent wouldn't tattle on her to her father. Since he had been taken off scavenging duty to work in the tinker's shop, he had less and less scrap metal brought to him. It didn't seem that long ago that Brent, Sweets, and Raven were scouring the forests around Silver Glen for pieces of the old world. Both of her friends worked in the mines now. Her father had given them grown-up jobs, as he said, because scavenging and berry picking was something to keep the older children entertained and busy.

Raven couldn't fathom not being able to go outside, to be stuck underground, under the sickly, glowing light.

She found a place on the other side of the worktable and leaned forward to watch Brent work. He had the arm apart in no time. It would have gone faster had he not stopped to admire each part. He sorted the pieces into buckets: gears, wires, valves, nuts, and things she didn't recognize. She found it hard to believe that all those parts fit into the space of the arm, and she found it harder to imagine how they would all work together.

What had the completed creature looked like? She tried to picture it—the monstrous human-shaped metal contraption, limbs plated with steel, brass, and copper, bolted together and steaming at the shoulders and hips.

"The old automatons were clunky," Brent said. "They were built for durability, not maneuverability. The newer ones have been streamlined, but the old ones like this arm were full of little parts and things." He pulled out a tiny gear that looked like two gears smashed together. "Oh, I already know what I'm going to use this for."

A memory came back to her, of a trader who had told them a haunting story about an automaton so finely built that he appeared human, but the eyes had given him away. They had been empty, wholly dark. Soulless.

"There was a whole automaton," she said casually, "but it was crushed by one of Wilyn's sanctums."

Brent gasped and dropped the scrap metal he'd been holding. It clattered into the bin. He blinked at her, his eyes wide. His lips formed the word "sanctum," and then he slowly pushed his goggles to the top of his head. His voice came out grave. "Raven, that's far beyond the border."

She cursed herself for the slip.

According to the Gray Elite's border laws, wandering automatons could not cross the border of an established town, but anyone caught outside those borders without the proper authorization was considered a refugee. The bigger the town, the higher the risk—as her father always said. Which was why the people of Silver Glen had taken to living in the mine, underneath the Gray Elite's border laws.

Raven crumpled under Brent's disappointed gaze. Sighing, she said, "I'm careful. It's not like I've got magic in my blood, or they would have caught me years ago, right?"

His frown deepened, and she cursed herself again. She had admitted to having gone beyond the borders more than a few times. She had, many times. Enough to know her chances of running into an automaton were slim.

Brent released an exasperated sigh. He knew there would be no talking her out of going back. "Just be careful. And don't try to bring back too much."

Brent fell into silence as he made his way deeper into the arm. The buckets slowly filled. Raven didn't move until an Alarm sang out a sweet tune, mimicking real birdsong. Booted footsteps made their way toward the back room.

A tall, lean bronze-skinned boy appeared in the doorway. He wore the top half of his dark brown hair long and tied back; the bottom half, he kept shaved. At the sight of Raven, a smirk stretched across his shapely jaw, and his sapphire eyes glittered. He wore scuffed leather boots, a dagger tucked in the buckles of each, and patched trousers. Another set of daggers were on his suspenders, half hidden by his unbuttoned vest. He'd rolled the sleeves of his white shirt to his elbows and tucked his hands into his pockets.

"Zander," Brent said with exasperation, "please explain the dangers of the woods to Raven."

Raven groaned. She didn't need Zander in the debate too.

Zander puffed his chest with importance. "Brent's right, Rae. Those iron beasts are more vicious than a hungry bear. Some have spears for arms that tear through a man's chest like a knife through a tomato." He withdrew a pistol from the leather holster slung low on his hip. "Next time you're itching to break the house rules, take me with you. I can keep you safe." He winked.

"Or I could run face-first into an iron maul," she deadpanned. "What do you want?"

Zander laughed. "This isn't your house, Raven. I can be in here if I want. I didn't come to see you. I have business with Brent."

She motioned at Brent, still meticulously picking apart the arm.

Zander frowned. "Just Brent, not you. Get out."

"This isn't your house," she chimed back at him. "I can be here if I want."

Zander chuckled, a retort on his tongue, but Brent spoke first. "I've finished the adjustments you asked for."

Brent set down his tools and reached underneath the worktable. He straightened, holding a cloth-covered something. He turned to Zander and pulled back the cloth to reveal a polished pistol.

"Here she is," said Brent.

Zander let out a sigh of longing and turned the pistol over in his hands. It was an old gun, hundreds of years old, but Zander and Brent kept it in good shape. The barrel was medium length and dark steel. The grip was dark red leather. Zander referred to his gun as *her* and had named her Birdie.

"There's my girl," he said lovingly to Birdie.

Birdie never missed her target, Zander would proudly tell anyone who would listen, no matter how many times he'd already told them or how often they had seen him shoot.

"Go test the new calibration," Brent advised, eyes fondling the gun. He knew Birdie as well as Zander did by now.

Zander didn't need more of a suggestion. His eyes roamed over Raven, and he said lazily, "Want to come see Birdie in action?"

She shrugged; she didn't have much more to do, unless she counted her chores, and if she had the choice between trying to infuriate Zander and making soap, she'd choose the first.

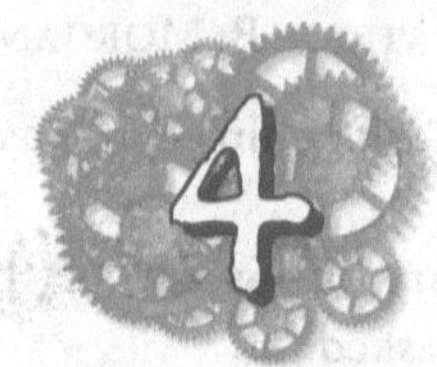

Zander, Brent, and Raven went to the shooting range, a shaded clearing up on the mountain, accessible by a mine shaft. The trees leaned toward the range, and their collective canopy shaded much of it from the sky. At the far end, hay bales, logs, and dirt-filled bags had been painted white, gray, and yellow. The colors of the Gray Elite. Most of the painted faces had comical grimaces, ogre teeth, large noses, and pointed ears.

Raven took up a spot near the front; Zander took a position a toe away from the ditch—the line separating him from the range—and Brent pulled open a fake tree trunk to reveal the control panel of the Cycle. With the pull of a lever, gears in the hidden track began to crank; steam hissed through the vents. The Gray Elite targets jittered to life and started to move along the tracks.

Zander pulled Birdie from her leather holster. He held her in one hand, his unnamed pistol in the other, and took a shooting stance—boots apart, knees slightly bent, body turned so Birdie aimed first. He let out a slow breath, blue eyes focusing with a predatory intensity that gave Raven a shiver. He looked ready to kill.

"Give me the count." Zander's voice mirrored his eyes: husky, deep, and focused.

Raven cleared her throat and raised her hand into the air. She held up three fingers and put each down as she called, "Three, two," and paused for dramatics with her index finger pointed to the sky. "One!" A fist in the air.

Bang! Bang! Bang! Birdie's blasts shook birds from the trees, scattering them in all directions. The Gray Elite targets absorbed the impacts, sending splinters and splatters of dirt into the air. Bullet after bullet, enemy after enemy, until Zander emptied both guns.

Not a single bullet missed.

Zander tossed a haphazard smirk over his shoulder at Raven. "One more for good luck?" He loaded a single bullet into Birdie without looking; he kept his stare on Raven. Her cheeks heated like they did sometimes when he looked at her, and with the blushing came a terrible embarrassment. Zander's smirk widened. Her blush and embarrassment intensified. Had he done that on purpose?

He snapped the cylinder back into place with a flick of his wrist and pulled his gaze off Raven to aim. As he pulled the trigger, Raven pulled the level on the machine. The belts pulling the targets jerked—

Bang!

The bullet missed.

"Oh?" Raven said haughtily. "Never misses?"

"You cheated," Zander spat. "You did that on purpose."

"What if I did? You can't expect your real enemies to parade in a conveniently predictable line."

Zander grumbled under his breath, and Raven pretended not to hear the name he'd called her. He reloaded Birdie one bullet at a time and slid her into the leather holster. He started to reload his second gun.

"Let's do a second round, Brent," Zander said, snapping the second gun's cylinder into place. He sneered at Raven. "Without cheating."

Raven opened her mouth to argue, but the trap door to the mine shaft opened with a creak. Sweets stuck her head out and squinted at the daylight. Her pale skin looked nearly white.

"There you are," Sweets said to Raven. "Your father is looking for you."

Raven's heart fell into her stomach, but she stood straight and set her hands on her hips. "What did I do this time?"

Sweets bit her lip. "Well, someone, not me, might have seen you walking through the mines with an arm over your shoulder. And, well, you know, word gets around."

"Someone's in for it," Zander taunted.

Raven groaned.

"Best not keep him waiting," Sweets said, her voice small. She shrank, letting the trapdoor creak toward the ground until only her eyes were visible. "He's in a bad mood today."

"Of course not." Raven kicked at the ground and started toward the trapdoor. She couldn't get out of this one. "When has he ever *not* been in a bad mood?"

"When were you born?" Zander asked.

She stuck her tongue out at him.

"And Zander," Sweets added. "Watch the bullets you use. The foundry's been slow this month."

He harrumphed his acknowledgment.

Raven followed Sweets back down into the mines. It took several steps for her eyes to adjust back to the dreary light of the fungi. They reached the main level of the mines, and Sweets vanished down a passage saying, "He's in his office."

Raven huffed. She could only imagine what he had to say this time. She made her way to his office in the middle of the mines, between the workshops and the living quarters. The door was shut. Raven straightened her shoulders and lifted her chin. Another lecture. She'd handled plenty of lectures. She could handle this one.

She knocked.

"Come in," came her father's reply.

Raven stepped into the office. Her father stood on the other side of his desk, an old wooden desk that had belonged to the mines, with his thick arms crossed and his trimmed beard barely hiding his scowl. Her stepmother, an older version of Lena in both looks and temperament, stood beside the desk.

"Ah, I must be going." Her stepmother kissed her father's cheek and then kissed Raven's temple. She lingered and whispered to Raven, "He means well, darling." Her stepmother left.

"Sweets said you wanted to see me?" Raven asked innocently.

"Close the door."

Oh... She knew that tone. Not good.

He wasn't just angry. He was *furious*. Raven gently pushed the iron door back into the frame. The latch clicked; the finality of it pulled her heart further into her stomach.

"Sit down," he said.

Raven sat in one of two chairs in front of his desk, both originally made of wood, both patched with metal. She started to slump forward but thought better of it. She held her shoulders square and crossed her ankles like her stepmother had taught her, and she folded her hands in her lap. She schooled her face into calmness and met her father's glare.

Her father was the overseer of the mines, of Silver Glen; he kept it running, and he kept the people safe and cared for. Sitting before him, Raven had no doubt how he had become overseer. He stood tall and broad and had an imposing presence. He radiated authority. As a child, Raven had wished that she would inherit that authority, that people would look to her as they looked to her father.

She didn't. They didn't.

Finally, he said, "You brought back an automaton's arm?" Though his brown-black eyes glared, his words were calm.

She nodded. "Brent said it was a good find. I watched him take it apart. There were loads of pieces inside of it."

"Where did you find it?"

She swallowed. "It was by luck. A bird tweeted, and I happened to spot it near to where I was."

"Which was where?"

Her fingers twitched. He knew exactly where the old temple was. He would know exactly how far outside the borders she had gone.

When she didn't answer, he growled, "Raven."

"By an old Wilyn temple," she said quietly.

He slammed his fist onto his desk, rattling the brass cup of quills and an ink bottle and knocking off a small tinker cat whose tail ticked with the time. It clattered on the stone floor of the office and rolled to a stop. Still, it clicked.

"You know where the boundaries are." His tone was venomous. "The automatons will not attack you within our borders, but outside them, they will cut you down on sight. That's their merciful punishment. Do you know what happens to the people they take back to the capital?" His eyes burned.

She twisted her hands in her lap. "You've told me."

"Then please, elaborate on what happens, what could happen to you. And then please, explain your reasons for disregarding those warnings."

She swallowed. Eyes on her fingers, she said, "When the automatons take a person to Lenhala, one is thrown in jail, killed, or sold as a slave."

"You know what fate would befall you? A seventeen-year-old girl?"

She didn't answer.

"If you were lucky, you'd be warming the bed of some military general."

He didn't say what befell the unlucky girls. He never did.

"I'm sorry, I—"

He slammed his fist down again. "You're sorry? Raven, the border laws might not exist underground, but they exist above ground, and you are not an exception to them. Going outside the borders is putting yourself in direct danger and not only defying the Gray Elite laws, but the laws of Silver Glen." He balled his fists. "What is wrong with you? Why must you continually do this to me? Your sister doesn't give me a fraction of the trouble you do."

Raven held her lip between her teeth to keep it from quivering. "You could stand to be more like your sister," her father had once told her after she had abandoned her chores to play in the summer rain.

She waited for him to admit it, that he preferred Lena over her, that she had been a mistake. She knew it; the whole mine knew it. Who could possibly prefer plain Raven, who did everything wrong, to lovely, perfect Lena, who did everything right?

Raven felt the tears welling behind her eyes, but she held them in.

"You've deliberately disobeyed me for the last time," he said darkly. "I've had it with you pushing aside the rules. Starting tomorrow, you're in the kitchen with your sister."

Raven snapped her gaze up at him. "What? No!" She jumped to her feet. "I won't do it again, I promise."

He shook his head. "I won't hear it. You've strayed too far." She tried to argue, but he held his hand up. "No. Tomorrow morning. The kitchen. Lena already knows, and your stepmother is going to be there to make sure you don't shirk your duties. It's high time you grew out of this wild streak, Raven. You're soon to be a grown woman. You're not a child."

With that, he turned his back. The discussion was over.

Raven stood on legs that didn't feel like her own. She set her hand on the door handle; then her father added, "Don't forget, you are on watch tonight."

Don't screw it up.

She let herself out of the office. She heard footsteps in the hall, but she didn't look up to see who. She didn't want to face them, in case they'd heard everything, and she didn't want anyone to see her cry. She started toward the living quarters, then turned down an empty hall. The tears pushed harder, wetting her eyelashes.

She headed for the quickest way out of the mines. When the ladder came into view, she bolted. She climbed as fast as she could and pushed through the trapdoor.

The calming breeze rushed through her hair and kissed her cheeks. She set the trapdoor back in place. Moss and stone had been affixed to the iron lid to hide it, but she knew how to get back in again. She started down the mountain to her favorite place in Silver Glen, where no one would tell her what to do.

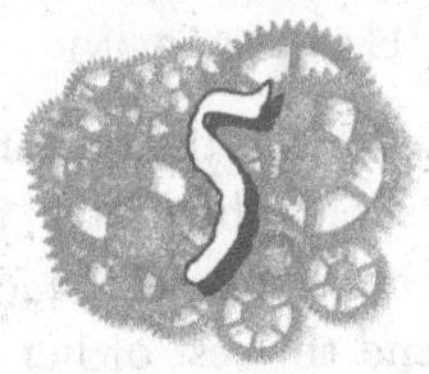

Raven knew the way to her tree. She could run it blindfolded. She weaved through the forest, her skirts rustling, her boots pounding on the dirt and grass. All around, the birds chirped, flaunting their freedom. They could fly about all day, wherever they pleased, while Raven couldn't even leave the boundaries of the mine.

Her tree—she had carved her initials into its thick trunk—stood a short distance outside the boundary. She came to the wooden fence that encircled their small corner of the kingdom and jumped over it in a single leap. Her boots hit the ground on the other side, and she ran all the way to her tree. It stood taller than the others, and its branches had grown in such an array that they begged to be climbed.

Raven climbed up and up and up until her head and shoulders burst through the topmost branches. Only then did she paused to catch her breath. Before her, the Hammel Forest sprawled to the horizon on rolling hills of blue-green. Above her, puffy white clouds lingered in the endless blue sky. The world went on forever.

Somewhere up there in the endless blue, sky cities roamed freely, going wherever they wished, whenever they wished. What would it be like to look down on the world from the deck of an airship? To live in one of the sky cities? The passengers were not confined to a life of hiding underground or in the cover of trees.

Raven knew there had to be more to the world than picking berries and surviving the winter. She knew there was more—Zander had proved it. Six months ago, he had escaped from Lenhala, the royal city of Rhynwier. He had shown up, ragged and dirty, in the middle of the night. But he never wanted to talk about it. Whenever someone mentioned Lenhala, he got a distant look in his eyes.

Somewhere to the south, Lenhala stood proud. A city of metal and stone stretching toward the sky. One day, Raven would like to see it. If only just once. Just to see what it was like, what the world could be like outside of the musty, dingy mines.

Raven inhaled the sweet scent of the outdoors, then slowly released it. The odds of her leaving Silver Glen were next to none, and her father would never permit her to leave. She would live here for the rest of her life, preserving food, tending to the children, and cleaning.

She climbed down to the fork in the tree and sat on the wooden plank she'd stolen from the workshop. She rested against the right fork and draped her legs off the plank, either side of the left fork.

She did not want to spend the rest of her life daydreaming about the rest of the world, but what choice did she have?

Raven sat, listening to the birds, the bugs, and the whispers of the forest, watching the sun make its steady path across the sky, until her hunger demanded she return for whatever grub the kitchens had made. She started down to the earth without enthusiasm. Her foot slipped on the hem of her skirt, and rather than grasp to hold on, she jumped the rest of the way down. Her feet slammed into the ground; the impact traveled up her legs and into her shoulders. Shaking it off, she started home.

Hands grabbed her shoulders and slammed her into the tree trunk, hard enough to knock the breath from her throat. She started to scream—a hand covered her mouth.

"You'll get their attention faster that way," growled a male voice.

She blinked—Zander had grabbed her. Her panic subsided and turned to anger. She tried to pry his hand off her mouth, but he didn't budge. His eyes flickered about the forest to her right, intent and focused. She mumbled for him to let go, and he shushed her.

She glared at him, and then she heard it.

A buzzing, not like bees or wasps, but a mechanical buzzing. Miniature gears clicking so fast, they hummed. An automaton.

The buzzing came closer. Her blood ran cold. Zander moved his free hand to his unnamed gun—he'd covered her mouth with the hand that would have grabbed Birdie. He slowly lifted the gun at firing lever and cocked it.

Her heart pounded. Her hands clutched Zander's. He wasn't shaking. He stood steady and sure. He wore his predator's face, a wolf ready to seize his prey, waiting, listening, and then—

The automaton came through the trees. Gears turned, thunking and clicking; steam hissed and gurgled. It looked like a birdcage with wings. The wings moved like a hummingbird's, so quickly, they blurred into a sheen of brass and steel. Steam issued from the bulbous head of the automaton, white-glass eyes turning in every direction, clicking as it searched. The body was a brass cage large enough for a grown man to sit in.

The automaton came closer, and Zander aimed.

Bang! The bullet smashed into the head, right through the left eye. It exploded into a spray of scrap metal. The wings sputtered. The cage crashed to the forest floor and stilled.

He didn't return the gun to his holster. For a moment, the forest quieted, and all she heard was the creaking and groaning of the dying automaton. Zander's hand slipped from her mouth, but she hadn't the words.

"Zander," Raven whispered, but he shook his head.

"Cage Birds travel in threes," he said. "We need to move. Now."

She nodded. Zander took point, and she followed a step behind. He walked with his unnamed gun at the ready, predatory eyes on the lookout. Raven scanned the forest as they walked, ears alert for the humming of mechanical wings.

The boundary fence came within sight, and for the first time in her life, her heart leaped at the sight of it.

And then she heard it—the hum of wings.

"Careful," Zander whispered. He adjusted his fingers on the gun and slowed.

How could she be careful when the boundary was right there? The automaton couldn't follow them over it.

They crept closer to the boundary, but Zander halted them. The second Cage Bird appeared in front of them, between them and the boundary—patrolling it, Raven realized. A rock fell into her gut. It hadn't been there when she had left. She would have seen it, heard it. Her chest tightened as she thought—it might have been there, and she had been too distraught to see it.

Another set of humming wings came from behind them. Neither Cage Bird had yet to spot them, but if they moved—

Zander aimed faster than Raven could blink. *Bang.*

She jumped; the Cage Bird's head exploded into scrap metal, and the body crashed to the ground. Zander spun to shoot the last Cage Bird behind them. He aimed over Raven's shoulder, and in the heartbeat that followed, his eyes widened.

The humming changed pitch.

"Raven!"

Cold metal hands fastened around her upper arms and yanked her backward. She yelped, but the sound evaporated as her back slammed into the bars of the cage, and the jaws of the Cage Bird snapped shut, shutting her inside.

Zander stood on the other side of the bars, Birdie in his other hand, both guns aimed at the Cage Bird, looking more like a predator than she had ever seen, teeth clenched, eyes wide and fierce. Angry.

But he didn't take the shot.

The Cage Bird started into the forest, away from the boundary fence. She shouted his name, but the Cage Bird moved too fast.

Raven's heart hammered. She kicked the doors, pushed them, beat them with her fists, but nothing worked. The cage wouldn't budge. Above her, the engine of the Cage Bird rumbled and clicked and crunched. The wings beat furiously, faster than before. Below her, the forest floor rushed past.

"No!" Raven slammed her hands against the cage doors one last time. The tears she had denied pushed against her eyes.

You've always wanted to fly, a dark voice in her mind said.

She sank to the bottom of the cage and brought her knees to her chest. Wouldn't her father be in a rage when he heard. A small amount of spiteful joy rose, knowing that Zander would be the one to tell him. Her father might even hit him. Too bad she wouldn't get to see it.

The Cage Bird lurched to the side, throwing her into the bars. It crashed into a tree with a sickening crunch of metal. It tumbled to the forest floor and rolled to a stop. The wings to her left had been crushed; the gears tried and failed to move.

For a moment, nothing happened. Her heart pounded, the sun glittered through the canopy, and the Cage Bird *clunked, clunked, hissed*.

Through the bars, Zander appeared. She'd never been as happy to see him. He knocked the butt of his unnamed gun into the jaws of the cage, and the lock sprang open. Raven crawled out from the cage, relishing the feeling of grass beneath her fingers. She stood on shaky legs, and when she stood clear, Zander shot the Cage Bird in the head, putting an end to the sputtering buzz of the remaining wing.

And then the forest was silent again.

Raven leaned against a tree trunk, hand over her racing heart. She could still hear the clanking of the Cage Bird's insides, the humming of the wings on either side of her, trapping her. Zander glared down at the Cage Bird with cold hatred, Birdie and his unnamed gun still in his hands.

With every heartbeat, her panic eased. Automatons, in Silver Glen.

If Zander hadn't been there... Then, another thought formed. Zander had been there, at her tree. "What were you doing?" Raven snapped at him.

"I could be asking you the same thing." Zander holstered his unnamed gun. A smirk replaced his grimace. "And after your father scolded you for wandering beyond the borders."

Her face reddened. It had been Zander in the hall.

"You should have shot it back there," she spat, turning toward the boundary. "You almost let it take me."

He holstered Birdie. His smirk lessened into something serious. "I didn't want to risk shooting you."

She laughed bitterly. "I thought you never miss."

"You'd rather I tempt fate? There was also the chance of the shrapnel taking out an eye or giving you a nice laceration." He ran his finger across his left eye.

She huffed, and they started back toward the boundary fence. They walked a while in silence, and then she said, "Thank you."

He made a small sound, and she knew he wore that arrogant smirk of his. "Good thing I followed you, or else you'd be on your way to Lenhala." A note of fear eased into his voice. "Raven, seriously though, Cage Birds have never come this far north. Don't leave the boundary without protection."

"You're saying I can borrow Birdie? I'd feel safer with her."

"No, you're not allowed to touch her," he said quickly. "But, if you are planning on leaving the boundary again, say something. I'll go with you."

She blushed at those words and turned her head so he wouldn't see. "My father would be angry that you'd suggest such a thing."

Zander chuckled. "He'd be angrier if he knew I let you wander into the forest alone."

She held her tongue. That way, Zander got to be the hero. She tried not to let it bother her. He *had* saved her from the Cage Bird.

The boundary came into sight, and she felt a relief and a burden. She also felt bruises forming along her shoulders and knees where the Cage Bird had crashed.

"No doubt, you heard my father take me off scavenging duty," she said.

Zander didn't respond.

She sighed. "I guess this means I'll be making soap and working with Lena in the kitchens."

Zander still didn't respond. He wasn't even looking at her. His intense stare looked through the forest, his hand resting on Birdie.

She yanked her attention away from him. She could ignore him too. She took a step toward the boundary when she felt it: a taut rope against the top of her foot. She glanced down. Thick wire stretched between two trees, into which she had walked.

A click—a *thwomp*—Zander grabbed her arm and yanked her back. She felt air move against her neck, and then a bolt embedded itself into the tree. Raven stumbled backward and lost her balance—a bolt had nearly gone through her throat! She fell, and Zander fell with her. Her back slammed into the ground, and Zander landed on top of her, his fist slamming into the ground beside her head.

She took a gasping breath—Zander's lips hovered a hair's breadth above her own. She couldn't move. Not because his weight pinned her, but because her limbs had turned to lead. She blinked, he blinked, and for a terrifying, exhilarating moment, she thought he might kiss her. For that same moment, she wanted him to. That terrified her more.

Zander blinked, then scrambled to his feet. She pushed herself up, face burning like fire.

She remembered—the bolt.

"What happened?" Raven asked.

"Someone set a trap." Zander touched the shaft of the bolt and followed the line it had traveled. He uncovered a narrow box attached to the opposite tree. The wire had been the trigger, releasing the bolt at her.

She took in the plain wooden bolt, and her face paled. "That's not one of ours."

Zander shook his head. "No. And, this bolt would have gone through your throat. The only animals in this area this could possibly be for are deer. Tell me, what else would a hunter use a bolt for?"

She swallowed. Understanding washed over her. "People."

He nodded grimly. "I was going to say, we should forget this happened and not tell your father, but this changes things. Come on."

Automatons and people hunters? Had they been in the forest that morning too? Raven followed a step behind Zander, glad to have him with her. She didn't want to tell her father about anything that had happened, but Zander was right. He needed to know.

Zander led the way to one of the trapdoors into the mine and waited for her at the bottom. In the dimmed light of the fungi, his dark brown hair appeared black, but his sapphire eyes stood out.

"Rae," he said, his voice soft. "Go on ahead. I'll talk to your father alone."

She hadn't expected that. Zander had never thrown aside a chance to get her in trouble. "Are you sure?" she asked.

"He's already yelled at you once today. I haven't gotten a good yelling for a few days. I don't want him to forget me."

She frowned. "Why? You used to thrive on my being in trouble."

He mirrored her frown. "Well, if you're so adamant, you can go with me. I'll let you explain why you were out there by yourself and how I saved your ass. Twice." He held up two fingers.

Her face reddened. Her stomach threatened to growl. "Fine, but don't make me look worse. I don't need him angrier."

He shrugged, and before he could change his mind, Raven headed toward the kitchens for something to eat.

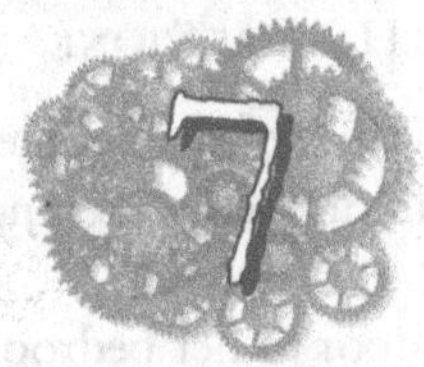

Raven headed through the cannery, not through the kitchen; she didn't want to meet anyone. No doubt, word of her insubordination and subsequent reassignment had spread. If she walked into the cafeteria, she would be greeted with pitied looks or *about time* stares from the older women. She still felt the puffiness of her eyes too, and she didn't want anyone to think she had been crying over it.

The cannery had quieted down since morning. The girls were gone, the blackberries had been processed, and the basket had returned to the stack in the corner. The smell of preserved berries floated through the air, tart and sweet, and it made her mouth water.

Raven slipped into the store for something quick.

"Back so soon?" asked Lena. Raven jumped; her half-sister stood on the other side of the storeroom, stacking jars of blue and red berry preserves. She gave Raven a knowing smile. "You missed lunch earlier." If Lena noticed Raven's puffy eyes, she didn't mention it.

"I did," Raven said.

Lena stood, waiting for an explanation. Raven bit her lip. She didn't want to tell her anything more than she had to, but she hadn't prepared an excuse for why she'd been gone. No doubt, Lena knew.

"I know this isn't the kind of job you want," Lena said softly. "But it's not so bad. At least we'll get to spend more time together. And you'll get to know everyone, and—I don't know—maybe you'll find a boy you like."

And settle down, she could hear her stepmother saying.

Raven shifted on her feet. She didn't want to have that conversation with Lena, with anyone. She placed a hand over her stomach. "Can you spare anything to eat? I'm famished. I'm on watch tonight, and I can't pass out from hunger, can I?"

Lena retrieved a few strips of dried venison, a stale slice of bread, and a bit of last year's preserves. Raven sat at the counter in the back while her sister worked, cleaning the dishes they'd used that day and giving Raven a quick rundown of all the chores in the kitchen. She included notes on how each worker had an important role, as to not make anyone feel less needed than another.

At Lena's behest, Raven washed her own plate and put it away. With a quick goodbye and a promise that the kitchen wasn't so horrible, Raven sulked back to her bedroom. Most of the people who called the mine home were still in the cafeteria, drinking and laughing after a day's work. Raven had no will to join them.

Raven shut the wooden door to her bedroom and let out a heavy sigh.

Her small room had only enough space for a narrow bed, a clothing trunk, and a bookshelf where she kept interesting stones, a few tinker toys, and what books she had managed to collect from traders. Raven collapsed onto her bed.

One thing she liked about her room was the ceiling. She had carved airships and stars into the stone and coaxed the fungi to grow in the lines so that the stars and airships glowed.

Kitchen duty. She'd much rather scavenge. There was so much more to see in the world than the ruins of Silver Glen, and she couldn't see any of it while stuck underground.

After the foot traffic of people returning from dinner quieted, Raven got up. She could put off her watch duty no longer. She grabbed her cloak, tucked one of her favorite books under her arm, and headed across the mines to the lookout tower.

The lookout tower jutted up from the highest point in the mines. On the outside, it looked like a thick tree. Its iron body had been covered with vining flowers, climbing ivy, and tree bark. From its top, the entire forest could be seen. Its purpose was to sound the alarm for danger, and someone stood on watch in the lookout tower night and day, every day of the year. It was a duty that they shared among the capable.

Raven's boots clicked on the iron steps, and the sound echoed up the tower's dark interior. On the last flight of steps, the last gleams of twilight gilded the lookout tower's landing in golds and blues, deep and mournful.

Carl was sitting at the desk, looking deathly bored. At the sight of Raven, he sat bolt straight and jumped to his feet.

Raven straightened her shoulders and put her hands on her hips. "I'm here to relieve you."

"Thank the Sisters," Carl breathed. He let out a wide yawn. He pointed to a basket. "My wife made biscuits. There's a few left. Help yourself."

"Thanks," she said.

With that, Carl made his way down the stairs. Halfway down, he started to whistle.

Raven sulked to the edge of the tower. She could see for miles, all the forest twilit and gleaming in dark golds. The pitiful town of Silver Glen sat nestled in the forest, vaulted wooden roofs dull, even in the twilight. The sun edged underneath the low-hanging clouds, turning them all purple and orange and pink. The summer haze glowed. A glorious sight. It made it look as though the very air glowed.

The colors dimmed, stars appeared one by one, and the night took control of the world. Millions of stars glittered from horizon to horizon. What would it be like to sail through them? To have the stars within reach? To fly between the stars and the clouds?

She let out a sigh and plopped down into the singular chair. A crossbow leaned against the wall, and a dozen bolts lay in a tall basket underneath the table. A chain hung from the warning bell, which, when pulled, would echo down the tower and into the mines. One ring for traders or visitors, two rings for everything else.

Raven had never rung the bell. She slumped onto the table and scanned for any sign of anything. She could still hear the buzzing of the Cage Birds, feel the metal hands close around her arms. She looked harder, but she saw no glint of metal in the night.

They couldn't cross the border anyway. The border laws didn't allow it.

But why had they been there? Had they wandered beyond their usual path? How had Zander known about them? Either he had followed her and spotted them, or he had spotted them and then gone after her. Either way left her stomach in knots.

But why?

The only thing Silver Glen had lay at its deepest point, far under the mountain. It was an ancient temple of the Three Sisters, one of the few remaining untouched by the war. Raven had never prayed or given an offering; few people still did, except for her stepmother. The ninny. The old temple was mainly used as a meeting for the council. Raven had always found its dark walls and dim light eerie.

Still, the attack that day had left her shaken. She watched, waited, and watched, but she saw nothing. As the night went on, time seemed to slow. Even the stars paused.

Raven felt the tug of sleep. To keep herself awake, she reached for her book. She propped her boots up on the counter and started to read. She'd read the book countless times; it was an adventure of a young boy named Leon Stark, who stowed away on a ship, thinking he would escape his life as a slave. However, the ship he boarded was a pirate ship, and through his adventure and bravery, he became captain.

Even though she knew the twists and turns of love and betrayal, she lost herself in the story. She stood with the boy on the pirate ship's deck as it shot out of the waters and into the sky, taking flight. She felt his awe as he saw the flying ship for the first time, when he felt the blast of the cannons, when he touched a cloud.

A bird cawed from the tower's roof, pulling her out of her fantasy. She blinked; the wind rustled the leaves. The moon had gone behind a cloud. She heard the flap of a heavy wing, then nothing.

She heaved a sigh. Tomorrow, the kitchens. She wouldn't step outside the mines again for a long while, not if her father had anything to say about it, and she would never see an airship—let alone ride in one. She would live and die in Silver Glen.

With that thought, she buried herself in the story once more. Her only escape.

Raven read until her relief came to take over the watch. She thanked him vigorously and then jogged down the stairs, yawning. She walked to her room in a sleepy daze, with sky cities and airships and pirate captains flying through her thoughts amid a flurry of adventure and romance. She tiptoed through the living quarters, which were humming with the soft breaths of sleep, and shut herself in her room.

She undressed and set her dress and her corset inside her clothing trunk. She slid her dagger from her boot and set it beside her bed. She always kept it and her boots within easy reach at night. It made her feel more prepared should something happen—not that anything ever happened.

She undid the clasp on her locket—the only thing she had of her mother's. It was a simple golden locket with a delicate floral pattern etched onto its front. She tried to open it, but like always, it remained shut. She'd never been able to open it.

She set her locket by her dagger. In just her chemise, she curled underneath the thin blankets.

In her mind, she could picture it: her own airship, a sky city unlike any other, of bright colors and with a full library. Flying through the stars. Flying alongside the clouds. Where magic existed, free as the wind, bright as a sunrise. High above the world, away from the Gray Elite, from their automatons, from their sprawling empire, from the shadow of the war.

She fell asleep to her fanciful thoughts, and too soon, a hand was shaking her awake.

"Jusaminmore," Raven mumbled, but the hand persisted.

"Now, child," came the deep, soft voice of the elder, Mel.

Raven snapped awake.

The older woman stood at the bedside, her silver hair braided over her shoulder, her dress the color of the darkness around her. Her piercing eyes reflected the yellow of the fungi.

"Mel?" Raven muttered, sitting up.

"Up, now," Mel urged. "There isn't time to chat."

Mel glided into the hallway with the grace of a ghost, and Raven scrambled to her feet. Had she overslept? Enough that Mel had come to fetch her personally? Guilt and shame coursed through her limbs like a dull ache, and she felt separate from herself as she hurriedly dressed. Raven rushed into the hall after Mel.

Raven yawned. She could have used a few more hours of sleep. She felt like she had barely gotten any at all.

All the other doors in the living quarters were closed. With every step, Raven's thoughts cleared of sleep. Mel did not lead her into the kitchens. She led her down, deeper into the mine, deeper and deeper. Raven's stomach flipped and flopped in rhythm with her hurried steps. What was wrong?

They walked deeper still. With no small amount of nervousness, Raven realized that Mel was leading her to the Temple of the Three Sisters. Her heart sank. Did this have something to do with the arm she had found? The arm she took from the ruined temple?

They descended a wide staircase carved from the dark gray stone. The stairs and the temple they led to were ancient, older than the mine, far older. The smooth steps and walls had no markings of carving tools, and Raven's stepmother often said the ancients had used magic to shape the temple. As she descended deeper, Raven felt a prick of fear that her stepmother might have been telling the truth. The stale air of the mine mingled with something else, something metallic and floral; the deeper they walked, the stronger the scent.

A chill sent gooseflesh over Raven's arms and legs. She hated going to the temple.

They finally reached the bottom of the stairs, and Mel led her through a set of iron doors. Each had been carved with a thousand interlocking whorls and starbursts. The main chamber of the temple held the statues of the Sisters, each carved from their respective stone: marble for Wilyn, sandstone for Minerva, and granite for Solen. The fungi grew along the walls and ceiling, shadowing the Sisters' stone faces.

Mel led Raven into a small side room without fungi. A single candle burned on a wooden podium. Raven didn't like how small the room felt and how full of shadows it was.

"The door," said Mel.

Raven quietly shut the door; her hands shook on the handle. To be called upon by the elder in the middle of the night...it couldn't be good. Raven turned, going through all of the possible things she might have done wrong, trying her best to hide her trembling nerves, when movement in the shadows caught her eye. A third person stood in the room.

Zander leaned against the wall, half hidden in shadow, with one foot propped against the wall and his arms crossed. His eyes met hers. The candlelight flickered shadows across his face, and his eyes appeared black. He wore a dire seriousness that turned Raven's blood cold.

She balled her fists in her skirt. Had Zander told Mel what had happened? Had he told her father? Her heart skipped a beat, then sped up like the beating wings of the Cage Bird. She wanted to shout her accusations at him, but not in front of Mel.

"Raven." Mel folded her boney hands in front of her. Her calm voice soothed a minuscule amount of Raven's anger toward Zander. "The time has come for you to prove yourself. The time of change is fast approaching; the winds have told me as much. From here, your decisions will shape your future, and ours."

Raven bristled. She doubted her decisions in the kitchens would shape anything, unless her food poisoned everyone in the mine. She glanced again at Zander. Why did he have to be here for this? He seemed to hear her thoughts; a smirk broke his serious mask, and he winked. She bit back the urge to stick out her tongue at him.

"Something was stolen from us this night, something of great value," said Mel. "It must be recovered at all costs."

Raven blinked at Mel; her surprise stole whatever thought she had had. "I'm sorry, what?" she whispered.

"We have been robbed," Mel said plainly. "I am charging you with finding the thief."

Raven gawked; surely, she still slept. Sleepwalking. That had to be it. She shook her head and rubbed her temples, trying to wake herself up. She glanced back at Mel, who hadn't removed her stare. Zander leaned against the wall, his eyes focused on Birdie.

Raven's stomach turned over, and panic set in. Had she missed something? "I'm sorry. I-I don't understand. What thief? What's been stolen? When?"

"When you were on watch," Zander said dryly. His sapphire eyes flashed from Birdie to her. He wore no emotion she could easily read. "A thief snuck into the mine, stole from us, all the while the person who should have sounded the alarm didn't."

Her heart skipped a beat. She had been reading. Under Mel's knowing glare, Raven's entire face flushed. Even Zander looked angry.

"I-I'm sorry... I didn't..." Raven glanced between Mel and Zander, shame weighing her shoulders down. She started to shrink but realized what Mel had said—that she would be the one to retrieve the stolen something. Raven jerked her chin up and straightened her shoulders. "I'll get it back. I'll have the thief by sundown. Just tell me what was stolen and from where."

Mel didn't look convinced. "The thief stole a relic from the temple, something as ancient as the stone and as valuable as the stars," she said darkly. She lifted her chin and looked down at Raven, making her feel even smaller. "The thief has already fled into the night."

Into the night... Raven gasped. "Outside?" The mere word sent a jolt down her spine and into her toes.

Mel was sending her *outside*?

Mel nodded. "Yes. Outside. You are familiar with the terrain. And since it was your negligence that allowed the thief access to the mines..." Mel hesitated to let those words seep in. "I am charging you with the relic's recovery."

The thrill of chasing down a thief rose and then subsided. "But my father's orders—"

Mel held up a hand to silence her.

"He does not yet know of this," Mel said.

Raven blinked several times. Surely, she had misheard. Mel would defy her father's orders?

Her confusion must have shown, for Mel said, "This is a matter of the utmost importance. I will speak to him come dawn and explain why I have sent you."

After she had gone—which wouldn't give him a chance to scold Raven for messing up her patrol or refuse to let her leave.

Mel was helping her.

Then, why did it feel like punishment?

Raven held her shoulders straight. "Yes, of course, I'll go. I might not have the thief by sundown, though. Is there anything to go on? A direction? A face to go with this thief?"

Mel's stern stare faltered a fraction, and something like exasperation slipped through. "I am not sending you alone."

Raven's hope withered, and realization settled in. She cast a glance toward Zander. He gave her a crooked smile and slid Birdie back into her holster.

"That's why I'm here," Zander said. "We're going together."

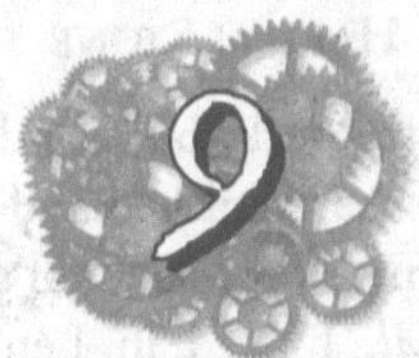

Something caught in Raven's throat, then she blurted, "Why must it be Zander?"

"Because I know the terrain better than you." Zander patted Birdie. "And as you know, you wouldn't survive out there without me."

She balled her fists in her skirts. "I could arm myself."

"It would take too long to teach you how to shoot," Zander said, stepping off the wall. "And our thief is likely heading to Lenhala. If we get stopped by Gray Elite, you're going to need me."

Raven fumed. "I will not."

"He is right, Raven," said Mel. "Should you encounter the Gracitan forces, they will require identification."

"Yes, but why does it have to be Zander?" Of all the people in the mine!

"Because," Zander said, his words grim, "I'm from the capital. I have papers. My name has meaning. It'd be easy to explain that I met a girl and ran away with her, and that's why I've been gone so long. It wouldn't draw suspicion. Otherwise, the automatons might think us refugees."

His words sank in. *I met a girl.* Raven paled, and the heat of embarrassment made her legs feel like sand. "You're saying we would be undercover as..."

"Lovers," said Zander, the word a purr on his tongue.

The sand in her legs liquified, and she feared she might melt into a puddle. She might have, had Zander not shot his arrogant, knowing smirk at her. Her embarrassment became anger. She couldn't believe this! Finally, her chance to see the world beyond this forsaken village, and she had to go with pigheaded, show-off Zander.

"Absolutely not!" Raven stomped her foot.

"Stomping isn't very ladylike," Zander murmured.

"Shut up," Raven spat.

He rolled his eyes.

"I am not going to play that game with this..." She couldn't think of a proper insult for Zander, at least not one she could use in front of Mel.

He raised his brow at her, waiting for it.

She growled and continued, "Why can't you send someone else?"

Mel sighed. She started to speak, but Zander spoke for her. "Because I know my way around." His sneer vanished and became a serious demeanor that Raven hadn't seen on him before; she didn't know if she liked it or not. "Because I'm *from the capital*. I lived in Lenhala." He hesitated, and a darkness came over his face. Then, he whispered, "I'm Gray Elite."

A heartbeat passed. Then two. Three.

"You..." Raven started, then paused.

She had to be sleepwalking.

Zander, a Gray Elite? Part of the military who had scattered deadly machines throughout the kingdom to hunt people like mice, who had destroyed magic and those who wielded it, who had forced the people of Silver Glen to live underground out of fear. Raven stepped back; her back hit the wooden door. She bent over, eyes on Zander's scuffed leather boots, the well-made leather boots that he had always worn.

She thought back to that day six months ago when she had first seen Zander. He was sitting in the trading post on the surface, a tankard of ale in his hands, talking to her father. His trousers had been torn and dirty. His shirt had slept-in wrinkles. His hair had been filthy. His sapphire eyes had met hers—full of defeat, ceaseless worry, and desperation. He had been withdrawn for the first few weeks, barely talking to anyone, and then he and Brent restored Birdie. Zander taught a few of the other boys how to shoot, and her father put him on scavenging duty.

He had started to talk more, and to make him feel welcome, Raven talked to him. She had sought him out a few times; she had asked him about the world outside the mine, but the details he gave were short. Eventually, she stopped asking. They talked more and more. She started to consider him a friend. He lost his shyness and wariness and relaxed into his cocky self, and while those eyes of his had been intriguing at first, every time he opened his mouth, she wanted to smack that smirk off his face.

All that time, Zander had been a Gray Elite? An enemy?

Zander wasn't smiling now.

Her voice came out small. "I thought you were an escaped refugee."

Zander's eyes lingered on her; then he shrugged. "It sounded better that way. If people knew I was a deserter, they would either turn me in for the money or kill me on sight."

Raven took a deep, steadying breath. None of this made sense. It all felt silly, strange, and she expected herself to be jolted awake at any moment by her sister, urging her to walk with her to the kitchens.

Zander's lips twitched upward.

Suddenly, she burned with embarrassment. "This is a joke, isn't it?" she asked, her voice wobbly. "You're pulling another joke on me."

Raven tightened her hands in her skirt, turning her knuckles white. Zander knew how badly she wanted to see Lenhala, to see the world outside this bloody village!

Zander frowned. "Rae, I'm not. Listen—"

She turned to leave, but Zander jumped between her and the door. He threw his arms out to block her path.

"Move!" Raven demanded.

Zander stood firm.

Mel's calm, quiet voice came from the other side of the room, "This would be a good time to explain yourself to her, Zander."

Raven looked over her shoulder at the elder. She stood half in shadow, the candle's light reflecting in her dark eyes. She was looking at Zander, not Raven, and the piercing look gave Raven a chill.

Zander huffed. "Fine."

Raven looked between Zander and Mel; something had passed silently between them. Another secret.

Zander took a deep breath, lowered his arms, and set his sapphire stare on Raven. Calmly, he said, "I was born in Lenhala. While my father served in the Gray Elite forces, he and my mother believed in the resistance against Regent Dunel's reign."

She blinked. "Resistance?"

"There are those who strive to rid Rhynwier of Gracita's rule and restore the kingdom to its former glory," he said. "They do so by freeing slaves, scrapping automatons, stopping the Gray Elite from expanding any more than they already have, and striking at the Gray Elite from the shadows. My father was a general to King Reginald, and my mother was a lady in waiting to Queen Katerina. Though they swore their allegiance to Regent Dunel, they remained loyal to their kingdom."

Raven hugged her arms around her chest. She'd never seen Zander so serious and so nervous at the same time. She didn't like it. It reminded her of that first meeting.

Zander looked down at his scuffed leather boots. "My father gave me something to hide as far away from Lenhala as I could," he said, his voice near a whisper. "Somewhere the Gray Elite wouldn't come looking for it."

"And you came here and hid it among the relics of the Sisters," Raven finished for him.

Zander nodded.

Her stepmother would be sick with shame at such an act. Raven shrugged and added, "Well, what is it?"

What could be so important that his parents would send him, an eighteen-year-old boy, to the edge of the world?

"I can't tell you," said Zander.

"Oh? Keeping more secrets?"

He frowned. "I don't know what it is. Only that it is very valuable and rare. My father sealed it in an iron box. I've never looked inside."

A part of her didn't believe him. She huffed. "Why me? Why not pick someone else to go with you?"

He gave her a lopsided grin. "Well, considering it *was* your fault for not paying attention on watch..." She swatted at him, but he jumped out of her reach. "And you are good at navigating the terrain. You're skilled at not being detected, at least, when you're trying. With a few lessons, you could pass for aristocracy."

"Why would I need to pass as aristocracy?" The word tumbled ungracefully from her lips.

His grin faltered. "Because that's the part of Lenhala I'm from." He took a step toward her. "This is serious, Raven. My parents put their trust in me to keep that box safe. I will get it back."

"But..." She gaped between Mel and Zander.

"We leave now," Zander said. "We need to be as far from here as possible when everyone wakes."

"Why?"

"Because I do not want your father sending a team after us," Zander said.

She wanted to ask if her father knew about this iron box, but Mel spoke first, "I agree. Now is best. Things have been packed. If you leave now, you will have several hours between you and here by dawn."

Raven sighed. Though the thought of such a journey thrummed through her veins, the idea of walking until dawn—several hours—exhausted her. Zander appeared beside her with a pack over his shoulders and another for her in his hand. She took it, glad she had dressed earlier, and slung the pack over her shoulders.

"Let's get on with it, then," she groaned. "You better have packed breakfast."

The walk through the mine didn't feel real. Zander led the way to the trapdoor farthest from the main entrance. Outside, the stars blinked, cool air blew down from the mountains, and the animals of the dark scurried, chittered, and hooted.

She could almost hear her stepmother croon, *Wilyn is watching. The stars are her eyes.*

"Where are we going?" Raven asked as she followed Zander down the hillside. She felt glad to have Zander leading the way, but she would never tell him so.

Zander looked up at the stars. "We need to head south for a day; then we'll head southwest along the river."

"I thought we were catching a thief?"

"We are. That's the best way to get to the old kings' highway, which is where our thief has most likely gone. We'll be able to catch up to him this way."

He started down the slope, and she started after him. Questions of his plan popped up, one after another. "But how do you expect us to find this thief?" she asked. "What does he look like? What if he didn't head south? What if this thing of yours was taken by one of the kids or moved so someone could clean underneath it and put somewhere else?"

Zander huffed. "Because it wasn't in a place anyone else but Mel went. *Hidden.* It's something the Gray Elite would pay dearly for. We won't be dealing with a common street thief, Rae. For someone to have snuck into the mine unnoticed and poked around enough to find the thing, we're dealing with an expert thief."

Raven wanted to ask about the contents of the box, but Zander's dark tone made her tongue curl against her teeth. He glanced back at her, predatory gaze piercing through her.

"Forgive me for having questions," she muttered.

He shook his head. They didn't speak again until they had reached the boundary fence. Raven quickly glanced around for any more Cage Birds. She saw nothing, nor did she hear anything strange underneath the scurrying and chittering.

"And," Zander continued, "we're going the same way our thief would have gone."

"And if he went east? Or west?"

Zander shot an annoyed glare at her as he lifted his boot over the fence. "Then, we'll take a nice trip together." He brought his other foot to stand with the other so that the fence stood between them. "From this point on, things will be dangerous. This is your last chance to turn around and beg Mel to put you back on kitchen duty."

Raven straightened her shoulders and held her chin under his disbelieving glare. "Isn't this why you asked me to come along? Because I refused to balk at danger?"

Zander's glare didn't relent. "There are worse things out there than Cage Birds," he said grimly. "Much worse. Bigger. Meaner. Ruthless. Trust me, I've seen the monster machines the Gray Elite have made."

She huffed. "You expect me to go running back to the mines with my tail between my legs?"

He shrugged, his serious mask shifting. "It's a fair warning. And"—he stepped aside to let her climb over—"it is your fault it got stolen."

She rolled her eyes and climbed over the fence. He held his hand out to her, but she ignored it and jumped to the ground instead.

They had walked a short distance when Zander said, "That trap you triggered earlier also suggested the thief would take this route."

"How so?"

"Because it had been set along this path, see?" He pointed to where the trap lingered against the tree. "It had been set so that if someone caught him and came running after him, the trap would distract or kill his pursuers."

She blinked at the trap. "Oh." She cleared her throat. She hadn't thought of that at all. "Well, then, I feel more confident about our direction."

Zander chuckled and shot her a smirk. She groaned and started to walk a little faster. He matched her pace, and they headed steadily south.

The sun slowly rose, and the inky shadows of the forest lightened from gray to misty blue to sun-warmed yellow. Raven had never been above ground during the sunrise, and she hesitated to blink lest she miss one of the colors of the forest. Beside her, Zander didn't seem at all fascinated with the waking world as the birds started to chirp, as the night bugs grew quiet, as the sun warmed the leaves and bushes and ever-shifting foliage. Fog rose in low places, small dips in the forest floor, and hovered above ponds and lakes. As the sun's rays tumbled over the treetops, the fog and mist burned with the sun's light until nothing remained.

It was beautiful, more so than she had ever imagined.

The sunlight made Zander's bronze skin glow golden, while it made her look ghostly white.

She had never been more than a few hours' walk from the border of Silver Glen, but the trees didn't look that different, nor did the bushes, berries, or rocks. She knew the landmarks around Silver Glen, and when she spotted new rock formations or trees she didn't recognize, a tingle of excitement worked its way up her spine. She spotted sparkling lakes and ponds through the trees, reflecting the rising sun's light.

Zander spoke little, mostly to point out possible traps or snares within the natural world and what plants to avoid at all costs. The farther they walked, the greater her exhaustion became. It weighed on her limbs, her mind, until she felt as though she moved through mud. She followed Zander's back between the sun-parched trees, alongside whispering creeks, and along ancient stones that might have been the remains of homes, waystations, or roads.

Finally, when she didn't think she could go on, they came upon a waystation. Its walls were rough-cut logs, its roof unevenly vaulted. Horses were tied in a small stable beside it, and a hammered metal sign advertised ale, wine, trading, and beds. A dirt path stomped into submission by generations of horses wound east and west; it vanished out of sight through the trees.

"We rest here," said Zander, and Raven hadn't the thought to argue.

They walked through the door of the inn. One side was devoted to a small tavern; the other side, a trading post. It smelled like stale ale and sweat. The trading post was a counter—a metal sheet held between two barrels. A woman stood behind the counter, sorting buttons by shape and size.

"Morning, ma'am." Zander put on a weary smile. "Is there a room available for travelers?"

Her crisp eyes flickered between Zander and Raven. "There's room."

"I have money," Zander added meekly, and he withdrew a silver coin from his pocket. "Is this enough?"

The innkeeper eyed the coin, then eyed them again.

Raven glanced at the coin—a silver coin with a hard-nosed face stamped onto either side. A Gracitan token. Raven held in her surprise as best she could. Zander had Gracitan money? Of course, he did. He was a Gray Elite, she reminded herself.

"I-I have trading also," said Zander, a strain in his voice she'd never heard before, a desperation.

His pleading voice worked on the woman; her brow curved in pity.

"The token is acceptable." The woman took the token and deposited it underneath the counter. She placed a heavy iron key on the counter. "Down the hall, second room on your right. Number two. Key works the water heater too."

"Thank you, ma'am," Zander said with a bow of his head.

The woman's eyes ran up and down Zander, then shifted to Raven. She took in her home-sewn dress, her leather corset, her dusty boots. "You both look a little worse for wear," said the woman.

Before Raven could reply, Zander spoke quietly, "We've been traveling most of the night." He glanced around the mostly empty tavern. A few men who looked like travelers were sitting at the far table by the open window. A group of older women, all knitting, sat on the other side of the room. None were looking in their direction.

The woman made a small hum.

"We were..." Zander paused, glancing at Raven. He wore fear in his eyes, and her heart thudded against her rib cage. He lowered his voice. "We were attacked last night, and I couldn't bring myself to make camp in the woods."

The woman's eyes grew softer. "There's been more trouble to the north recently. Bandits or worse?"

"Cage Birds," he whispered.

The woman pulled her bottom lip into her mouth. She gave a subtle shake of her head.

Zander swallowed and glanced his sorrowful eyes at Raven. "One nearly took Rae." He reached out and took hold of Raven's hand, giving it a gentle squeeze. She nearly ripped it away from him but then remembered their roles. Lovers. She let him hold her hand and tried to look at him with what she hoped was kindness, while pretending her heart didn't flutter at the touch.

"It could have been worse," the woman whispered. "I've had travelers tell me they've seen Goliaths in the woods."

Zander made a small sound of shock. He shook his head in disbelief. "No," he whispered. "Sisters, there's getting to be fewer safe places in this kingdom. Soon, Gracita will have us all enslaved."

The woman nodded. "You'll want a warm meal later, I suppose. We don't have much, but my girl and I can cook up a fine stew from the ingredients the wood offers. Wilyn hasn't abandoned us entirely."

"Thank you," Zander said.

"Take care," said the woman. "I'll send word when the meal is ready if I don't see you."

Zander thanked the woman again, and then he led Raven down the hall. An iron number two had been nailed onto the lopsided door. He unlocked the door with a heavy clunk and pushed it open. It was a small room, but a room. Raven walked past him and dropped her pack onto the floor before collapsing onto the metal frame bed that took the majority of the space.

"I'm exhausted," she grumbled.

He dropped his pack on the floor and threw his jacket over it. "Don't hog the bed; scoot over," he grumbled.

She blinked and pushed herself onto her elbows. Indeed, their room had only a single bed. Two pillows. One blanket.

Her face burned. "There's only one bed?"

He put his fingers to his lips and hissed, "Because we've lovers, remember? *My love?*"

She swallowed and glanced down to the bare wood floors. "Maybe you should sleep on the floor."

He half laughed. "Why should I sleep on the floor?"

"Because you're the gentleman," she said flatly.

He lifted a brow at her and laughed—his low laugh sent a shiver down her spine. "I'm a gentleman, she says," he said, a smirk on his lips. He unfastened his holsters and hung them on one of the brass coat hooks nailed unevenly on the wall. He sat down on the other side of the bed and started to unbuckle his boots. "I'm sleeping right here. You are free to sleep wherever you see fit."

Zander reclined back on the second pillow and let out a sigh of relaxation.

Raven glanced at the floor; it looked horribly uncomfortable. Beside her, Zander's face had already relaxed, his chin dipped to the side—asleep. Or pretending, like he had done for the past six months, like he had done with the innkeeper.

Raven sat up, untied her corset, unbuckled her boots, and set them on the floor. She unclasped her locket and slid it inside one of her boots so she wouldn't lose it. Gritting her teeth, she climbed underneath the blanket beside Zander. The space between them felt too small, and she could feel the heat coming off his body. She could feel him there, breathing, his heat pressing against her back.

Despite the oddity of his proximity, she tried to find comfort. She needed sleep; she was exhausted. Sunlight seeped through the wooden shutters on the narrow window, making the room much brighter than her bedroom back at Silver Glen. She had never before tried to sleep in the sunlight. When she closed her eyes, the shadows were tinged with orange and gold.

"The Gray Elite will pay for the capture of anyone with magic," Zander whispered. "There are some who would eagerly turn in strangers for a chance of a few tokens."

"Is that why the innkeeper was hesitant?"

"Yeah. But when I told her about the automaton almost taking you, she got that sympathetic look in her eye. She's not one of those." Zander shifted, and the whole bed shifted with him. The metal frame creaked. When he spoke, he sounded closer. "People are wary of strangers. People are quick to point out magicians. The Gray Elite have turned the people against them. People are terrified of magic now."

"Why is that?"

"Anyone caught harboring a magician will also be put to death," Zander said grimly. "Even if they knew nothing about it."

Her heart skipped a beat. "That's awful."

"I didn't say it wasn't. Gracita is serious about stomping out magic."

"Why, though? It never made sense to me."

"To prove their machines superior," he said bitterly. "And, Gracitans, by nature, can't use magic. My father used to say they feared it, so they strove to make themselves stronger, and when they could, they invaded Rhynwier. They are always striving to make sure magic doesn't come back."

"Come back?" Raven rolled onto her back. Zander had rolled onto his side, facing her. His exhausted sapphire eyes met hers.

He half laughed. "Magic isn't something you can stomp out, though the Gray Elite try. They see magic as a disease and think killing all those with it will make it go away. But that's now how magic works."

"How does it work?"

He didn't answer immediately. His gaze turned curious and searched hers. Those eyes fell to her lips, and her heart stopped. "They don't know," he whispered, and his gaze returned to her eyes. "No one does. And the Gray Elite want to keep it that way."

They stared at one another for a long moment; then Raven turned her gaze to the ceiling. She didn't ask any more questions; Zander didn't offer up any more history. Soon, gentle snores came and went with the rising and falling of his chest. Soon, exhaustion pulled her far into sleep.

Raven woke feeling better rested than she had in a long while. Her body had never felt more relaxed. She didn't want to move. She inhaled, and the scent of dirt and sweat filled her nose. Sunlight gleamed on the other side of her eyelids, warm and welcoming. Birds flitted about, tweeting and chirping to one another. Voices drifted from somewhere. Outside, maybe.

Then the night before came back to her.

The inn, she realized. She blinked her eyes open. Judging by the golden sunlight streaming in through the gaps in the shutters, it was afternoon. She'd slept most of the morning. She inhaled, filling her drowsy chest with the stale air of the inn, and rolled onto her back.

Her arm grazed something warm. She turned her head; Zander slept beside her. Right beside her. Her arm grazed his. It took a heartbeat and a half for her to feel the heat from him pressing into her, and another heartbeat for that heat to flush her face bright pink. She moved her arm away quickly.

Zander shifted but continued to sleep. Gentle snores escaped his parted lips.

Trying her best to ignore the rapid thumping of her heart, Raven carefully scooted off the bed and tiptoed into the small adjoining bathroom. Shutting herself inside, she heaved a breath.

Copper pipes of varying sizes ran along the back wall, connecting the water basin, the toilet, and the showerhead tucked into the tiled corner of the room. Underneath the main water tank, the heater looked like something Brent would salvage together from scrap metal.

She unbuttoned her dress and hung it over a wooden chair. She laid her underdress on top of it, followed by her socks and underthings. She stood on her tiptoes to turn on the water heater, but it had no knob or level. Only a keyhole.

Of course, the key. It started the heater.

Raven reached for her clothes but stopped. It would be a burden to redress only to undress a few seconds later. And Zander was likely still sleeping. She glanced around and found Zander's overshirt hanging off a hook—he must have gotten up sometime in the night and left it here.

Slipping Zander's shirt over her naked body, Raven tiptoed back into the bedroom. She spotted the heavy key at once, sitting on the small table at the foot of the bed. She closed her hand around it, and then someone cleared their throat.

She whipped around, holding the key out like a dagger. Zander stood by the open window, canteen tilted toward his lips. Water dribbled down his chin, and his eyes had gone wide.

A fire burned through her cheeks. She wore nothing but his shirt.

Zander gaped at her, unblinking, while the water dribbled from the canteen and onto his undershirt. Raven yanked the hem of the shirt as far down as it would go, but her knuckles still only grazed the tops of her thighs. It covered the necessities but left her legs bare. Zander's wide eyes wandered up and down her exposed legs, and her skin prickled under his gaze. She had never seen *that* look on his face—hunger.

She flushed from head to toe. "Stop looking!" she hissed.

He blinked several times. His parted lips curved into a mischievous grin, and he said, "If you didn't want me to look, you shouldn't have come out half naked."

Her skin felt like fire. She stormed back into the bathroom and shut the door. She thrust the heavy key into the water heater. With a hard turn, the heater started. Steam hissed through the pipes, heating the water in the tank.

How dare he! Her skin burned, and one look in the broken mirror told her she'd gone entirely red. She yanked off his shirt and left it on the floor.

She didn't wait for the water to heat all the way. She pulled the chain to release the water into the shower's pipes; it streamed out of the head. She welcomed the cooler water against her burning skin. After that episode, she needed a cold shower.

When Raven reentered the bedroom wearing her dress, Zander was gone. She combed her light brown hair and braided it back. She tied up her corset and slipped on her boots, taking care to make sure her dagger was secure. She was slipping her locket underneath the collar of her dress when the door opened, and Zander sauntered through.

His eyes ran along her body before he met her gaze; her cheeks burned. He cocked a grin, and if she had been holding something, she would have thrown it at him.

"Dinner's nearly ready." Zander shut himself in the bathroom.

She sighed through her nose and opened the shutters. She could see people coming and going from the tavern and trading post. There weren't that many more people than in Silver Glen, and they all looked ragged and weary. The few houses and buildings she could see looked to have been there a long time, the wooden logs weathered to gray, nails rusty and orange, shutters lopsided, and fences patched in several different shades of newness.

It looked like the ramshackle surface town of Silver Glen, a ghost of its former self. Another town the one-hundred-year war had torn through. Another town the Gray Elite had left to rot.

At the thought of her home, her chest tightened. Her father would know she'd left by now. Zander too. What had Mel told him? Had he sent a search party to retrieve them? Had Mel convinced him otherwise?

The mines would be better off without her, said a mean little voice in her head. She didn't hold an important job. Maybe that was why Zander had chosen to take her along—the mines wouldn't miss her.

Zander stepped out of the bathroom. His hair was wet, and his shirt clung to the water between his shoulder blades. He sat on the bed beside her, and she feared he'd bring up that he'd seen her nearly naked.

"Here's the plan," he whispered, and her chest loosened. "During dinner, I'll keep everyone in the tavern distracted. You sneak into the other rooms and see if our thief is staying here."

"And if he is?"

"Then, you steal back the box."

She huffed. "What kind of plan is that?" He frowned, and she added, "What kind of thief would leave his goods lying about? How am I supposed to know which room to search? How am I supposed to steal it back?"

"Then, I guess you'll have to go through their things," he said. "We don't have much choice. We need that box. I don't know how else to search without holding them all at gunpoint and demanding they empty their pockets. That won't go over well."

She nodded. As much as it pained her to admit, he was right. "You expect me to knock? The doors will undoubtedly be locked."

Zander threw her a smirk. "I know how good you are at picking locks."

At that, she didn't balk. Brent hadn't invented a lock that she couldn't get through. At his smirk, her cheeks burned, and her pride swelled.

They went to dinner together. More people lingered in the inn than before, everyone in the little town it seemed. The innkeeper, the woman who'd given them the key, and her husband and daughter ran the place. Her husband looked like a much more agreeable person, laughing and talking to anyone within range of his booming voice, which was most people. He clapped Zander on the shoulder like an old friend and gave him a wide, friendly smile that Zander returned.

Zander and Raven accepted steaming bowls of wild stew and joined a local couple at a table. It was a logging town, they quickly discovered. It had the best supply of white oak and red pine, but the Gray Elite had stifled business when their machines took over. They preferred metal to wood, and the logging industry had declined.

The view of the Gray Elite was poor here, just as it had been in Silver Glen. As the loggers and farmers began to drink and talk, Raven understood why Zander had been nervous about spending Gracitan tokens; no one liked the Gray Elite, and several promised horrible deaths to any unsuspecting Gray Elite foolish enough to be caught alone.

Raven didn't contribute to the talk. She kept her eyes on her stew, looking carefully at the chopped meat and roots. Rabbit, maybe?

One hundred years of war had taken its toll on Rhynwier, and the past fifteen years had only been worse. The Regent, Marco Dunel, had brought poverty to the countryside while building up life for the rich and powerful in Lenhala and making Gracita's people richer.

Rhynwier suffered while Gracita prospered.

Raven ate the entire bowl, though her stomach clenched. She handed her bowl back to the innkeeper, hoping the older woman wouldn't notice how badly her hands were shaking.

"How are you holding up, dear?" asked the innkeeper. She glanced at Raven's hands, then at her eyes.

"My nerves," Raven whispered—her stepmother had often complained of her nerves.

Zander joined another table, the one in the thick of the talking. Raven excused herself. She entered the hall as the room exploded into drunken laughter. Zander began to spew a joke of his own, his words slurring.

He hadn't drunk near enough to be drunk. Then, she realized, he was pretending.

Raven tiptoed to the far room in the hall, the room with an iron number three nailed to the wood. As good of a place as any to start. She slid a steel hairpin from her hair—pins that Brent had gifted her—and easily picked the lock. She slowly let herself inside, eyes watching the room and the hall; she did not want to explain herself should the room's occupant come around the corner.

She didn't see the box in any obvious places. She went through the pockets of the smelly overcoat, the small leather bag, and every conceivable hiding place in the room. No iron box. With every moment that passed, every burst of laughter from the main room, her heart beat faster.

She locked the door from the inside and slid back into the hall. She looked through the other three rooms, but she found no iron box. She did find coin, both silver Gracitan tokens and copper Rhynwierian marks. Her hand clasped around the coins, and she fought a slither of greed to take them.

No. She had seen the people in the town and the people passing through. She couldn't steal from them. They needed their money more than she did. Not even the book of plants she found in the last room. If she stole it, she wouldn't have anywhere to put it.

She found many things among the possessions but no iron box. By the time she slipped back into her and Zander's room, a bawdy song about a bar wench had most of the tavern singing along, and her heart pounded deafeningly loud.

When Zander finally returned to the room, his voice was hoarse from singing and shouting. He cleared his throat and looked at her expectantly.

She shook her head. "Nothing."

Zander let out a sigh. "Then our thief's not here. He's moved on, I'd bet."

"Then, I suppose that means we should as well," she said.

He nodded.

That night, just as the sun began to set, they set out south, toward the old highway. Zander traded a few things for rations and first aid supplies, making Raven wish she had taken a few in her pilfering.

"Stay safe in your travels," said the innkeeper. "I wish you luck. Watch out for Cage Birds and Goliaths."

"Remember," said the innkeeper's husband, "the Goliaths might look tough, but they can't swim."

Raven and Zander headed out into the summer night. They followed the dirt path into the woods. She wanted to know what a Goliath looked like, what it sounded like, but she and Zander moved too quickly to talk. The forest slowly changed, and she spotted more and more maples and fewer pines. In the dark, she spotted things moving through the underbrush: coyotes, deer, and who knew what else. She took a small relief in knowing that Zander could shoot a deer between the eyes at a hundred yards. She'd seen him do it.

Finally, they stopped beside a lake to eat and drink. The moonlight reflected off the surface of the water, broken into constantly moving slivers.

In the quiet, Raven found her chance.

"What is a Goliath?" Raven asked, breaking her dried venison in smaller, easier to chew chunks.

"It's an automaton shaped like a man, only taller and wider and meaner. They have empty chest cavities to store people inside, but they more often kill on sight," Zander said flatly, eyes on the dried meat in his hands. He glanced around as if one might appear. "They are one of many automatons the Gray Elite used during the war."

Zander stared out over the water. The moonlight made his sapphire eyes glitter and his hair appear black. A shadow of stubble darkened his jaw. Beautiful, if she had to put a word to it. Handsome, without a doubt, even if she'd never admit it to him. It would only make him more arrogant. He turned his glittering eyes to her, and her heart skipped a beat.

She looked out over the water. "What if we don't find our thief?" she whispered. She didn't need to speak very loud. Aside from the animals scurrying and bugs chittering, there was little noise. Crickets sang from the rushes alongside the lake, as did a chorus of frogs.

"We'll find him," he said, his voice hard.

"You're awfully confident about it." She tossed another chunk of venison into her mouth.

A soft sigh escaped his lips. "You'd rather give up and sulk back home? Raven, we have to find that box, and we will." A shadow of desperation darkened his tone.

She believed him, but a part of her thought him mad to worry so much over a box whose contents he didn't know. "Do you think our thief knows its value?" she asked.

"He would have to." Zander leaned back on his elbows and stared up at the starry sky. "Either he knows, or he's guessed. It would have taken a good thief to sneak into the mines and out again, and any good thief wouldn't have come all this way unless there's a significant payout waiting for him."

Raven tossed a bit of fat from her dried venison into the shallows of the lake. The moonlight rippled. "I wonder what could be inside that's so valuable." The mystery of it tingled at the back of her mind.

An owl hooted in a nearby tree.

Zander sighed. "I don't know. I do know it's something the Gray Elite would pay a fortune for. It's powerful, priceless, and rare."

She whispered, "Is it magic?"

He didn't answer. After a long moment, he stood. "Come on, we're wasting time."

She nodded, regardless of her doubts and questions. Chasing a thief through the wooded countryside of Rhynwier trumped mashing blackberries into preserves and scrubbing the same pots and pans every night.

They topped off their canteens under a small waterfall and set off through the moonlit forest. Through the canopy, Raven spotted the endless stars. She watched for the moving shadows of airships, but she saw none.

Raven and Zander came to the old highway just after sunrise. Before the war, before the Gray Elite seized control of the kingdom, the old highway had been a main artery of transportation. It weaved through the major towns, leading all to the capital of Lenhala. Raven looked up and down the road, but she saw no other travelers. Way ahead of them, she thought she saw dots of something moving, but she couldn't tell.

She and Zander started south. The forest had grown closer to the highway, shading it from the sun. The years without care had left the road cracked, faded, and in some parts, fallen in. Weeds and bushes and trees ate at the edge of the road, crumbling it.

The highway ran beside a wide river, where fishing boats leisurely graced the water. Villages spotted the bank, and each one had the same rundown homes and lopsided fences, children playing in the shallows, jumping and splashing. It reminded Raven of the river near Silver Glen where, in the warmest days of summer, they had swam as children.

The water was safe. Automatons could not get wet.

"Down south, where the river is widest," said Zander, "there is a city built over the water."

"Over the water? Is it floating? Like a ship?"

"No. It's built over the river like a bridge. Ships pass underneath it."

She tried to picture such a place, but it looked ridiculously impractical in her mind. "What keeps it from falling into the water?"

"I don't know, another marvel of the Gray Elite's craftsmanship and desire to prove themselves above the laws of man and nature," Zander said bitterly.

Raven didn't ask any more about the floating city. Instead, she asked, "Have you ever seen a sky city?"

"I have."

"Have you been on one?" Curiosity bubbled in her stomach.

"Yes."

She bit her lip. "What was it like?"

He glanced at her, and when he beheld her childlike wide eyes, he smiled. "It's like being on a ship, only once it's in the air, it doesn't come back down. It's always moving, and it feels like it too. The turbines are always going, and the noise they make is deafening. Sleep is hard to come by."

She glanced into the cloud-speckled sky as if one might appear on the horizon. An entire city in the sky. Her heart ached to see such a sight!

"You want to see one that badly?" he asked. He knew of her desire; she had told him once, months ago.

"I want to live in one."

Zander frowned. "They're more confining than the mines."

"But they never stay in one place," she said in awe. "It would be marvelous to go to sleep in one city and wake up in another. Every day an adventure."

"Most sky cities have a path they follow," Zander said. "And the ship goes where the captain deems, which is greatly influenced by where the city's baron wants them to go, which is greatly influenced by where the Gray Elite wants them to go. It's not the freedom you think it is."

She pouted. "You're marring my dream."

"I'm adding reality to your dream," he said. "Sky cities are where barons and admirals hide their friends. They're more clubs than communities."

"I still think it would be thrilling to live in the sky," she said.

He chuckled. "You're just sick of living underground."

She did not disagree with him. His truths about the sky cities did not dampen her spirits entirely, and she refused to let them.

By midday, they came to the next town. It sat beside the river and had a number of rickety wooden docks and the near-overwhelming smell of fish. Raven didn't mind the smell; her feet ached, and her stomach begged for something other than venison jerky and water. The inn sat beside a blacksmith, and the whole inn smelled of white-hot iron, sweat, and smoke.

Zander paid for their room with Gracitan tokens. He acted the same as he had before; he played the role of the pitiful traveler weary from an escape of Cage Birds. This innkeeper did not whisper of Goliaths. He glared at Zander, at the coin, at Raven, but he slid them a key to one of the rooms, which Zander accepted with gratitude.

"I'd keep an eye out if I were you," Zander whispered, locking the door. "I don't like that innkeeper. He's suspicious."

Raven nodded, though she felt too exhausted to care much what the innkeeper thought.

Again, their room had a single bed. Neither said a word as they shed their outer layers and crawled under the musty-smelling blanket. Outside their narrow window, hammers beat iron and steel into submission. Over and over and over.

They slept until midafternoon. They washed up in the small bathroom, ate muddy-tasting fish at the tavern next door, and that evening, while Zander rolled the locals into a drunken song, Raven went through the rooms at the inn. After searching each one, she returned to their room without an iron box, but with a few Gracitan tokens, healing ointment, bandages, and a bag of almonds. She had taken things they could use, not things they would have to barter with; she didn't want the owner of the stolen item to recognize it.

She tucked the stolen items into their packs and then sat down on the bed. It surprised her how easy taking the things had been. She had assumed she would feel guilt, but she didn't. She reasoned with herself that she hadn't taken anything that would ruin a person or starve a family; she had taken small things. Things a person might not miss.

Raven waited, but still the drunks in the tavern sang. The sun set, the crowd in the tavern filtered out into the night, and Zander didn't return.

She began to pace. Had something happened? Had someone recognized him as Gray Elite? Had that innkeeper ratted him out?

Her heart beat faster with every passing moment.

Finally, she heard Zander's drunken voice drift down the hall of the inn. A pair of boots scuffed and shuffled; another pair walked steadily.

"This is great," Zander slurred. "I haven't had so much fun. I shouldn't go back to the city." He hiccupped. "You country folk know how to live."

"Aye," said a male voice. "That we do. You'd be welcome here if you're thinking of staying. Talk to me in the morning. There's always work for able-bodied men."

It took a moment to place his voice—the innkeeper. He spoke softer than he had when they'd arrived.

"Weren't there more people here?" Zander hiccupped. "I remember more people."

"We get people coming and going on the highway," said the innkeeper. "Not as much as we used to, though."

"What 'bout that fellow with the braids? Reminds me—" *hiccup* "—of my little brother."

"Oh, that one left before dinner. Odd fellow. A bit shifty. You're better off without talking to that one," said the innkeeper. Keys jingled. "Ah, here we are."

The door swung open. The innkeeper shuffled through, supporting a drunk Zander.

Raven didn't have to pretend to gawk. Fury bubbled. She jumped to her feet, hands knotted in her skirt. "What happened?" she demanded.

"What d'ya mean 'what happened'?" Zander hiccupped.

The innkeeper helped him over the threshold and then let go. Zander teetered, and Raven dashed forward to catch him. He leaned fully onto her, hot breath on her neck, and she grunted as she supported his weight to the bed. They made it to the bed, and Zander flopped. The metal frame squeaked.

Zander let out a sigh. "I drank a little bit," he mumbled.

"A little bit too much," laughed the innkeeper.

"Thank you for bringing him back," Raven said, patting Zander affectionately, though she felt like smacking him. While she had been looking for the box, he'd been drinking. Really drinking. She let her hand rest between his shoulder blades. The heat from his body soaked into her hand.

The door closed, and the innkeeper headed down the hall.

Zander hiccupped and rolled onto his back.

Raven stood and hissed, "You're useless."

"Useless?" he whispered, slur gone. He propped himself up with his elbows. "I can hold my ale better than that, Rae. Find it?"

She blinked. His eyes were no longer watery or unfocused. He looked at her with the alert intensity he always had. Of course. Pretending. She felt foolish for believing his act.

She fisted her hands in her skirt. "No."

She didn't tell him about the other things she'd taken. He would find out when he opened his pack; then she would explain.

Zander swung his legs to the floor. "Then, I'm willing to bet our thief left right after dinner."

She opened her mouth to question him, then realized. "The man you asked the innkeeper about."

He nodded. "I saw him at the last stop too. He's traveling alone and light."

She blinked, disbelieving that Zander could be that crafty. "And he's on the move," she said. "So, we'll be on the move. Good thing I've readied the packs."

Zander grabbed his jacket from the hook on the wall. "Right. We leave immediately."

"But you're drunk," she said. "Won't that look suspicious if you leave sober?"

"Drunk men make horrible decisions every night." Zander buttoned his jacket unevenly, slid his pack over his shoulders, and then sauntered with all the grace of a drunk man.

Raven grabbed her own pack. *Pretending.*

Zander had been right; though the innkeeper looked at him with heavy disapproval, he didn't force him to stay another night and sleep off the ale. He simply shook his head at Zander and gave a nod of sympathy to Raven.

As they left, she heard him mumble, "Poor woman. I'd hate to deal with that drunken bastard."

She let the door close behind her and followed Zander into the cloudy night with a smile on her face. She knew Zander had heard the innkeeper too.

They traveled through the night and into the morning. The stars faded one by one. The eastern horizon glowed blue-gray, then pink, then orange; then the golden-yellow sunlight spilled over the tops of the trees, burning away the pockets of lingering fog and dew. From a high point, she could see for miles. Villages and farms dotted the countryside, connected with dirt roads and circled with boundary fences.

They passed a field of golden wheat where automaton Harvesters worked. With scythes for hands and chests made for storing, the machines worked faster than humans could. Their bodies were silver against the golden wheat, their movements identical and monotonous. Steam hissed out at uneven intervals.

Raven stared—she had only ever heard of Harvesters.

"Another marvel of the Gray Elite," murmured Zander with distaste. "One Harvester replaces ten workers, and that's ten workers without a job and ten families without money or food."

She hadn't thought of that. Her marvel turned sour. Indeed, she didn't see a single human worker in the fields.

They continued on, skirting villages and fields in case humans or automatons spotted them. They kept to the forest paths that paralleled the highway when they needed, avoiding clumps of people and towns that sat on the highway. Zander explained that the towns that supplied better things for the Gray Elite received better supplies in turn.

"So the towns here have more incentive to turn in refugees," he whispered.

Still, they walked.

The sun neared the midpoint in the sky.

"My feet are killing me," Raven complained. They didn't hurt that bad, but she only wanted to take a short break. To rest, to breathe, to let the sweat along her spine dry.

"We're running out of time as it is," Zander said, though exhaustion underlined his eyes and snapped in his words.

Slowly, the sun reached the midpoint and started an impossibly slow slide to the west. Raven couldn't stand it anymore. Her stomach was grumbling, and her feet really did hurt.

"I'm exhausted," she said. "If we don't stop soon, I'm going to pass out in the middle of the road."

Zander growled and spat an insult under his breath. The next town they came to was larger than the others; several hundred people called it home. The lingering scent of freshly tilled fields tickled her nose as Zander led her to a shady inn off the main street, down a narrow side road with barely enough room for two people to walk side by side.

Raven hesitated outside the inn's lopsided, weathered, and discolored front door. It looked to have once been painted white, but the paint had streaked and peeled and flaked.

Zander rolled his eyes. "What? I thought you were tired," he growled.

"Yes, but, are you sure about this place?" She eyed a spiderweb in the corner of the roof. A fat spider sat waiting.

"Yes." He entered the inn without another word.

Raven hesitated but followed. She kept her eyes on the spider—she feared that if she took her eyes off him, he wouldn't be there when she looked back. The inn looked as questionable on the inside as it had on the outside. Smoke lingered against the ceiling, blown from a group of men with wood-and-copper pipes in their mouths. An odd smell lingered, sweet and warm and bitter all at once. Raven tried to place the smell, but she couldn't.

Zander approached the innkeeper, a hunched man with narrow, suspicious eyes. He took the silver token without question and handed them a bent room key. Zander dragged her to their room and quickly shut them inside. The room didn't look like it had been cleaned. The linens were stained, the floors needed sweeping, and instead of a bathroom, it had a water basin in the corner. A moth-eaten curtain the color of mildew hung against the wall, the only privacy for someone using the water basin. That strange smell lingered in the room, like it came from the very wood.

"It's disgusting," Raven said. "I think I'd rather sleep outside."

"If you were a thief, where would you stay?" Zander said. Exhaustion nipped at his words. He dropped his pack to the floor. "A thief trying to keep a low profile wouldn't stay at a decent inn. He'd go to one like this."

Zander pushed aside the ratty curtain over the window, the sunlight illuminating a strip down the middle of his face, and then he let the curtain flutter back into place. Dust swam through the dim air like snow.

She shrugged off her pack and set it by his. Sisters, how her shoulders ached. "What's that smell?" she asked, sniffing. "It's like sweet cloves and mint."

He half laughed. "Don't breathe it in too deep. That's opium."

She blinked. She'd only heard of the drug, but she'd never smelled it. She took another quick sniff of the air. "It smells like winter candy."

"It's laced with—" he stepped closer and dropped his voice "—magic."

Her heart thumped at the word.

"Oh," she said. Did that make it better? Worse?

"The men downstairs were smoking it, and I'm willing to bet the tavern next door is a den." Zander glanced again out the window. "And, if I had extra coin and a betting attitude, I would bet that our thief will stop by before he goes."

She tensed. "You want to visit an opium den?" A magic-opium den.

"They're illegal," he said. "So people who have no problem with illegal activities often visit them. Thieves, criminals, magicians. You can find them all in an opium den."

Her heart leaped. "Magicians?" she whispered.

He nodded. "With magic being illegal, the magicians left have had to find other ways to make a living. They can't exactly be farmers or fisherman. The automatons would find them," he whispered. He shot her a sideways glance.

She put the thoughts together. "They become criminals?"

"Drug dealers, back-alley healers, problem solvers," he said casually, waving his hand between them. He smirked, though his exhaustion pulled the humor from his eyes. "Consider it a lesson on culture."

They slept into the late afternoon, ate at the tavern, and after a few seedy conversations, Zander got them access to the opium den next door. There were no doors from the street. The only way in or out was through a secret door in the tavern, guarded by a man sitting on a barrel. He wore a dark cap low over his eyes, and at first glance, he looked asleep. But as Raven and Zander approached him, his dark, beady eyes took them in faster than she could blink.

The opium den was darkly lit and not much bigger than the tavern. Mismatched tables and chairs scattered the mezzanine and the sides of the main floor. A few dozen people lingered about the den, some inhaling from bowls, some smoking pipes. Most wore ratty clothes or dark cloaks; none looked like upstanding citizens. Their calm chatter resounded like the chittering of evening bugs, constant and natural.

Three lanterns hung from the ceiling and gave off a pale lilac light. Metal bowls of burning opium were scattered around the room, each producing a different color of smoke; the streams of smoke slithered up to the ceiling and mingled without mixing, creating an ever-moving rainbow. It hid the ceiling, and Raven had the strangest urge to drag her fingers along the smoke, but she withheld her urge and kept her arms at her sides.

The den smelled like cloves and mint, and underneath it, she detected a scent she could not identify. *Magic*, she whispered to herself. Magic smoke. What would happen if she touched it?

Zander ordered them drinks, and Raven tried her best not to cringe when the cheap ale touched her tongue. They took seats on the mezzanine, not too close to any opium smoke, and Zander joined a table of cards. Raven lingered beside him, sitting close enough that their hips touched. She pretended to be interested in his gambling and his easy talk with the others, but her eyes wandered. Her imagination went with them.

She spotted scantily clad women and men who wore vests with nothing under them and easy smiles on their faces. She spotted scrawny thugs and big thugs, beady eyes and watchful eyes. Could one of them be their thief? How many of these people were magicians forced into a life of crime?

In her mind, she invented magician criminals who thrived in the underbelly of the kingdom, breaking laws and serving their own kind of justice for the right price.

While Zander gambled and talked, a band appeared down below. They set up on a little stage and carried strange instruments of brass and strings and an assortment of drums. They began to play a haunting, somber tune; her eyes drifted to the smoking bowls, whose streams seemed to undulate with the music.

Were there more bowls than before? She didn't remember seeing the pink smoke or the pale blue or the sunrise orange—so many colors!

Her eyes met those of a blonde girl across the mezzanine. She sat on a man's lap with his arm draped over her thighs. The girl winked at Raven, and Raven winked back. She didn't see the harm in it.

She took another sip of her ale. It wasn't so bad after the first sip or two. She could barely feel the burn of it.

There *were* more bowls—the smoke rose thick in plumes of purple, pink, blue, orange, and red. It rose up and up, ever-changing, swirling, colliding into new colors she had never seen before nor imagined.

Zander was laughing, a low and steady sound. It reverberated in her chest, down her ribs, and into her hips. The drums were beating low. People danced on the main floor, over and under and all around. They looked to be having so much fun. She wanted to have fun too. Why shouldn't she be allowed to have fun? A flash of yellow caught her eye, and she met the golden eyes of the blonde on the other side of the mezzanine.

The brassy instruments began to play a rhythmic chime like she'd never heard, and those strings pulled her to the first floor. She joined the other dancers, clustered together, all dancing as one. The blonde girl from across the mezzanine joined her and wrapped her slender arms around Raven's waist.

The drums beat, the strings chimed, and Raven felt the music pulse through her veins just as the smoke filtered through her lungs. It made everything better. With the bodies clustered so close together, she felt the life beating around her. All hot skin, loose hair, colored smoke, and the beat.

The blonde tipped her mouth to Raven's ear, and her warm breath mumbled something that pushed a laugh from Raven's throat. The blonde smiled at her and pulled Raven closer.

Raven didn't know when Zander had arrived, only that he had. He pushed himself between her and the fun blonde, who vanished into the dancing crowd. Zander brushed Raven's hair away from her ear and spoke low, hot words; his breath tickled against her skin.

Whatever she told him hadn't been his desired answer, and his grip on her shoulders tightened. She tried to pull him into a dance, but he didn't budge. Why did he have to be such a stick-in-the-mud? He said something, but she couldn't hear him over the beat. She tried again to dance with him, but he pulled her flush against him and then pulled her off the dancefloor, away from the crowd. She stumbled, but he held her upright.

The smoke thinned, the music quieted, and then cool night air met her sweaty skin. She could still feel the beating of the drums in her blood.

Zander grumbled.

Raven caught sight of the stars; they were dancing, throwing themselves about the inky sky, and watching them, she fell backward into Zander's chest.

"Look!" She pointed to the dancing stars. "They're dancing too."

"I shouldn't have let you out of my sight," Zander growled. He sounded tired, why did he have to be tired? They could have danced all night.

She wobbled, but Zander's hands on her waist guided her forward, into the inn and into their room. His grip loosened, and she twirled to face him. A dizzy spell overtook her, and she latched her fists in Zander's vest to keep upright.

"Don't you puke on me," he warned.

She laughed, and the dizziness passed. Sisters, had he always been this handsome? Giggling, she ran a hand along his unshaven jaw, her fingertips over his lips. She caught his hot exhale on her fingers. She grabbed his shirt collar and brought those lips down to her own.

His hands on her waist twitched, then he pushed her away from him. She stumbled back and fell onto the bed. Zander stood above her, predatory gaze looking down at her. That gaze stirred the heat surging underneath her skin.

"Go to sleep," he growled.

"But I'm not tired." She tugged off her boots and started to pull at the ties of her corset. She yanked it off and tossed it over her boots. Dust whooshed from the floor. "You don't want to sleep either."

"Oh, I don't?"

"You want to have fun, don't you?" she asked, reaching for the laces on her dress.

Zander's eyes followed her hands.

"You love fun!" She worked the laces loose, to the bottom of her breast bone.

Zander's eyes widened.

He grabbed her wrists; his fingers brushed the material of her dress. Heat from his skin seeped through as easily as water. "Don't."

"Why not? I thought you wanted to? Aren't you always bragging about how talented you are with girls?" She tried again to pull at the laces, but Zander held her hands firmly. "Come on, Zander," she purred. "Show me."

He didn't answer. With a rough tug and a push, he tossed her to the other side of the bed. He growled, "Go to sleep."

She landed on the pillow, his pillow, that smelled of him. She hugged it to her face to smell it better. Oh, how soft! Had it always been so soft? Then, she couldn't let it go. Her limbs became unresponsive, and her mind shut down.

Raven woke with a pounding headache. She blinked several times before the world came into focus. She slept on her stomach. Zander slept on his back beside her. Zander inhaled like he might wake, but his eyes remained closed.

Why did her head hurt so much? She rolled onto her back and put her hands to her temples, and then the night before came speeding back at her with merciless guilt and shame.

The magic-opium den. The blonde. Zander.

Sisters, she'd tried to undress in front of him. She'd tried to seduce him. She'd *kissed* him.

Please, let it be a dream, she begged. *A horrible smoke dream, a fever dream, anything!*

But as she lay there, she knew it had been her own hands, her own mouth, her own want powering her ludicrous actions. But Zander had stopped her. He had grabbed her hands before she completely embarrassed herself. He hadn't jumped on her offer like she thought he would. He'd declined it, said no.

Face burning with embarrassment, she rolled onto her other side, away from him.

He had shoved her away last night, twice. He had been appalled, disgusted, and furious. She'd heard it in his voice. Why shouldn't he be? He had lived in the capital. He had met far more attractive and appealing girls than her, with refined manners and educations and gowns of silk and velvet and whatever else. She was the backwater girl, stupid enough to fall for the magic-opium. Plain. Forgettable. Useless.

Zander inhaled again; this time, his breathing changed. She heard the subtle shift of the pillow. She felt his stare on the back of her head, but she refused to acknowledge it. Zander shifted again. He got out of bed. His socked footsteps walked across the wooden floor, then stopped. With a twist of a creaky knob, water sputtered into the basin. The curtain swished along the track.

Raven rolled onto her back; Zander had shut himself behind the curtain. Sighing, she sat up and hugged her knees to her chest. Her head pounded like nothing else. She rested her forehead against her knees. The world tilted slightly around her, churning her stomach in unfriendly ways. She squeezed her eyes shut and sat like that until Zander pulled back the curtain.

"Wash up," he spat. He headed to the door. "We leave immediately."

He shut the door a little too hard. The sound thudded against her skull.

Great. Not only did she feel sick, Zander was mad. She couldn't blame him; she was mad at herself for letting the smoke get to her too. Mad and embarrassed that Zander had witnessed the whole thing.

Raven carefully peeled herself out of bed and washed her hands and face in the freezing water. She readied her pack and met Zander downstairs. He was leaning against the wall, glaring at the main door. He handed her a biscuit and then left the inn without another word. She followed, the biscuit feeling like sand in her mouth.

The sun had risen, and the world was slowly waking up. Bakeries were opening windows to let out the steam and the favorable aromas of their ovens to entice customers. Women and children flocked to the water pumps, buckets and pitchers in hand.

Zander didn't speak again until they'd left the little town behind.

"We lost a night of travel," he said. *Thanks to you*, is what he didn't add. He didn't need to. She hadn't gone through the other rooms either. Had Zander?

All around them, birds chittered away. Each tweet felt like a nail being driven into her skull. "Well, you could have warned me," Raven said in her defense. Or that it would feel like her brain was melting the next morning.

He spat, "I didn't realize you'd never encountered opium smoke."

"In Silver Glen?" She half laughed, and the shake of her lungs radiated into her head.

He huffed. "It wasn't entirely your fault. That girl you were dancing with, the blonde, she's what they call a Trance. She had you under her spell too."

A magician? Raven barely could remember the girl's face. She remembered her hair, bright yellow-gold.

"Trances work their magic to put people in trances, like their name suggests. They can then do with them whatever they want, sell them to brothels, rape and rob them, whatever," Zander said bitterly. "You're lucky I spotted you in time, or you might be halfway to a brothel by now."

She gripped the leather strap of her bag. Shame warmed her cheeks, but luckily, Zander walked in front of her. "I'm sorry," she mumbled.

Zander growled in annoyance. "Just pick up the pace. We don't have time to lose."

They returned to the highway. They didn't speak to one another until the sun had risen to the center of the sky, shortening shadows to puddles and lifting the temperature into a slightly uncomfortable warmth. Raven tugged at the collar of her dress and undid the top button. It helped but only slightly. The river rushed; she longed to strip herself of her cumbersome clothes and jump into the water, like they'd done as children. But the idea of Zander seeing her naked burned through her skin worse than the sun.

"Stop," warned Zander.

She tore her eyes from the glistening river. Zander had slowed his pace. It didn't take her but a moment to find out why. Up ahead, a monstrous automaton of dark bronze and steel stood on the roadside, checking the few travelers along the road. The automaton stood twice as tall as a man, its arms and legs jointed for elbows and knees, and steam hissed out at regular intervals from its thick neck. A man walking beside a donkey-pulled wagon loaded with barrels shrank from the automaton's red eyes. It watched the man pass.

"It's a Detector," Zander whispered. "It's looking for someone."

Her skin felt clammy, and the sweat turned cold. She whispered, "Who?"

Zander eyed the Detector warily. "I'd rather not find out. Let's avoid it. This way," he said, motioning her to the roadside.

They left the highway as the Detector turned its red-eyed gaze down the road toward them. They entered the safety of the forest and walked quickly, leaving the highway and the Detector behind. Zander guided her through the thickets and over tangled tree roots. Raven hadn't missed navigating through the brambles and bushes. Their quick scramble from the Detector tore her skirt in several places.

He guided them south, past the Detector, where they would walk parallel to the highway in the shallows of the forest.

"Was it looking for you?" she asked, fiddling with a large tear at her thigh. Luckily, the thorn hadn't reached her skin.

"I don't know," Zander said, but the hitch in his voice said otherwise. "I don't want to give it a reason to question us. The Detectors aren't regular automatons. They can detect faces."

Detect *faces*? Raven did not like the sound of that. "Do you think they would have recognized you?"

"Like I said, I'd rather not find out."

"I thought you were somebody in the capital," she taunted. "I thought you were one of the Gray Elite?"

"Who's been missing for six months. I'd rather not call attention to myself. That would call attention to where I've been, what I've been doing, and why I left."

And draw attention to that which he had been tasked with hiding. It made sense, although his answers seemed dodgy.

They were crossing over a dense trap of tree roots when Zander suddenly stopped. Raven nearly walked into him.

"What?" she spat.

He held up his hand to shush her. The predator's gaze returned to his face, and he scanned the forest before him.

Rolling her eyes, she turned to scan the direction he couldn't readily see. She saw the forest, sunlight through the shifting leaves, and then she noticed. The birds had gone silent. The bugs had too. The summer forest had gone deathly, unnaturally silent. She looked harder and listened.

There, through the rustling wind, she heard the clomping of metal feet, the clunking of gears inside a mechanical body, and the hissing of steam.

Her heart skipped a beat. In her mind, she pictured the Cage Bird, but the Cage Bird hummed. Whatever approached them walked—or stomped, rather—through the forest. Could it be another Detector?

Zander slowly pulled Birdie from the holster. He stepped closer to the thick tree, and she mimicked his stance. The tree hid them, but it narrowed her line of view too.

Cautiously, she started to climb the tree. Zander spat a whispered warning, but she ignored him. She climbed into the branches, high enough to see for a considerable distance. She spotted brass-colored movement, clomping through the trees, maybe a hundred yards away. The automaton walked on two legs. Four arms sprouted from its thick torso, and a monstrous, squat head sat upon its bulky shoulders. Red eyes scanned the forest before it.

"Goliath," Zander whispered from below.

Raven swallowed; the name fit the contraption. It stood twelve feet fall and thrice as thick as a large man. Its legs stomped through the underbrush, crushing roots, tearing weeds, and snapping saplings without faltering. It ripped through the thick roots of an oak, and at the ripping of the green wood, Raven felt her mouth go dry.

What could those feet and arms do to human flesh and bone?

"Move," warned Zander. "Slowly. It hasn't seen us."

She climbed down as quietly as she could. They made their way around the tree, heading the opposite direction of the Goliath. It stomped on, and they crept around it. Raven took the lead with Zander a step behind. He held Birdie, ready to defend.

Raven heaved a breath as she stepped around a thick three—and right into the path of a second Goliath.

The beam of its eyes found her and glared bright red, nearly blinding her, and all at once, steam hissed from its shoulders and hips, gears thrust into one another, and the machine came to life. It had been waiting, she thought with horror. The Goliath's four arms rose, each ending with three-pronged claws. The metal prongs twisted and clicked together.

"Stay where you are," said the harsh mechanical voice of the Goliath.

"Run!" screamed Zander.

Raven threw herself out of the way of its massive arms. She hit the forest floor as the hands came together where she had been standing. A bullet zinged off the metal, but the Goliath didn't stop. She staggered to her feet in time to see it stomping toward her, the bullets from Birdie bouncing off its metal hull with high-pitched dings.

"Raven, go!" Zander shouted at her.

The other Goliath ran toward them, red eyes coloring the forest in blood, each footfall an earthquake. Zander drew his unnamed gun and fired at the incoming Goliath. The bullets bounced off the hull. One found purchase with a crack of metal, but the machine didn't stop.

"Zander!" Raven cried.

"*Go!*" he shouted.

One of the Goliaths started toward her, and she hoisted her skirts and started to run as fast as she could. She heard Zander do the same. She dodged trees, jumped over roots, and the Goliath ran after her, shaking the ground as it ran, too close for comfort. Nothing stopped the machine—it stomped through the bushes and knocked down saplings; it moved around the larger trees with stomach-flipping ease.

Its mechanical voice said, "Stay where you are. Do not resist."

Raven ran, ran, ran. Her side ached, and her breath turned ragged. She ran toward the sound of gushing water. Automatons hated water. The trees thinned, and she came to an old mill; a stone bridge arched over a wide river, where a similar mill sat on the other side. The Goliath stomped behind her, repeating, "Stay where you are. Do not resist."

Raven ran across the bridge. Halfway across, her boot caught on a loose stone. She fell and scrambled to her feet. Panting, her side aching to split open, sweat turning her clothes damp, she turned to see the Goliath; it stood on the bank, its metal feet an inch from the bridge's stone.

It can't cross, Raven thought hopefully.

And then, to her disappointment, the Goliath stepped onto the bridge.

She glanced down at the river. *The Goliaths might look tough, but they can't swim.* The Goliath was gaining with every heartbeat, its feet thundering on the old stones. As it reached the incline, the old stones began to crack and crumble under its weight.

She started toward the opposite bank, the bridge shuddering under her steps. She didn't make it. The bridge lurched downward with a vicious *crack*—the age-old mortar giving, the stone cracking apart. The lurch sent Raven careening into the stone railing.

Below, the water gushed at a good speed, but not too fast as to drown her.

The Goliath came closer. Its arms extended, steam hissed as the panels of its chest cavity began to open, and its hands turned to scoop her inside.

What choice did she have?

"Stay where you are. Do not resist."

As the bridge cracked underneath the Goliath's weight, Raven jumped into the river.

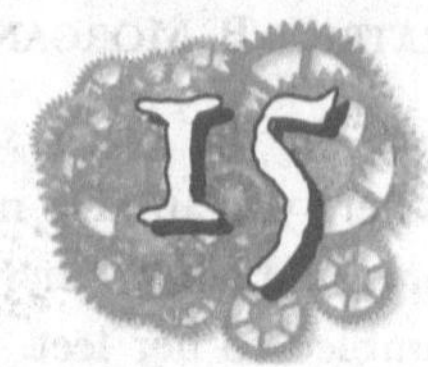

The cool water surged through her clothes, her nose, her mouth, her hair; it tugged her along faster than she had anticipated. The bridge collapsed, sending stones and the Goliath into the water below. The Goliath struggled, its voice a waterlogged croak, its steam chambers drowning, its gears gurgling. One of its eyes flickered out.

She fought to stay afloat, and soon, she stopped caring about the submerging Goliath and started to worry about her own survival. She tried to swim to the shore, but the water tugged her back in, under, and sideways. She heard the water gushing around her, but soon, that gush turned into a roar. A crashing roar that made her heart sink further into her soaked boots.

Raven found an old tree lost in the river and latched onto one of the thicker branches, scraping her arms against it, tearing through the sleeves of her dress. The Goliath approached, fixed its remaining red eye on her, and clamped onto the tree branch she held. The dead branch snapped, sending her and the Goliath back into the river's current.

The Goliath's metal hand clamped down on her arm, pulling her closer. Her already frightful panic turned white-hot. She twisted her feet up and slammed her heels into the automaton's chest with all the force she could muster. A shock zapped through her feet, up her legs, and into her hips, but her arm slipped out of the Goliath's grip, and she pushed herself out of its easy reach.

She and the Goliath surged downriver. The rushing came closer, fast.

A waterfall. She hadn't been able to see it from the bridge. As it neared, as the rushing and crashing water grew deafening, she knew she would not make it over. In her adventure books, waterfalls always ended in rocks, sharpened by water to deadly points.

She didn't have time to panic, time to wonder—over the falls they went.

Her descent ended nearly as quickly as it began; her back slammed into solid stone, knocking out what little breath she had left. Down below, a crash echoed above the roaring waters.

The automaton.

Water splattered her face, and she lifted a hand to shield herself from it. She had only fallen a few feet. Gasping for the breath she had lost, she turned onto her shaking hands and knees.

"Sisters," she gasped.

She had landed on a stone lip that jutted out from the waterfall at an upward angle, dividing the water without being submerged. Had she reached the falls anywhere else, she would have plummeted.

Cautiously, with limp fingers, she looked over the edge of the lip. The Goliath had fallen a considerable height, and pieces of it continued to float downriver. The majority of the automaton had been speared on a sharp rock, one of many that lined the bottom of the falls. Raven flattened herself against the stone. That could have been her. Should have been... She shook that thought and pushed it away. Not now.

Raven looked to either side. There was no way off the rock but to jump down, and that would be a death sentence. She couldn't go back up either.

Stuck. She might as well have fallen.

"Looks like you're stuck," came a girlish voice from behind her, shouting over the falls.

Raven started and whipped her head around. Behind her, standing halfway through the falls, was a head. Goggles blurred the eyes, and flaxen hair was plastered to the head.

The flaxen-haired stranger gave her a wide smile. "Come on this way. It's easier than going down."

The head vanished through the waterfall. Heart pounding, Raven inched her way to where the head had gone. She shut her eyes and crawled through the waterfall. To her amazement, she crawled through the water and found herself in a space large enough to stand up in. The sunlight filtered through the waterfall and lit the space in constantly moving shades of blue and silver.

The goggled girl stood waiting for her, no older than sixteen. She wore clothes fit for adventure; boots tucked with daggers, close-fitting trousers, a belt packed with daggers, tiny glass vials, and a canteen. She wrung water out of her shoulder-length hair.

Raven stood on shaky legs. "Thank you," she said over the roar of the falls.

The girl motioned for Raven to follow and started down the passage. Some of the rocks looked natural, but others looked to have been carved. Raven glanced over her shoulder; the passage connected the two banks. A secret, man-made tunnel.

They walked through and came out on a grassy patch a short distance from the waterfall.

"You're lucky to have landed there," said the girl. "I've seen what happens when someone goes over the falls. It's not pretty."

"Like the Goliath," Raven added.

The girl nodded. "Exactly, only much messier." She stuck out her gloved hand. The leather had scratches and nicks. "I'm Ivy, by the way."

"Raven." She shook the girl's hand. She had a surprising grip, or maybe Raven's hands shook too much.

"What are you doing out this far, Raven?" Ivy wiggled the goggles off her hazel eyes and looked Raven over. Freckles dotted her nose and cheekbones. "You lost?"

"I am now," Raven said. "I ran from the Goliath and ended up in the river."

"You mean you jumped to get away from it," Ivy corrected with a smile. She winked. "I saw you jump in. Smart move, considering it wouldn't have been worth a damn in the water, but dumb, considering you were so close to the falls. I saw it grab you. Normally, those things grab and don't let go, but the water saved you there."

"I was thinking about surviving the Goliath, not the falls," Raven said, her cheeks heating.

Ivy nodded, glancing toward the falls where the machine had met its end. The girl didn't look like Gray Elite or a threat, but could she be trusted? What other choice was there?

"Understandable," said Ivy. She set her hands on her hips and studied Raven. "But what are you doing out this far? You don't look like you belong out here. No offense, but..." Ivy gestured to Raven's soaked and tattered dress.

She decided to use Zander's sympathy card and said meekly, "We were...on the highway. We went into the forest, and the Goliaths found us."

"Us?" Ivy raised a brow.

Raven's heart squeezed. She nodded.

Ivy hummed and put her gloved hand to her chin. "Well, no one else went over the falls, and I didn't see anyone else. But, that's not saying your other half won't show up."

Raven's face burned at the wording. She started to correct Ivy but didn't. She and Zander *were* supposed to be lovers.

"Come on, Raven," Ivy said. She started up a beaten path that lead up to the top of the falls. "Your other half might be in trouble. Regardless, you'll need something dry, or your feet will start growing stuff."

Suddenly, her wet toes felt vulnerable.

She followed Ivy up the incline. They didn't go back to the mill. Instead, Ivy took her along a nearly invisible path through the forest. They walked and walked, and Raven's feet squished with every step. Ivy's hair dried into buttery blonde, wavy and dirty from the waterfall.

The trees grew thicker and thicker until some of the trunks had grown into one another, creating a monstrous tree whose branches twisted in every direction. The further they walked, the more ingrown trees she saw, until she saw nothing but them and the path wound between them.

"Here we are," Ivy said. They came to a twisted trunk with knots all along its bark. Ivy fingered a few of the knots, then pushed the one in the center. A trunk beside them opened with a hiss, revealing a wooden ladder inside a metal chute.

Ivy started up, and Raven staggered behind; her wet shoes slipped on the rungs. At the top, Ivy pushed open a wooden hatch, and sunlight spilled into the space.

"Hey, I brought a new friend back with me," said Ivy cheerfully as she crawled through the hatch.

"What?" came a male voice.

Raven neared the hatch, but before she could crawl out, a hand fastened around her upper arm. The grabber pulled her up and out, and her feet landed on solid flooring. Blinking, she saw the grabber—a large man in his thirties, brown-black beard and watery green eyes. He did not look happy to see her.

"You working for the Elite?" he demanded.

Raven blinked. "No."

He studied her, his piercing eyes looking deep into hers. He leaned away, arms crossed over his barrel chest.

"You a spy?" he asked.

"No," Raven answered, shaking her head.

"You a magician?"

Her heart thumped at the word. "No."

"Oh, don't be mean, Tay." Ivy stepped around the larger man. "She ran from a Goliath, got lost, fell in a river, and then almost went over the falls. I think she's earned a dry pair of boots and a snack or, at least, a place to nap while her boots dry out."

Tay glared daggers at Ivy, but he released Raven's arm. "Fine. But she's your charge, Ivy. You bring the strays home, you keep them in line. If she's led those machines to our doorstep, it's your fault."

"Noted," said Ivy, though she didn't sound worried.

Raven blinked and took stock of her surroundings. They'd climbed into a treehouse whose roof comprised of leafy branches woven so close together, they appeared solid; only small bluebirds and sunlight came through. The walls were wooden planks, metal sheets, and woven cloth and reeds, as were the floors.

Ivy slung her arm through Raven's and led her through the main room and down a hallway with an arched ceiling of tightly twisted tree branches. The ground gradually rose and fell, like they had built the floor from tree to tree. Ivy brought Raven into a hallway with a series of rooms with doors of multicolored cloth. "This is a guest room," Ivy said.

Raven wandered inside and sat down on a wicker chair.

"Yours for right now. I'll get you something dry to wear and something to eat. Then, we can find your other half."

The panic of the Goliath attack brought Raven to her feet again. "I have to find Zander." What if the Goliath had taken him? What if the Detector had found him?

"Zander?" Ivy blinked. Her brow furrowed.

"He's the guy I was traveling with. The Goliaths split us up."

Ivy leaned against the doorway, eyes looking at something far away. She blinked and asked, "What does he look like?"

Raven began to describe him, his dark hair, his blue eyes, his bronze skin, his lean and muscular build, his height and weight, his arrogant smirk and attitude. Ivy listened, eyes focused on the wall. She gently tugged her leather gloves off and tucked them into her back pocket.

When Raven had finished, Ivy said casually, "Don't worry about him. If he's out there, we'll find him. No one knows these woods like we do."

"Who are you?" Raven hadn't intended for it to come out so bluntly, but Ivy didn't balk.

"We've been called Forest People, but we call ourselves the Dwellers," Ivy said proudly. "Now, you need to get out of those wet clothes. I'll be right back with something dry. And I've got to tell Niall that there's a Goliath out there to be salvaged before the river takes it away."

With that, Ivy vanished back through the maze of tree branches. Raven sat down and removed her wet boots and socks. A bluebird chirped in the canopy, its black eyes flickering down at Raven.

Her stepmother's warnings about birds came to mind, but Raven shoved them aside. She unlaced her corset's slippery strings and dropped it to the floor. The thud frightened away the bluebird, and it fluttered away to find a quieter branch to sit on.

Raven unbuttoned her dress and let it flop onto the floor. The sun shining through the canopy warmed her bare, chilled skin like a blanket by the fire, and she relished the feeling. She pulled her wet chemise off her skin to stand fully in the sun. She rebraided her hair up into a bun to keep it off her neck.

By the time Ivy brought back a fresh set of clothes, Raven had nearly dried. She gladly dressed in the blousy shirt and close-fitting pants. Ivy brought her an old corset with new strings. It was shorter than her other and smelled vaguely of musty autumn leaves. It contained less boning, allowing her a wider range of movement. She liked the dark blue and handsome brass grommets.

Raven tucked her dagger through the loops on her pants. Ivy provided her a pair of slip-on shoes.

"Looks like it fits you well enough," said Ivy, eyeballing Raven's new clothes with a serious eye.

"It feels easier than a dress," Raven said, twirling in place and admiring the snug fit of the trousers. Moving through the forest would have been so much easier in pants.

Ivy nodded. "I've never been one for dresses myself. Too much weighty fabric going all over the place, getting caught on chair legs and bushes and tripping me."

"It's all I've worn," Raven told Ivy. She glanced at her soggy, discarded dress. The jaunt through the forest had cut and shredded the material and left the hem a tattered mess. Rags. "My father believes in tradition." As did the rest of the Silver Glen, but she kept that admission to herself.

Ivy shrugged then set her hands on her hips. "That's how the cities are too. Boring and stuffy. I prefer it out here in the wild. It's free."

That meant Ivy had been to the cities. Before Raven could ask, Ivy pulled her back into the hall. She followed Ivy through the Dwellers' camp and into what looked like a mess hall with mismatched wooden tables and chairs. A few of the chairs had legs made of tree branches—some still had bark on them. Ivy scrounged up a quick meal of nuts, berries, and a dried meat Raven didn't ask about.

"I sent for Niall and passed word along about your missing boy," Ivy said, gesturing to the open door of the mess hall.

"Did I hear my name?" asked a young man of eighteen or nineteen. He had tan skin and intelligent brown eyes; his shoulder-length hair had been braided and tied back in a thick bundle. He spoke fluently, his voice smooth and calm. A streak of grease ran along one cheekbone. His eyes fell on Raven, and he gave her a small but friendly smile.

"You did," Ivy said. "Raven, this is Niall, the best mechanic and tinker this side of the Himata River. Niall, this is Raven. I found her in the woods after she and a Goliath nearly went over the falls."

Niall chuckled, a soft sound. "Did she now?"

Niall sat at the table, and while Raven ate, Ivy told him about the Goliath and the falls. Niall listened patiently, his face schooled into calmness. When Ivy finished, he leaned back—his gaze turned to one of calculation and excitement.

"Sounds like a job for the Extractor," said Niall.

Raven didn't ask, and Ivy didn't provide an explanation; it sounded like a machine. After she ate, she followed Ivy and Niall to a lower section of the treehouse, one that looked less organic that the others. Wooden walls, floors, and ceilings had been hammered together with iron nails. The low lighting and musty smell told Raven they had gone underground. A cave.

It felt oddly familiar.

The narrow wooden walkway opened up to a cave, one with a mouth shaded by hanging moss and ivy. The sunlight slipped through in a misty green-gray. Within the cave, several machines lined the walls, their steam vents and engines quiet. A dock, she realized.

Niall walked over to one of the machines, a squat machine with a thick chest. The Extractor. One hand was pronged; the other was a drill. From the design of the arms, it looked like several more hands were hidden inside it, ready to be changed for whatever Niall needed. He climbed into the open driver's seat, and Ivy and Raven climbed in behind him, resting in the tight quarters, their legs stretched out on either side of his seat.

With the pulling of a few levers, the Extractor rumbled to life. The limbs shuddered, steam hissed through the pipes and vents, and with Niall's gentle touch at the controls, the Extractor took a step toward the moss-hidden cavern mouth, and when they approached, its thick hands parted the moss as easy as if it were human.

On the way to the waterfall, Niall quickly named off all the useful parts the Goliath would give him, all the upgrades and repairs he could make, the new inventions he had been thinking about. He talked the entire way to the waterfall, only being interrupted with comments and questions by Ivy.

Raven had little to say. Sitting in the Extractor, listening to Niall and Ivy, it reminded her of when she, Sweets, and Brent had more time to spend together, before her father deemed them old enough to work, before their friendship was interrupted by chores and duties.

The Extractor navigated the forest floor with surprising nimbleness, not unlike the Goliaths. Raven scanned the dense forest, but she didn't see any sign of people, and no sign of Zander.

At the thought of him, her heart squeezed.

Raven heard the roar of the falls before she saw them. The Extractor walked to the rocky shore, and Niall leaned over to see the Goliath better.

"Look at that," said Niall, his voice awestruck.

Ivy let out a whistle.

At the bottom of the waterfall, the Goliath had been impaled by a water-sharpened rock. It had gone through the softer metal between the breastplate and the collar, and it would have impaled anyone who had been inside the chest cavity.

Raven imagined Zander trapped inside the chest of the other Goliath, and her heart shuddered. The Goliath suddenly seemed a waste of time.

Raven and Ivy stood to the side while Niall used the Extractor to fish the Goliath's parts from the river. Like the Goliaths, its chest was empty. It lifted the parts with one hand, supported itself with the other, and swallowed the parts. They clanged inside of its chest, one after the other, until the largest parts of the Goliath remained. Then, the Extractor lifted the Goliath's hull in its arms.

Niall returned to the shore and looked expectantly at the girls.

"You go on ahead," Ivy called over the Extractor's engine. "We're going to do some manhunting."

Niall didn't question her. He gave them a parting wave and started back through the forest for the hidden cave. Ivy pulled Raven toward the rocky incline that led to the top of the waterfall.

"Manhunting?" Raven asked once they reached the top and the roar lessened somewhat.

"We're going to look for your other half," Ivy said. "Let's retrace your steps. We might find some clues."

Raven nodded and walked beside Ivy as they made their way upriver, past the broken bridge and rundown mill and into the forest. Raven walked back to where she thought the Goliaths had appeared—she wasn't sure. She had done a lot of running, and the forest looked the same in every direction.

They wandered through the forest without a sight or sound of Zander. With every glance through the trees, Raven's gut twisted. Had something happened to him? Had the Goliath gotten to him? She shivered at the thought of him crammed into the chest of the machine, on his way to slavery for the Gray Elite. Or worse. Sisters only knew what the Gray Elite did to their deserters.

Or he had left her behind and gone after the thief. He'd been mad that she'd cost them so much time, and he might have seen his chance to finally be rid of her—she'd done nothing but slow him down.

She didn't know which scenario made her feel worse.

"Hey, don't worry." Ivy snaked her arm around Raven's shoulders and gave her a squeeze. The warmth in her eyes pushed away Raven's hopelessness. "We'll find him."

Raven wished she felt as confident as Ivy sounded.

They made it to the highway, and by then, Ivy had begun to frown. The Detector still guarded the road, watching all travelers.

The machines had been looking for Zander, or Zander had suspected they were. That's why they had gone into the woods. The more she thought about it, the more it made sense. Her gut agreed too.

The sun started its downward fall into the west, and Ivy guided her back into the dense part of the forest. Raven walked in a daze. Her body felt separate from herself.

They hadn't found him. Zander was gone. Either he had gone on without her, or he had been captured. If he had gone on without her, she wouldn't be able to catch up to him. She wouldn't know which way to go or where he would have gone. If he had been captured, she couldn't go after him. She couldn't fight off a Goliath or go into Lenhala to find him.

She didn't know the way back to Silver Glen. Without Zander, she was on her own. Maybe...it wouldn't so bad. Ivy was friendly. Niall was nice.

By the time they reached the Dwellers' camp, the sun touched the west and painted the forest in golden hues and deep purples and rich blues, and while Raven would have liked to stay outside and watch the colors change, she couldn't bring herself to do it. Her body felt numb. She followed Ivy up the ladder.

Her stomach felt like upheaving itself with worry for Zander, whatever his fate. If only she'd been stronger against the opium smoke, they would have had the thief by now. It was her fault. Useless.

She lifted herself into the treehouse to the sound of male chatter. It came from a curtained-off room from the main space, and Raven paid little attention to it. She felt like lying down for a few weeks until the world felt right-side up again.

"Well, look at that," said Ivy, her voice cheery. She stopped, and Raven nearly ran into her. "We were scouring the forest for you, you know."

A familiar voice chuckled, though he didn't sound very humored. "Sorry, I got distracted when your friend here decided to blow up the Goliath and nearly me with it."

Raven snapped her attention up. There, sitting on the other side of the curtain that Ivy held back, was Zander. He looked worse for wear, with a cut on his chin and a split lip, but alive. Alive. Here.

The dark-headed young man sitting beside him laughed. He had what looked like grenades attached to his suspenders. He leaned forward and slapped Zander on the shoulder. "Sorry 'bout that, mate. I didn't think the boom would be *that* bad."

Laughter resounded from half a dozen people, but Raven didn't see them. She saw only Zander, there—alive. His stare met hers, and the floor tumbled out from under her feet. He looked her over, and his smile faltered. A hint of his anger returned.

She balled her fists. She saw the accusation on his face, the blame. How dare he blame her for this! She wasn't the one the Detectors had been looking for. And while she had been hunting him down, worried for his safety, he had been here, lounging about with the Dwellers like old friends. Her stomach twisted with jealousy and bitterness.

"Glad to see you're okay," he said flatly.

"You as well," she said as calmly as she could.

Ivy glanced between her and Zander, then cleared her throat. "Rae and I did quite the jog around the woods. We're famished. Bye." She let the curtain fall back across the doorway. She snaked her arm with Raven's and pulled her away from it. "Well, that solves that problem. Thirsty? Gab makes a mean cider from the Gompa fruit."

"The what?"

Ivy took her into the mess hall and pulled a dark bottle from one of the cabinets. She poured a yellow liquid into two steel goblets. Raven brought it to her lips and sniffed. It smelled sweet like juice but like something else too. Ivy took a sip, and Raven mimicked her. It tasted like...she didn't know, but she liked it. She drank mostly in silence, while

Ivy talked about the mysterious fruit they'd stumbled across decades ago—Gab had perfected the cider recipe soon after.

Ivy tapped the side of her goblet. "So...you and Zander nearly got eaten by Goliaths."

Raven nodded. A part of her wished he had been. "I'm sure he would rather I had been."

"That's harsh, even for Zander."

"He's mad I keep slowing us down." Raven sighed. She didn't know how much to tell Ivy, though she seemed trustworthy enough. She had saved her from being stuck on that ledge, given her dry clothes, and shown her hospitality. She couldn't be that bad.

"You tired?" Ivy asked. "I've got a spare cot in my room if you'd rather not sleep alone in a strange place."

Her first thought went to Zander. "I'm not sure what Zander's plans are. I'm sure he'll want us to leave immediately."

"No," came Zander's voice from the doorway.

Raven glanced at him from over her shoulder. He leaned against the doorway and wore a grim expression. Niall and the boy with the grenades lingered in the room behind him. Waiting.

"We leave first thing tomorrow. Get your rest." Zander turned around and followed the other two down a hall and out of sight.

"Well, I guess that settles it," Ivy said. "Come on. I'll get you settled in."

Raven followed Ivy down another hall and into a part of the tree where stars peeked between the branches. She led her into a room with one well-used cot and one not-so-well-used cot. After finding some spare blankets, Ivy showed her to the women's privy. The pipework looked similar to that used in the towns, only better kept. A Goliath's claw arm had been made into a wall hook.

Raven returned to Ivy's room and sat on the edge of her cot. She glanced up at the twinkling stars between the branches. A night breeze fluttered by, brushing against the leaves.

"What do you do if it rains?" Raven asked.

"There's a shield that goes up," Ivy said. She pointed to the far side of the room where a brass cover curled—when unwound, it would cover the room like a roof. "The water runs into the network that feeds the trees and us."

"Incredible," Raven said. She undid her shoes and vest and laid back on the cot. She brought the blankets up to her chin. "It must be nice to sleep under the stars every night."

"Where do you usually sleep?"

"We live underground," Raven said. "I had nothing to look at but stone."

Ivy hummed. "Sounds stuffy. You're free to stay here, you know. We'd welcome another pair of hands to help out. Always something to do or fix." She quickly added, "You know, whenever you and Zander are done with whatever it is you're doing."

Raven thought about it. The Dwellers were not that different from her friends and family, however far away they were now. If she went back to Silver Glen, she would have a lecture and a half waiting for her, and a kitchen job. She might never see the sun again, or the stars. Lying here, looking up at the stars, she thought about living with the Dwellers instead, living in the freedom of the forest.

But she knew she couldn't. She couldn't leave her father and stepmother like that, or her sister. Silver Glen was her home, like it or not. She couldn't just forget about it.

Then again, a tug in her chest reminded her of the things she had stolen from strangers, how easy it had been. Would it be just as easy to leave Silver Glen and never look back?

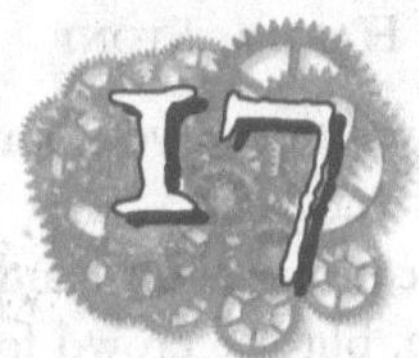

Raven fell asleep dreaming of sky cities, their brass and copper hulls gleaming in the moonlight, their leathery balloons painted to match the gold of morning, the steam of the engine puffing out cloud after cloud. She dreamed that she had been invited to a ball aboard such a ship, a grand ball of gowns and suits and ice swans.

An automaton band played from a suspended stage above the dance floor, their brass limbs caressing finely crafted strings. Underneath them, a music box added a harmonious melody. She dreamed of the music, magical and heavenly, something that could only have been played in the sky cities, only this far above the world.

Raven danced with faceless men in fine suits of all manner of colors. The amber windows cast the dance floor in strips of gold that flashed by as she danced.

Oh, the colors! The music! She traded partners, one after the other, as women in beautiful dresses joined her on the dance floor. Around and around, she twirled to the sound.

Her new partner reached for her hand, and she set her other on his shoulder. He held her closer than the others and smelled of gunpowder and steel. His sapphire eyes met hers.

"Zander?" she asked him.

He lifted a brow in that cocky way of his. "What? Didn't think I could crash a party like this one?"

"You can't even dance," she said. "Why are you here?"

"What do you mean I can't dance? I've been dancing since I could walk." He led her through the steps and didn't miss a single one. He moved with effortless grace.

"Well, now you're just showing off," Raven said.

Zander laughed, that soft chuckle of his that sent a prickle along her skin and a warmth underneath it. At her blush, he gave her his charmer's smile. "What do you mean? You're supposed to like me, Rae. We're lovers, after all."

She let out a sigh and whispered, "We're just pretending, Zander. I don't like you like that." Suddenly, everyone in the ball was looking at the two of them. No one spoke. "Zander, keep dancing, everyone is looking."

He laughed. "What do you mean you don't like me like that? Come on, Rae, you know that's not true."

Her face burned, and she dropped his hand. She took a large step away from him. She wanted to run, but the crowd formed a fence around them, shoulder to shoulder, blank faces—all of them.

Zander puffed out his chest and gave her his arrogant smile. "Come on, Rae, stop ruining the party for everyone. We've already lost enough time as it is."

Something cool touched her face; one of the swans had started to melt. It tilted dangerously forward. She reached to shield herself from the falling beak, and—

Raven snapped awake to see Ivy standing over her. She held a cup in one hand, and several cool drops of water dripped from her fingers, which she suspended over Raven's forehead.

Ivy gave her a wicked smile of greeting. "There you are," she said. "I kept trying to wake you up the old fashioned way—you know, by talking—but you kept mumbling. Some dream, eh?"

Raven wiped her face on the blanket and sat up. "Yeah, I was in a sky city. At a party. The ice swan started melting on me."

Ivy glanced at her fingers and laughed. She patted them dry on her shirt. "Figured. Anyway, we've got breakfast ready for you and some supplies. Zander's eager to get going."

Raven washed up in the privy, then followed Ivy into a small mess hall. Zander was already seated. At the sight of him, her face heated. She kept her eyes off him and on the plate the cook placed in front of her.

She picked at her food and tried to eat most of it—she'd never been a big breakfast eater. She found the glass of warm tea much more satisfying. On her second cup, she chanced a glance at Zander. He hadn't eaten much better, and he kept his eyes on his plate. He had that intent stare again. A heartbeat and a half passed, and then Zander felt her gaze. He looked up; all of the dream came back to her.

But he didn't give her one of his charming smiles. He looked like he wished the Goliath had taken her, anxious, a little unsure, and frustrated. "We leave as soon as we're done. The Dwellers have been kind enough to give us supplies."

"That's good."

"Eat up," Zander said, pushing his food around his place. "You'll need your strength, and I can't guarantee a warm meal after this."

She didn't eat much more. Neither did he.

Fed, dressed in fresh clothes, and with a pack on each of their shoulders, Zander and Raven followed Ivy, Niall, and Thalame—the boy with the grenades—through the treehouse and down a second ladder inside a fake tree trunk. This one led deeper than the other and exited among thick tree roots. Niall held an old-fashioned lantern, and the five of them walked single file down a cylindrical metal tunnel—an old pipe. A layer of dirt and pine needles softened the bottom of the pipe and evened it out for easier walking.

Raven walked behind Zander. Thankfully, he couldn't see her eyes on the back of his head. He hadn't said a word since breakfast, and he had kept his face straight-lipped and unhappy. Still mad. How could he still be mad at her? Of course...this entire ordeal was her fault.

Guilt sank deep into her bones.

The tunnel led out into a cavernous platform. The ceiling and walls were mismatched hammered metal of varying shades of copper, bronze, steel, and iron. Several panels curved, some had windows, some doors—parts of old machines.

"Ah, here she is," said Niall, his voice proud and bright. "My little Hellcat."

Raven blinked. She had been looking at the walls and nearly missed the most obvious thing in the room—a metal monster resting upon tracks, its face pieced together from metal scraps to make it look like a predatory cat, only longer and narrower. She spotted bits of Goliaths and Cage Birds and automatons she didn't recognize in its body. The top half was open to the air, and three rows of differently colored leather seats rested inside it.

Raven stepped onto the base of the car's platform and glanced down the tracks. They vanished down a tunnel barely wide enough for it, its metal sides spotted with rocky walls. About a hundred yards down, the lights vanished into a circle of darkness.

"Where does it go?" she asked, her voice echoing off the walls.

"Where we're going," Zander snapped. He climbed into the first row of seats. Niall joined him, taking a seat at the commander's wheel. "Get in."

Raven climbed into the middle seat with Ivy, and Thalame sat behind them. Niall tucked his lantern underneath the control panel; its light illuminated the front of the car, shining through the metal bars, giving it fangs and fire-eyes. A Hellcat, indeed.

Thalame leaned forward between Ivy and Raven, a wicked grin on his face. "You're gonna want to put your belt on." His rough voice strained with anticipation.

She found a leather belt at the corner of the seat. A metal hook on the end fastened into a buckle on the other side of her hip. Thalame gave her a quick run-through of how to tighten the belt.

"Why, exactly, do I need to wear this?" Raven asked.

Thalame grinned wider. He winked. He leaned back and fastened his own belt. Ivy was fastening hers, as were Zander and Niall. Raven drummed her fingers on the leather seat.

Ivy gave her a knowing glance and whispered, "It's not that bad. I remember my first time. Screamed myself hoarse."

Raven shot a worried look at Ivy, but as her mouth opened, the car underneath her rumbled to life—gears vibrated against each other, belts hummed, and the engine pumped, gurgled, and spat—then purred like an automaton cat. Steam hissed out of from underneath the cat in quick white shoots.

"Here we go!" shouted Niall. He wore an unmistakable grin.

The car started forward, its feet hooked onto the tracks. A little faster. A little faster still; then—Ivy threw her hands into the air—steam burst out, metal screeched, and the car shot forward into the darkness.

Raven's back slammed into the leather seat. The impact stole the scream from her throat.

Ivy let out a whoop; Zander was laughing, the sounds of them both barely audible over the rush of air and rumble of the Hellcat. The Hellcat's light barely lit the tunnel walls; metal and rock and rust flashed past and gave the sickening impression that the tunnel was shrinking. Air rushed by at tearing speed, whipping Raven's hair from its braid, lashing the strands against her cheeks. She squeezed her eyes shut, but the darkness felt only a little better.

The tracks began to turn and tilted; the Hellcat leaned dangerously sideways. Raven gripped the leather seat, biting into it with her nails, hard enough to hurt.

"Yeah!" Ivy shouted, her voice moving too fast to echo.

The tracks leveled. The Hellcat rumbled down the tracks at feverish speed, never slowing, turning this way, that way, speeding along the dark tunnel with only the light from the Hellcat's metal monster face. After a time, the panic wore off. Talk was impossible over the roar of the engine and the whip of the wind. Only the occasional scream of joy and fit of laughter sounded, though none came from Raven.

Then, at last, a light at the end of the tunnel. Niall slowed the hellcat with the switching of levers. A screech of metal and a punch of steam, and the car jerked and jostled its way into the light.

It was a platform not unlike the one they had left, only smaller. The top of the cavern had holes that allowed the sunlight to filter in, along with incessant dripping and vines. The sunlight filtering through seemed impossibly bright. The walls of the platform were mostly carved rock and natural rock—it must have been a cavern once. It reeked of mildew and stagnant water.

The car came to a final halt, and Ivy undid her belt. Raven fumbled to undo hers; her hands shook.

Zander jumped out of the car and started at once for the bulkhead on the far side of the platform. Thalame appeared beside the car and held his hand out for Ivy and then for Raven. She took it; his hand felt considerably sturdier than her own.

Booth feet on solid ground, she mumbled, "Thank you."

Ivy beamed, hands on her hips, grin wide, hair wild. "Well?"

A creak—Zander was unlocking the bulkhead.

"It's not what I expected," Raven admitted. She swallowed. Her throat felt dry.

Ivy laughed. "Beats walking, don't it?"

Raven nodded, though she didn't know if she agreed or not. A nice calm walk through the woods sounded pleasant after that experience. Yet, at the same time, she wouldn't turn down another ride on the Hellcat.

"Well, this is where we leave you to it," said Thalame, a farewell mixed into his words. He climbed into the backseat and lounged against it, hands behind his head.

Ivy hopped into the front seat with Niall. She said, "It was nice to meet you, Raven, but Thalame's right. I hope you find your thief."

Thief? Raven blinked; Ivy knew about the thief?

Zander inhaled sharply. He stood with his body halfway through the bulkhead door, his face twisted in a grimace. "Enough talk," he growled. "Let's go. We're on a time limit."

"Bye," Raven said to the Dwellers. "Thank you for all your help."

Thalame brushed it off, Ivy grinned, and Niall gave her a nod. Zander then grabbed her arm and yanked her through the bulkhead. He shut the door and twisted the wheel into a locked position. The Hellcat roared on the other side, spitting to life. With a whoop that sounded like Ivy, it shot out of the tunnel.

How many more platforms did the Dwellers have scattered around the underground? She didn't have the chance to ask, for Zander stomped down the dimly lit tunnel. Raven jogged to catch up with him, leaving an arm's space between them.

"I would have liked to say a better goodbye," Raven said.

"Life's too short for goodbyes," Zander spat. "Now, come on."

She heaved a sigh of agitation. "Where are we going?"

"Niall's Hellcat saved us a day's travel," Zander said. "Our thief is staying in the town above us. This is our last chance to catch him, Rae. We can't afford any more *mistakes*."

She clenched her fists. She caught the emphasis he put on "mistakes." As in, *she* couldn't make any more mistakes.

"How do you know that he's staying there?" she asked.

"Because it's the quickest route to Lenhala," he said flatly. "I talked it over with the guys back in the Dwellers' camp. They agree. They...have smuggled the occasional person or object into and out of Lenhala, and this town is the best bet. Plenty of holes to hide in. Black market connections."

"But—"

"Stop talking," Zander snapped. "You walk slower when you're talking."

She huffed and stomped after him. He led them down a short tunnel, then up a ladder that rose into a fake tree similar to the one that led into the Dweller's treehouse. She climbed out after Zander, and he shut the tree; the fake tree blended in so well with the trees around it, if she hadn't been looking at it, she wouldn't have noticed it.

Zander led her into a town bigger than any of the others they had stayed in. The main streets were paved stone, not dirt or gravel, and the shops bore colorful window displays and welcome signs. People walked along the sidewalks, meandering through the shops and talking—a gentle hum lifted through the air.

Zander didn't stop or even pause; he kept moving through the alleys and streets, and with each street, the town grew less impressive and more questionable. The paved streets gave way to narrow dirt streets, the colorful displays became dingy glass storefronts, and the people were less inviting. They came to a narrow street with stalls instead of stores. Blankets and clothes had been strung over the rooftops, shading the street in shadowy shapes. People wore cloaks and scarves, most kept their heads covered, and Raven felt horribly exposed. The chatter became a low murmur, full of whispers and strange words she didn't understand.

They passed stalls that sold carved trinkets, stalls that sold bottles of liquid and bottles of smoke, stalls that sold shimmery cloth, stalls that sold leather-bound books without titles, and stalls that didn't have any merchandise at all—no signs announced store names, items for sale, or prices. They passed a stall whose vendor wore a head-to-toe black robe. The table before him held all manner of sickly looking blades that curved, hooked, split, and scooped. The handles, she realized with a pitting of her stomach, looked like bone.

The bone-knife vendor shifted, and in a drawling voice like dry grass, he said, "Fancy a test of my blades, lass?"

Beady black eyes settled on Raven, and she felt her skin go cold. Zander's arm appeared beside her, and his fingers fastened around her elbow. He pulled her away from the strange vendor, further down the shaded market, and onto a wider street. He didn't stop until he reached a dark weathered building with a single sign hanging from rusted hooks that advertised: *Inn.*

Zander pulled her onto the porch of the inn and pulled her closer to him. Startled, she flattened her hands against his chest, ready to shove him off. Before she could shove, he bent forward and pressed his mouth against her ear, his breath hot as he whispered, "Don't speak to anyone." His words tingled against her skin and sent a shiver down her spine. "Don't look at anyone. Don't take anything anyone offers you. Act like you know what you're doing, where you are, and that you belong here."

She thought of the strange vendors they had walked through, and embarrassment flushed over her skin; she must have looked like a startled deer. Stupid. Useless.

She couldn't formulate a response, but Zander didn't require one. He straightened, hooked his arm with hers, and led her into the inn. Inside, the stench of beer, human stink, and smoked meat cogged her throat. On the first floor, six or seven tables littered the dark space. Five cloaked men were playing a game of cards in the corner, each smoking; purple and pink smoke slithered up from their table. Two women were whispering to each other, sorting buttons like coins.

Raven looked away before she could make eye contact and held her chin high like she belonged there, though she held tight onto Zander's arm. She held her tongue while he paid for a room; he gave the innkeeper the name Hamilton rather than his own.

"All we've got open are the upstairs rooms," said the toothy innkeeper. "Downstairs is full."

Zander glanced to Raven and drawled, "Is an upstairs room all right with you, Linda?"

Raven nodded.

He paid with silver Gracitan tokens, and the innkeeper didn't bat an eye. He slid across a rusty key. Zander led Raven up a set of rickety stairs to their room. A dull, broken number six had been nailed to the warped wood. Inside, Raven set her pack on the dingy floor. It felt marvelous to have it off her shoulders.

Zander closed the door and then sat down on the bed. He lowered his head into his hands and let out a frustrated sigh. "That market was a black magic market," he whispered.

Her heart skipped a beat. She inhaled sharply. "A black magic market?" she repeated. A black market for magic, or a market for black magic? She supposed they were the same.

Zander kept his stare on the opposite wall. "Because magic is illegal, magic dealers and magicians have had to go to the black markets in order to make a living, and as you saw, most of them belong in the black market," he said, rubbing his temple. He pulled the tie out of his dark hair and raked his fingers through it, loosening it. It fell near to his shoulders. "That vendor who spoke to you, that was a bone-knife dealer; they make their blades from human bones."

She swallowed; she had thought those a myth.

Zander leaned forward, head in his hands, and groaned.

"I'm sorry," Raven said quietly.

Zander peeked through his fingers at her, blue eyes weary. He dropped his hands. "For not talking that long?" A slight smirk broke through his grimace. "I thought you'd be purple in the face by now."

She huffed. "For losing us so much time."

"It's fine." He looked away from her and to the small bathroom. "Can't do anything about it now. We're here, and we're close, and we'll get him."

"How do you know he's here?"

He fixed his stare on her, then looked away. He stood and walked into the bathroom. "I saw him walk in here. He's here." He turned on the water. "It's here. Tonight, I'll distract; you search."

He shut the bathroom door, and she couldn't voice her concerns about his plan. She hadn't seen anyone walk into the inn before them, but she hadn't been paying that close of attention. Maybe he had. Zander had seen him before, not her. She wasn't even sure what the thief looked like. Zander had mentioned a man with braids to one of the innkeepers, but braids were not uncommon.

She let out a sigh and unbuttoned her jacket. She hung it on the hook beside the door and picked Zander's up from where he'd thrown it on the bed and hung it beside hers.

It didn't matter how Zander knew the thief was here. She would find the box tonight, or they wouldn't find it at all. Not with Lenhala so close. No mistakes, she told herself.

No mistakes.

With Zander in the bathroom, Raven had time to collect her thoughts and rattled nerves enough that she dreaded the coming night. No mistakes.

Zander walked out of the bathroom with his hair down and the top three buttons of his shirt undone, exposing the hollow of his throat and his collarbone. He pushed the curtain from the small window, and his intent eyes scanned the street outside.

"What are you looking at?" Raven asked, picking at a stray string on the quilted bedspread. The square under her hand looked to have once held a button.

"Nothing," he said too quickly. She narrowed her eyes at the back of his head. He let the curtain fall back into place, shutting out the sunlight and letting the dingy shadows grow. He caught her stare and sighed through his nose. "This is our last chance."

He blinked, and underneath the agitation, the snarkiness, she saw something else, something she hadn't noticed: fear.

Zander took a deep breath and paced once from the window to the door. He ran his hand through his hair.

"We'll get it," she whispered, though she knew such a thing was outside of promises.

"I know the thief is here," he said quietly.

"But—"

He held his hand up to silence her. "I...know that the deal is going down tomorrow. Here. In town. And...I know that the thief is staying here."

"How?"

He fixed his eyes on her, bottom lip between his teeth—thinking. He knew, but he didn't want to tell her.

She pulled her legs up to her chest, easier in trousers than a skirt, and guessed, "Did the Dwellers know?"

His gaze sharpened; then he nodded. "They've got connections all over the kingdom, and some in the next. They're not just people who live in the woods; they're spies and scouts too."

"Do you know them? From before?" When he had lived in Lenhala as Gray Elite.

"Yeah," he said, barely audible. He looked again to the closed window. "Look, I'd rather not discuss this here," he said quietly. "We've got too much at risk, and I need to get down there and put on an act."

"Well, at least you won't have to pretend to be stressed," she said, trying to make him feel better, but the smile she faked didn't look like it worked.

"I'll go down there as the drunk husband whose wife"—he pointed at her—"is pissed off at him." She frowned, but he didn't let her speak. "People won't ask why you aren't down there with me or why you're okay with me getting smashed."

"Why are we fighting?" she asked, if only to further the story.

He thought for a second, then said, "Because I lost all our money gambling. That way, any thugs down there looking for a quick token won't look twice at us."

She let out a dark chuckle.

"Oh?" His brows rose. "Would you rather go down there and distract a tavern full of thieves, assassins, mercenaries, and other such lowlifes while I search through all the rooms?" He waited for her answer, and when she held her tongue, he said, "That's what I thought. I'll stick to what I'm good at, and you stick to what you're good at."

"You're good at being a drunk, and I'm good at going through other people's things?"

He frowned. "That's one way to put it."

He was good at *pretending*, she told herself. And she was good at going unnoticed.

They slept into the late afternoon. Raven woke up numerous times to strange sounds in the hall, creaking boards that sounded as though someone had entered their room, and she woke up in fear of seeing a black-cloaked figure standing at her bedside. In the narrow double bed, she felt Zander's heat against her back, and though she would never tell him so, his presence settled her nerves each time she woke.

She woke once more with finality and knew she would sleep no more. Her nerves returned in anticipation of the night to come, of what she would be doing in just a few hours. Beside her, Zander slept on.

The sun gradually lowered in the sky, and the town chittered with people and summer bugs as the evening arrived. The cicadas sang louder here than they had in Silver Glen, as though they sang right outside the window. Maybe they did. The sunlight seeping through the shutters turned from golden yellow to bronze. The black magic market a street over buzzed with activity, hushed and secret.

Zander rolled onto his back and let out a sigh. An awake sigh.

"What are you thinking about?" Raven whispered.

"How I'm going to be dead if we don't find that box," he whispered back.

Raven rolled onto her back and turned to face him. She hadn't taken off her locket, and it slid across her chest as she moved. The dim evening light warmed Zander's face but shadowed it at the same time. His eyes were closed.

"I'm sorry I've been short with you," he whispered. "I'm worried about what might happen if we don't get to the thief before he makes the deal. If that box slips into the capital, it'll be gone forever. If we don't find it tonight, then it's over. It'll be too late."

"It's not your fault he stole it," Raven admitted; it had been hers.

Zander's lips turned upward, a slight smile. He opened his sapphire eyes and sought hers. "Thanks for taking the burden of blame, Rae." His smile turned a shade brighter, truer. "I... Thank you for coming with me. This would have been harder without you."

His fingers graced the back of her hand, and then he laced his fingers with hers. Could he feel the heat that rose at his touch? Hear the lurch of her heart as it skipped a beat?

"I'm sorry about what happened at the opium den," she whispered. Shame and guilt warmed her face, but she couldn't look away from him.

Zander chuckled. "I wanted to dance in the street with you." His eyes glittered. "If we hadn't been running short on time, we would have."

"When this is over," she said, holding onto that warm gaze, "we can dance wherever we want."

His smile widened and warmed, and she melted at the sight. He squeezed her hand and brought it up to his lips. He placed a chaste kiss on her knuckles. His eyes turned mischievous, and the sight sent a hot tingle over her skin.

"When this is over," he said lowly, "I'll let you kiss me all you want."

Her face burned, and Zander laughed. He kissed her knuckles again and returned her hand to the bed but didn't let go of it.

"I'm so glad you remember that night in such detail," she said, her voice a pitch too high.

"Oh, I remember," Zander affirmed. "*Every* detail."

Her face burned hotter still, and she rolled away from him so he couldn't see it, slipping her hand out of his. Laughing, Zander propped himself up on his elbow and leaned over. He placed a warm kiss on her temple.

And her heart flip-flopped nearly out of her chest at the sensation of his lips against her skin.

"It's okay, Rae. I should have kept a better eye on you that night, warned you about what might happen. I forget you don't know all the things that I know." He set his hand on her shoulder. Its warmth seeped through her sleeve. "But I'll do better from now on. I'll keep you safe. I promise."

"How can you promise that?" she asked.

He raised a brow.

"If I throw myself headfirst into danger, you're going to throw yourself in after me?"

He smiled wickedly. "As the Sisters as my witness, I'll throw myself into the Underworld after you."

She rolled onto her back to see him better. He wore no humor, only sincerity, and by the Sisters, a light pink tinted his tan cheeks.

"That's quite possibly the sweetest and strangest thing anyone has ever said to me." She let her gaze fall from his eyes to his lips. Just once.

"Don't ever say I haven't been nice to you," he said, his voice lower. He started to lean toward her, and she knew she wouldn't stop him. He leaned closer, his breath on her lips, and then—

The dinner bell rang, a ghastly, intrusive sound that made them both jump. Just like that, the moment between them dissolved.

Zander leaned away, blinking rapidly. He cleared his throat. "Time to go."

"No mistakes," she said.

Zander got out of bed first. He slid on his boots and his vest. He stepped to the window and lifted the curtain an inch or so, just enough for him to see out without too many people seeing him do it. He let it fall back into place. Dust motes fluttered from the material.

"Okay," he said, buttoning his jacket. "Wait until I start singing 'Jim Goes Fishing.' That's the signal that our thief is downstairs, leaving his room exposed."

She nodded and sat on the bed. Zander left, and in a few long minutes, she heard him laughing with several other male voices. Within the hour, the crowd below had increased, and the drunken chatter began. She paced. She peeked on the street outside, where the evening crowd strolled about, arm in arm in their best dresses and clothes. Through the alleys, she spotted the nicer streets, nicer dresses, and funny hats.

What would it have been like to grow up in a place like this instead of Silver Glen? On the outskirts of the capital instead of north of nowhere? Where the automatons didn't hunt fugitives and refugees like game. Where people just lived. Where they didn't have to hunt for their food or make their homes in an old mine to protect themselves from turning into slaves.

If she had been born in Lenhala, rather than Silver Glen, would she have craved the wider world so much?

Zander had grown up in Lenhala, and he knew so much more about the world than she did. Zander knew about the Dwellers. He knew about the Gray Elite. He knew about all the automatons they'd encountered and more. Seeing the world for herself made her feel...small. She'd been hiding in a small corner of the world while all of this was happening, while places like this town existed with all its shops, people, and events.

And he had almost kissed her. She brought her fingertips to her lips, where a ghost of his breath lingered. And he hadn't been high on magic opium either.

Sighing, she walked into the bathroom and washed her face and hands in cool water. Her reflection in the dirty mirror was a blur of pale beige, unremarkable.

Wait. Why did she care what Zander thought of her? Why did she care if Zander thought her simple or stupid? She didn't! She shouldn't, yet deep down, she knew that it bothered more than she wanted it to. She'd fled Silver Glen with Zander in hopes of an adventure, and here she was, worrying about what he thought of her.

She took a deep breath of the humid air in the bathroom, mixed with the opium-laced air vented from below, tinted with stale ale, smoked meat, and human stink.

They would find the thief, get back the box, and then head back to Silver Glen. All would return to normal. She would return to her new job in the kitchens, and Zander... What would her father do to him when he found out what he had done? That he had talked Raven into leaving with him? Of course, if this box was as important as Zander said it was, her father had to know about it. He knew about everything that happened in Silver Glen, above or below.

And...maybe Silver Glen wouldn't be so bad if Zander was with her.

Raven returned to the bedroom and ate from the rations, including the last of the almonds that Zander hadn't mentioned. When he had pulled the bag from his pack, he had blinked, then continued on as if they had always been there.

He knew she stole them, but he hadn't said a word about it.

She tossed a few almonds into her mouth and watched the sunlight sink deeper into orange, then purple. She lifted the curtain. The town was lit with lanterns, but to the east, a white glow warmed the horizon enough to black out the stars above it.

Lenhala, the capital and royal city of Rhynwier. Even from this distance, its sparkling towers of glass and steel glowed like gold and silver in the twilight. How amazing it must look at night, all lit up. She had heard through traders that Lenhala was always lit up, day and night; there were stadiums and parks that glowed as bright as day during the night.

Raven had loved the trips to the surface with her father to meet the traders, but when she had gotten old enough to ask questions, her father had refused her pleas to go with him.

He didn't want her asking questions. The mines were secret, he had told her. If the Gray Elite found out about Silver Glen, they would come charging in. As a child, she had accepted that story without a doubt, but as she grew older, she knew her father had made it up to keep her from talking to the traders. To keep the world and her separate.

The sun sank lower. Lenhala grew brighter. Bright enough that it outshone Wilyn's Star. The little town glowed too, with all its shop windows, apartments, stacked homes, and lanterns, but not like Lenhala. How must it be to live in a world that never goes dark?

The ruckus downstairs grew more drunken by the minute. She heard Zander's bawdy laugh, and every so often, a horde of male laughter would fill the entire inn, belly-shaking and beer-aided. Raven took a deep breath and sat on the bed.

Waiting.

Any moment, Zander would start singing.

Unless he didn't. Unless the thief didn't show. Unless the thief had gotten smart and stayed in his room.

A horrible thought struck—what if the thief kept the damn thing on his person?

That thought didn't stick too long, for it hadn't crossed her mind a moment before Zander's drunken slur drifted up the stairs:

> *Jim goes fishing every day.*
> *Jim goes fishing every night.*
> *Jim goes fishing.*
> *Boy what a sight!*

Raven was on her feet, treading lightly to the door. She fastened her hand around the handle.

A cacophony of voices sang with him:

> *Jim goes fishing to escape the wife.*
> *Jim goes fishing to forget his strife.*
> *Jim goes fishing,*
> *But forgets his knife!*

Raven crept into the lonely hall of the inn's room. "No mistakes," she repeated to herself. No mistakes.

Raven slipped into the hallway without a sound. She repeated her search of the upstairs rooms, picking the locks with her steel hairpin, sorting through the sparse belongings. Zander hadn't been kidding about the type of people staying at the inn. She found vials of strange liquid, bags of teeth that looked sickeningly human, runes carved in stones, and an old doll the size of her thumb, with black eyes.

She didn't dare take anything from the rooms; her gut warned her not to.

Three of the six upstairs rooms were occupied, and none contained the little metal box. Which meant she would have to go downstairs.

Raven started down the stairs one at a time. Zander led the drunken tavern through another bawdy bar song, this one of mermaids. She reached the second to last step as they began to sing a verse about the mermaid's peaked breasts. Raven's entire face burned. That Zander knew such a song infuriated and embarrassed her.

A man stepped out of the third room. Raven froze; she didn't have time to move—he stepped around the staircase. Their eyes met. He was of average height, lithe but thick with lean muscle. He had dark skin of the southern kingdom and eyes like coal. His black hair had been done in dozens of thin braids that fell halfway down his back. He wore close-fitting clothes, a lightweight leather cuirass and trousers adorned with knives and daggers. His sharp eyes did not gleam with ale or glint with malice.

He halted before the staircase, just out of sight to anyone on the main floor looking toward the back hall. He leaned onto the banister, his movements easy with grace. A stark aftershave wafted along with him. Closer, he didn't look that much older than her, maybe twenty.

"Judging by the disgusted look on your face, you must be that drunk's wife he keeps going on about," he said, his voice smooth and pleasant.

She swallowed. "I-I didn't know he knew such songs," she said meekly.

He looked Raven up and down. "How long you two been married?"

She bit her lip, withholding the answer. That wasn't something she and Zander had discussed. She hadn't planned on meeting anyone, explaining herself, or talking.

He shook his head, frowning. "I take it, it's not been very long, then."

She didn't answer.

His quick eyes darted to the doorway to the main floor, where another verse dedicated to women's body parts had all the men singing, and a few women by the voices. "I heard him say you hadn't known each other long." His eyes returned to Raven.

"Not long enough," she said quietly. She balled her fists on the knees of her trousers. She was starting to think she didn't know anything about the real Zander at all. All that he had done, the singing, the flirting, the lying, the pretending. "I'd known him to be a scoundrel and a braggart, but..."

"You thought you could change him?" He shook his head in pity. "Word of advice, little bird, men don't change. No matter how much yelling or pouting or withholding a woman does, men don't change." He pointed toward the door. "Women do, though. Not for worse, but they do change with age."

"Please, don't tell him you saw me here," she said quietly. "He'll only make a scene about it."

He considered her, his clever eyes searching her face. "How old are you, bird?" he asked.

"Seventeen."

He frowned. "Not old enough to marry. Some people got strange ideas about marriage. Especially the rich. They think it's like game pieces, marrying off children like they sell off property or stock. I lucked out by growing up poor."

"You're married?"

He shook his head. "I've got a girl back home, but we're not legal. Can't afford the wedding, the license, or the taxes that would come along after. But we don't need a piece of paper to tell us that we can be together. Love doesn't have to be certified."

She nodded. "That is a nice way of thinking about it. I wish more people thought that way."

He chuckled, and his black eyes glittered. A certain joy brightened his entire face, and it made Raven think of Lena. "You know, bird, you don't have to stay with that scoundrel. I've got connections. I could get you passage out, somewhere better. Somewhere you won't have to worry about pleasing that scum or how many kids you'll have. The south is still outside Gray Elite rule, and it's a good place to start over. My people could find you a job, a place to stay, maybe even some friends. Ever see the sunrise over the gulf? It's a beauty, let me tell you."

She looked at the man thoughtfully; though her marriage to Zander was a ruse, the proposal of a new life outside of Rhynwier, beyond the Gray Elite, was enticing. She could leave it all behind and start new somewhere else. She could leave Zander, the box, Silver Glen—start over with a new name, a new life.

But...she couldn't leave Zander.

"Tell you what." The man reached into his pocket and withdrew a coin. "If you ever change your mind, follow the stars to Wayward Point. Go to the white brick building, called the Destiny Show, and present this coin to the doorman. Tell them Conrad sent you. You'll find help inside."

He set the coin in her palm. It was not a silver Gracitan token or a copper Rhynwier mark; it was a wooden coin. Both sides had been carved with an elegant circle with a diamond inside of it.

"Thank you," she said, gazing up at the man.

He nodded. Without another word, he returned to the main room. The song never fluctuated.

Raven took a deep breath, tucked the coin into her pocket, and started down the hallway. She picked the lock on the closest room, let herself in, and quickly went through the personal effects. Nothing. She repeated with the second room, but still nothing. She hesitated at the third door, the door Conrad had come from. She skipped it and went to the fourth room, then the fifth. No box in either.

She stood in front of the third door. Conrad had been nice to her. Going through his things felt wrong.

Still...

No mistakes. This was their last chance.

She picked the lock and slipped inside. Like the others, the room was sparsely decorated. Water trickled in the bathroom. The same stark aftershave lingered in the air. Her panic rose; she had no defense if Conrad returned and caught her going through his things. She doubted he would be as friendly the second time.

The song shifted to another, and she began her search with trembling fingers. She looked in the obvious places first, under the pillow, in the small dresser, and finally, she turned to a shabby leather jacket. She started to search through the pockets—there were dozens of pockets inside it—more than any other coat she had ever seen.

Why did one man need so many pockets? Did he go around handing wooden coins to all the girls he met? She found all manner of things, tokens and marks, buttons, necklaces, rings. What in the world did—

Her thoughts slammed to a halt as her fingers closed around a cool metal box in one of the jackets's deeper pockets. Her heart slammed into her ribs, and she gently pulled it out.

A small iron box. No more than an inch wide. The metal had dulled with time and age and looked like something Brent would have thrown into his Scrapper.

This? *This* was what she had come all this way for?

And then she realized—the man who had given her the coin, the man who had been so pleasant and friendly—he was their thief. Conrad the Thief. A professional thief.

No sooner had that thought passed, than booted footsteps sounded in the hall. She quickly tucked the box into her pocket and rearranged the jacket. The footsteps stopped in front of the door, and a key shoved into the lock.

Her heart stopped—she hadn't the time to plan. She dropped to her knees as silently as she could and rolled underneath the bed. She covered her mouth to quiet her breathing, and the door to the room opened.

The thief's boots walked inside—the only part of him visible. It was Conrad, if that was indeed his name. He marched to his jacket and yanked it from its hook.

"Five tokens a night," he mumbled. "The whole inn's not worth five tokens."

Raven's heart threatened to beat its way out of her chest and expose her to the thief. What would he do if he found her under his bed? Nothing good.

The thief let out a sigh and something crunched—bread, she realized, as he began to chew. He reached down, and his dark fingers fastened around the strap of his satchel. Raven held her breath despite her thundering heart. He straightened, hauling the satchel out of her view. He left as quickly as he had entered.

Raven stayed under the bed until her heart slowed, then clawed out on shaky limbs. Dust clung to her clothes and hair, but she hadn't the time to worry about it. Out. She needed to get out and to the safety of her own room. Before anyone else came looking. She double-checked the box in her pocket and then let herself back into the hall.

The thief had gone. The only other person in the hall was a balding man who held onto the waist of a whore. Her eyes were horridly painted in red and black, and her dress dipped dangerously low in the front. Neither of them paid Raven any mind, and she skittered up the stairs and shut herself into her room. She twisted the lock, and as metal slid against metal and settled with a *thunk*, something like relief spread over her shoulders.

No one came thundering up the stairs after her. She took each breath as it came and pressed her forehead against the backside of the door. After a long moment, she shut herself into the small bathroom. She stripped herself, dusted off her clothes, and washed in cool water. She set the box on the basin, within sight.

The box didn't look worth hiring a thief over. It looked like junk. But the Gray Elite had hired someone like Conrad to find it, so it had to be worth something.

Raven turned off the water and stood to dry. Without the rushing of the water, she could hear a few people still singing downstairs. It sounded as though ale had gotten the better of a few of them. Outside, through the slatted vent above the water tank, a fight had started. She listened to the sound of fists colliding with flesh, the grunts and groans of injuries, the cheers of drunken onlookers. Her heart thumped, and she thought of Zander. She listened harder to the voices and picked his out of those still singing.

As dry as she cared to be, she dressed and braided her hair and carried the iron box into the bedroom. She sat on the bed and turned it over in her hands. It felt warm to the touch. She didn't see a way to open it. The metal was seamless. She rattled it; it was not empty. Something was inside, although it didn't move. It had weight but not more than a few ounces. What could be so valuable as to go to all the trouble of stealing it? And then stealing it back?

Or was it the mystery of the thing? No one knew what was inside, and the mystery made it valuable.

The singing downstairs faded with a final song, and Raven tucked the box into her pocket. Patrons were filing into their rooms in the inn, and others were meandering outside. The drowsy, drunken chaos drifted with them, sputtering out into the night. Footsteps sounded on the stairs, but the owner walked past her door. She released a breath. The door to the room next to hers opened and closed; then a body collapsed onto the metal frame bed with a heavy thump and creaking metal.

Another set of footsteps sounded on the stairs, sloppy and uneven. Drunk. The feet made it up the stairs and fell into her door, and she jumped at the sound. She drew her legs up and closed one hand around the dagger in her boot.

A key hit the wood around the handle, a drunken man's thrust, and after several attempts, the key slid into the lock. It turned slowly, and then Zander stumbled inside. He shut the door louder than he should have, then fumbled to lock it back.

He turned his drunken gaze on her, his eyes swimming. He swayed dangerously back and forth but somehow made it to the bed. He flopped with the grace of a stone, landing on his stomach. He released a deep, ale-laden breath. Raven leaned back onto her pillow. Zander opened his eyes and met hers. He couldn't stay focused.

"I drank a little too much," he said, slurring. Really slurring, not pretend-slurring. His breath reeked of ale, stout and too sweet.

"Then go to sleep," Raven whispered. She eased onto her side. "I'll tell you the good news in the morning."

He blinked several times; then he smiled wide. It lit up his drunken eyes. He let out a bark of a laugh and slung his arm over her side. "Really?"

"Really." She pushed his hair out of his face. He started to speak, but she pressed her finger against his lips. "Shh, you're drunk," she whispered. And his breath stank. "You're talking far too loud. Go to sleep."

He hugged her against his chest, warm and rhythmic with his heartbeats. His clothes had soaked in the smoky tavern stench, but Raven had no immediate desire to move.

Zander fell asleep quickly, his lips slightly parted, his ale-laden breath warm on her temple. When he had fallen deeper into sleep, she slithered out from underneath his arm and shut herself in the small dark bathroom. She washed her face in cool water.

She gripped either side of the metal basin, her hands shaking.

She had found the box. She should be happy. But her stomach twisted.

She reached into her pocket and fastened her hand around the iron box. Warm to the touch. Just iron, she told herself, but something deeper inside of her didn't believe that. Something else, something more.

Back in the bedroom, the moonlight gleamed through the holes in the curtain. She tiptoed to the window and pushed the curtain aside. Beyond the lights of the town, Lenhala glowed bright on the horizon. A man-made star.

She removed her boots and Zander's boots and slipped back underneath his arm. He didn't even stir. She took a deep breath, spiced with Zander's ale-laden exhales, and tried to find sleep.

Raven tossed and turned most of the night, waking up at every sound the inn made, fearing the thief would burst through the door, anger twisting his face. Would he get to wherever he was going, discover the box gone, and know she had taken it?

A hand touched her shoulder, and she jerked awake at once. Her fist collided with her assailant, and he let out a grunt.

"Shit," Zander spat.

She blinked

Zander sat back on his heels, rubbing his cheek. "What the hell was that for?"

"I-I'm sorry," she said, clutching her fist to her chest. "It was a reflex."

He glared like he didn't believe her. "Well? Do you have it or not?"

She reached her pocket and pulled out the little iron box. Zander's eyes widened, and his hand fell from his jaw. With a sharp inhale, he gently lifted the box from her hands and turned it over.

"Is this it?" she whispered.

He nodded without taking his eyes off the box. "Yeah." He closed his hand around it and met her gaze. His awestruck expression fell into a frown. "What's wrong?"

She blinked; had she made a face?

"Did something happen?" he whispered. He motioned to the box.

She bit her lip, then told him how she had met the thief on the stairs and how he had nearly caught her. Zander's brow crinkled. She left out the thief's name and the wooden coin he had given to her. She didn't feel like explaining it to Zander. Not right now.

After a moment of silence, Zander set the iron box back into her hands. "Hold onto it with your life." He scooted off the bed. "We should get out of here as quick as we can." He stood too quick and wobbled. He threw out a hand to catch the wall before he fell, then put a hand over his eyes and let out a groan. "Sisters," he mumbled.

"Well, that's what you get for drinking so much," Raven said.

Zander shot her a deadly glare as he walked into the bathroom. Raven pulled on her boots and readied the packs while Zander washed up. With them ready, she walked to the window and opened the curtains. The fresh morning sunlight burst in, warming her face while the cool breeze kissed her cheeks.

She took her turn in the bathroom while Zander stood outside the door, tapping his foot, munching on hard bread, murmuring for her to hurry. When they, at last, left the inn, Zander walked at a clipped pace, winding their way around the black magic market.

"Are we heading back through the tunnel?" Raven felt a jump in her chest at the thought of riding the Hellcat again.

"No."

"Why not?"

"Because there's no way of knowing where it is within the tunnels," Zander said, motioning toward the ground. "There's no way of contacting them with enough time for them to get here. We're on foot for a while."

Raven sighed. The idea of walking back to Silver Glen filled her with dread. "That's so far."

"We just need to get back to Oun. It's the town we skipped with the Hellcat," Zander said. "When we get there, we can send word to the Dwellers."

"Oh, that's not dreadfully far," Raven said, though she didn't know for certain.

"Now, hurry up," he grumbled.

They retreated through town and toward a path that led through the forests to Oun, rather than take the main road. According to Zander, too many people would see them on the main road. Zander led the way, and it left Raven able to look around. People were getting to work around the town, fixing homes, tending to animals, and opening shutters and shaking feather dusters. Somewhere, fresh-baked bread and sugary sweets wafted through the air, making her mouth water.

Zander paused, and she got a second look at a man sweeping dust from the stoop of a store—he wore plain clothes, and his hair had been shaved close to his scalp.

A slave, she realized. Bile rose in her throat.

At the sharp bark of a woman, the slave retreated back into the store, his face devoid of emotion. Zander started forward again, and Raven followed, feeling sick. She had never seen a slave before.

They crossed another street and wound through a narrow alley. Raven glanced down the street to see if other slaves were working, when her eyes met those of a young man standing at the open door of a nicer inn. His dark hair was short and slicked back, and he wore the yellow and gray uniform of the Gray Elite. He was speaking to a well-dressed innkeeper; behind the innkeeper, a slave stood silent, obedient.

She had never seen a Gray Elite before, at least, not in uniform.

Her stomach twisted into knots. She tore her eyes away from the Gray Elite and focused on Zander's back. He gave no indication that he had seen the young soldier. He wound through another alley, up a street, and through another alley.

They were passing a sheep farm on the outskirts when her stomach growled too loudly to ignore.

"We'll get something to eat when we get to Oun," he said.

"Why not now?"

He didn't answer immediately, then growled in frustration. "Because we need to get out of here while we can."

The knot in her stomach tightened. Had he seen the Gray Elite? Was he following them? Looking for them? Her thoughts churned her anxiety and fears, and her hunger got pushed to the side.

The sun vanished behind a cloud as they started down the winding forest path to Oun. The path rose and fell with the hilly terrain, far more than it had to the north. Rocks jutted out from the ground in some places, a few creating shadowed coves. The sun came and went between the clouds, dousing them in bright light and then shade and back again. The sun rose higher and higher, and the temperature rose with it.

By the time Oun came into view through the trees, her stomach had grown viciously empty, and sweat stuck her shirt to her back. Oun was set on a hill, and the final incline nearly did her in. Zander led the way through the simple wooden shacks and stone homes. She walked a step behind him, and he guided her around a larger stone home to a small clearing.

She lost her breath at the sight.

Because Oun sat on a hill, the land before it dipped downward and gave them an uncrowded view of Lenhala. It rose in the distance, gray and faded blue, its white and metal towers reaching for the sky. It almost sparkled in the light.

"I've never been so close," Raven whispered to Zander.

"And hopefully, it will be the closest you ever get," he said with distaste.

They walked into an open-air food counter, and Zander paid for a simple meal of smoked meat, sliced brown bread, and cheese. They took their late breakfast outside in the shade of a tall oak, and she ate without talking. She finished all of her food, but Zander picked at his. At her stare, he ate a little faster.

"Why are you so nervous?" Raven asked him as they filled their canteens at the bar. "We did what we needed to."

He nodded, though his eyes were elsewhere. Raven looked back to Lenhala. It looked like another world, where metal ruled over stone and dirt, where the machines weren't cobbled together with ancient parts, where girls didn't have to work in the kitchens because of their overprotective fathers.

A part of her wanted to run away to the capital, or to Wayward Point—wherever that was. She didn't want to drag her feet back to Silver Glen and give up the possibilities of the world before her, of adventure, of new people, of sights she'd never dreamed of. Of all the places she had seen, the inns and taverns and houses, Silver Glen was by far the shabbiest, smallest, and loneliest.

"What are you thinking?" Zander asked, tearing off pieces of bread.

"That it would better to be a slave in paradise than a king in hell," she said.

He frowned. "Lenhala looks nice, but it's a different kind of hell."

He continued his slow eating, and Raven glanced back at the little town. A flash of yellow and gray caught her eye, and her stomach dropped into her groin.

The same Gray Elite she had seen that morning now stood at the very food counter they had visited; the man at the counter pointed in Raven's direction, and the Gray Elite turned. Their eyes met. He gave her a warm smile, but something sinister lay beneath it.

"We're being followed," she whispered.

The Gray Elite started toward them, walking with the learned grace of one used to combat. A saber hung off his belt, and a fine leather holster hung off the opposite hip.

Zander glanced over his shoulder. His eyes settled on the stranger, and he jumped to his feet—food abandoned. His straight-line mouth fell into a grimace, and he looked ready to kill. His fingers twitched toward Birdie, and Raven pushed herself onto shaky legs.

The Gray Elite stopped in front of Zander, who'd gone a shade too pale. Raven studied the uniform. He wore dark green decorations on his shoulders, signifying him as an officer. Raven felt her own skin pale; an officer of the Gray Elite had followed them, looking for them. Raven thought to the box in her pocket and fought the urge to curl her fingers around it.

The officer's small smile stretched wide. He looked Zander up and down and then threw his arms out wide. "Zander, it is you! I half thought the reports to be false." He spoke elegantly. The officer's gaze slid over Raven. "And you're not alone. The reports were right on that account too."

Zander took a step closer to Raven, his fists clenched. "Hello, brother," he said, though he didn't sound happy about it.

Brother? Raven looked between the two. She saw resemblances: their jaws, their noses, their dark brown hair, the shape of their eyes; they looked like brothers, but where Zander had sapphire blue eyes and bronze skin, his brother had charming brown eyes and beige skin. Zander stood with a lethal grace, while his brother held himself like a soldier.

"Aren't you going to introduce me to your..." his brother motioned toward Raven, and she bristled at the subtle distaste in his tone. She knew at once, she didn't like him.

Zander turned to her, unhappy in every sense. "Raven, this is my older brother, Baxter. Baxter, this is Raven."

"Raven," said Baxter, her name a purr on his tongue. His eyes slid over her, and she felt his assessment happen before she could speak. He took in her disheveled clothes, her loose braid, her dirty boots—and gave her a small smile full of snobbish pity. Her cheeks burned. He held out his hand for hers, and she cautiously gave it to him. His fingers curled daintily around hers. He placed a quick kiss on the back of her hand. "It is a pleasure to meet you."

"The pleasure is mine." She had the urge to wipe her hand on her trousers. His fingers twitched as though he thought the same.

"Where have you been?" Baxter asked, clapping Zander on the shoulder. "I was worried you'd gone somewhere you shouldn't have, and someone got the better of you. I cringed every time the news came, fearing I'd hear your name in the passages."

While Baxter spoke elegantly, he spoke with a learned charm, a practiced insincerity. With every word he said, Raven liked him a little less.

"I've been fine," Zander said, his words clipped. He brushed off Baxter's hand. "I've been busy."

Baxter's gaze slid back to Raven. "I see. I never thought you would be the type to run off with a girl, but I'm not surprised. I daresay that Mother will be overjoyed." He started to say something else, but he hesitated. His eyes roamed over Raven's state of dress once more.

"While it's great to see you, we need to be going." Zander took Raven by the arm and tried to lead her around his brother, but Baxter sidestepped to block their path.

"Just like that?" Baxter's brown eyes widened, feigning insult. He put a hand over his heart. "You wound me, Brother, to just leave again. Please, come home first. You look like you could use a few good meals and a few good washes too."

"I'd rather not." Zander tried again to step aside, but Baxter blocked his path.

"You've been gone six months," Baxter said, a plead on his tongue. "Half the city thinks you're dead."

Raven swallowed. Half the city? Lenhala was *huge*. Was Zander that well known?

"It's not a good idea," Zander said. "It'll only cause a stir."

Baxter laughed. "Since when have you worried about causing a stir? I thought you loved stirring?"

Zander huffed.

"Just for a few days," Baxter said. "Show the world you're alive and well, and then you can be on your way. This way, the Gray Elite won't be shoveling resources into finding you."

Zander gritted his teeth, and his hand tightened on her arm. So the Detector *had* been looking for him.

"Fine," Zander spat.

Baxter's smile widened, and he led the way to the main road, where a fine horse-drawn coach sat. Raven blinked; the horse was not a horse at all, but an automaton. It had been built to resemble a horse, its metal coat a shined brass. Rather than a mane, glass globes of dark red lined its neck. A driver sat on the front of the coach in a red coat with brass buttons and slicked-backed hair. The inside of the coach was a rich black leather and buttoned beige velvet. Baxter sat across from Zander and Raven, and with a knock on the coach's wall, the automaton horse hissed and roared to life.

The coach started forward, and the Detectors guarding the road didn't give them a second glance.

Baxter leaned back into the leather seat, his posture lazy but alert. Beside her, Zander sat straight as an arrow, his hands digging into the leather. Baxter peppered them with questions of where they had been, who they had seen, and why; Zander answered each with a non-answer. It didn't seem to bother Baxter. If anything, he seemed amused. His overly sweet tone irritated her, and by the look on Zander's face, it irritated him too.

From the window, Raven watched the capital come closer as Zander dodged Baxter's nosy questioning. They started through the outskirts of dilapidated homes, shoddy farms, and lean-to shacks. A stone fence kept the road separate from the outskirts. No one seemed to notice or care about the coach passing by. Some of the workers had shaved heads; some did not. Slaves and working poor.

As the coach trotted closer to the city walls, Raven noticed dots above the city; the dots became steadily larger, and then, with no small amount of surprise, she realized what they were. Airships. Hundreds of them, darting back and forth, up and down, all over the sprawling city. There were airships of every shade of metal and design; some looked like dragonflies, others like bullets with balloons, and others were coaches with winged automaton horses.

They produced a gentle roar that blended together into one endless engine purr, fluctuating as the wind shifted, as the airships moved. Raven couldn't take her eyes off the airships—so many of them! The part of her that had carved airships and stars into her ceiling wanted to shout, but as she glanced back inside the coach to find Baxter watching her with interest, that desire faded into embarrassment. She calmed the smile that had stretched her lips wide and forced her attention away from Zander's brother.

The outskirts became ramshackle buildings of dirty stone, weathered wood, and rusted metal. Farms shrank. Homes grew taller and cleaner. Each street they passed grew a little sturdier, a little prettier, and a little richer. By the time they arrived at the outer wall of Lenhala, the houses were taller, grander, and of clean metal and washed stone.

The gates of the city halted their advance, but with one look at Baxter and a flash of his shiny bronze badge, the guardsmen bowed their heads and allowed them passage.

"Right away, Lieutenant," said the man at the window.

Raven glanced at Zander. His lips had gone pale and tight. His knuckles were white on the seat. He eyed the guardsmen like a cornered fox eyeing wolves.

The car passed through the iron gates and into Lenhala—indeed another world. The buildings were smooth stone, metal, and glass, in all manner of colors. This close, the city was not pale gray and white, but a rainbow of purples, reds, blues, and all colors in-between. Splotches of green burst between houses and on top of them—gardens and parks. An endless cacophony of sounds flooded through the coach's windows, of people, of automatons, of airships—engines, chatter, laughter, clanking hooves, shouting—all the rhythmic heartbeat of the city.

And the people! She'd never seen so many people at once, walking along the wide sidewalks, riding in coaches drawn by all manner of automaton animals. She spotted several beautiful horses, bears, cats, and a winged creature she'd never seen before. The automatons came in every color of metal she could imagine, more colorful than the city. The coaches themselves were encrusted with gems and jewels, bright and shined, open and closed.

It all came with a metallic scent, underlined with perfume and grease.

She glanced at Zander, and he gave her a small smile.

"I take it this is your first time in the city?" came Baxter's carefully worded question.

"Yes," Zander answered for her. He didn't elaborate. He met Baxter's eye, and the conversation ended.

Raven swallowed. Baxter had been watching. After that, she tried her best to hold in her glee at all the wonderful things she'd never seen before.

Baxter explained that Lenhala had been built on a hill, and each district rose higher than the one before it. The first district was unremarkable; the second district held smaller businesses; the third and final district, which rose the highest on the hillside, housed the military, the palace, and the Gray Elite.

She wanted to stick her head out of the window to see the tall buildings of steel and stone for herself, but she held it in. She sat firm in the seat and watched the first and second stories pass her window. The steel was shined to a gleam, giving it the sparkling nature, and white and gray marble had been engraved and carved with all manner of things to give each building a dozen things to look at.

The people dressed finer than she had ever seen or imagined. The women wore silks and hats and heels and corsets and walked like goddesses. The men wore fine suits and jackets and shined shoes. She spotted several women carrying fans; she saw one woman tuck the fan into her dress's sleeve, where it vanished.

Raven thought of her clothes. Her trousers had been slept in, her shirt wrinkled, and her vest suddenly felt cheap. Compared to these people, she was nothing but country trash, uneducated and un-pampered and stupid to the ways of the city.

The coach took them through the heart of the third district, past grand halls and buildings so high, they left much of the street in shadow, for which blue-white lanterns had been lit along the sidewalks. It felt so...otherworldly.

"Welcome to Lamp Light Way," said Baxter.

"Because it's in the sun for only an hour each day," added Zander. He motioned to the lamps. "The lamps are lit day and night."

"It's lovely," Raven said.

"Lamp Light Way is the main street in the third district," said Baxter, his tone light and airy. "Symphony Hall is here, as well as the more prominent residences toward the south end."

They passed what must have been Symphony Hall, a grand structure with stone and marble. A theater, she realized. A large theater.

They drove down Lamp Light Way, through the otherworldly shadows and blue-white light, to the south end Baxter had mentioned. Grand mansions and palace-like homes dotted the street, fenced in with stone and metal and wrought iron, with magnificent gardens and orchards.

It looked like a place for gods to live, she thought.

And then, the coach slowed. It turned into a gated drive. The property's black marble and wrought iron wall rose twenty feet, ending in sharp points. The wall was as beautiful as it was intimidating. The house beyond it stole her breath—a palace of pale red stone, white marble, and light wood. The front garden sprawled with apple trees, peach trees, and red maple.

Zander looked nearly sick. Raven nudged his hand with her small finger, but he didn't budge.

The coach pulled alongside the gatehouse so that the window of the coach and the window of the gatehouse were parallel. A well-dressed man in a uniform of pale red and gray stuck his head out.

"Ah, afternoon, Lieutenant," said the man.

"Afternoon," said Baxter's calm voice.

The gateman glanced at Zander, and his pleasant smile faded. He blinked several times. Baxter cleared his throat, and the gateman stumbled back to the gatehouse. With the pull of a lever, the gates began to open with a soft squeal of metal and the silent thumps of gears. The coach pulled through the open gates and down the drive to the looming mansion at the other end.

"Where are we?" Raven asked.

"Welcome," Zander said quietly, his voice rough, "to Winchester House. It's my home."

Her breath came out in a disbelieving gasp. Zander had said he came from the aristocracy, but she hadn't expected *this*. He lived in a house as big as the entire mining system of Silver Glen! He didn't look happy at all to be home; he looked nearly sick. The color had faded from his cheeks and neck.

The coach pulled into a steepled garage the size of a tavern. Though the stench of oil and cleaning polish lingered, the room was immaculate. The tiled floor was spotless, the wooden beams dust-free, and every tool and contraption had a place on the shelves. Four stalls lined one wall, three of which contained a coach and its automaton animal. One coach was solid black with a gleaming steel horse, another was a stunning sky blue and pulled by a white wolf, and the third was ivory and pulled by a golden cat. A servant stood on the far side. He stopped whatever he had been doing at the workbench and bent into a deep bow.

The coach pulled into the empty stall and hissed to silence; the driver opened the door. Baxter stepped out first and then held out his hand to Raven. Behind her, Zander hissed a curse. His brother didn't seem to notice.

Raven gently placed her hand into Baxter's and stepped out of the coach. Zander quickly appeared at her side, between her and Baxter. A subtle glare passed between brothers. Baxter led the way across the garage and to a set of brassy double doors.

"I'm sure you are both famished," Baxter said. "I'll call Demetri for—"

"I can do it myself," Zander interrupted.

"I only thought—"

"I'm not a guest," Zander spat. He curled his fingers to fists. "I know my way around. This is my house too."

Baxter looked like he wanted to argue that point, but didn't. He nodded. "I'll meet you in the Orange Lounge for lunch, then?"

"Fine." Zander didn't sound enthused.

Baxter walked through the double doors, and Zander slowed his pace as to not be right behind his brother. He then led Raven through the same doors, through a breezeway lined with floor-to-ceiling windows, flowering ferns, and bright gold and red tile, and then into the house.

The air darkened, despite the tall windows. Dark wood paneling and red walls made the space darker and somber.

They entered a parlor. The ceilings were twice as tall as Zander, half dark paneling and half elaborately painted red and a slightly darker red. Zander didn't give her time to gawk; he pulled her through a set of wide, dark wooden doors with massive bronze handles. He pulled her down the hall, without a word, and up a grand staircase to the second floor.

Everywhere she looked, she saw elaborate paintwork on the walls; metalwork on the chandeliers, door handles, and curtain rods; and woodwork on the banister, panels, and doors. She saw candlesticks of silver, bronze, and copper, each a masterpiece. She followed close behind Zander through the second floor, up another grand staircase to the third floor. She had never seen so many paintings and spindly tables!

Despite the house being as big as the mines, she saw only one person inside—a woman in the same uniform as the gateman and the garage attendant, cleaning the rosewood picture frame of a large woman in pink. She didn't look up when Zander and Raven walked past.

Servants. He had *servants*.

She caught glimpses of the grounds through the tall windows. She spotted leafy green fronds and bright flowers that angled around a gray stone and iron gazebo as well as a sparkling fountain the size of a small pond.

And he'd left all this for lonely Silver Glen?

Zander led her through a set of wide doors into what, at first, appeared to be a sitting room; then she saw the pocket doors on the left and right. A grand fireplace of marble looked like it hadn't been used in a while, though everything looked pristinely upkept. Zander shut the doors behind them and heaved a heavy breath.

"Sisters," he breathed, setting his head against the polished wood of the door.

Raven meandered into the spacious sitting area and ran her hand along the back of a red and gold chair. "You live here?"

"I *lived* here," he corrected. He leaned away from the door and rubbed the back of his neck. His sapphire eyes took in the room with disdain. "The bathroom is to the left. The bedroom to the right."

She blinked; then she realized. "Is this your room?"

"It was." He met her eyes and frowned at her expression. "What?"

She shrugged and motioned to the fancy chairs. "It's so unlike you." Unlike her too. She had never stood in a room so nice, and it made her feel beyond insignificant and unworthy. Especially in her dirty boots and wrinkled trousers.

"Exactly." He diverted his attention to the walls, which were painted in shades of blue rather than the red that prevailed in the rest of the house. "Clean up while I try to find something else for you to wear."

"What's wrong with this?" she asked, motioning to her slept-in trousers and blouse.

His eyes looked her up and down, his lips set in a straight line. He met her gaze; not even a shadow of humor lit his eyes.

She felt something deflate in her chest. "I'm kidding." She started toward the bathroom. "Find me something nice."

Zander sank into the chair closest to him and hung his head, running his fingers through his dirty hair. Raven meandered to the pocket doors, finely crafted of dark wood and elegantly carved with lines and panels. She tucked her fingers into the smooth brass handholds and pulled the doors apart.

The bathroom on the other side was as big as the sitting room. White and gray tiles covered the floor and walls. The ceiling had been painted a sky blue. A brassy chandelier hung from its center. A grand bathtub took up the same amount of space as her entire bedroom back home. A separate shower stood away from it. On the other side, a toilet sat behind a blue and white folding screen with delicate gold metalwork.

She turned the faucet on the bathtub for warm water, and it spilled from the waterfall spout halfway up the wall. She found soap in the cabinets that smelled like jasmine and shampoo that smelled like apples. The towels were soft beyond reason and wide as blankets. She readied the items on the table beside the tub, stripped herself of her clothes, and stepped into the hot water.

Oh! She had missed a good bath—the washings she'd had along the way hadn't done the body justice. To be submerged in the water, to let it soothe and pull out the aches and worries—nothing compared.

She washed and soaked until the water cooled, then wrapped herself in the soft towels. She combed her hair and left it down to dry. She started to reach for her dirty clothes to return to the sitting room, but she spotted a beige robe hanging beside the door. Silk. She pulled it around her shoulders—she had never felt material so soft! Like water woven into thread.

The bath put her in a much better mood. She returned to the sitting room and found Zander slouched in a different chair. His listlessness had faded, and he stared into the empty fireplace with that intensity of his—thinking.

"You could do with a bath too," she said.

"There are a few dresses for you in the bedroom," he said without looking at her. His eyes focused on something she could not see. "I didn't know what size to tell them, so there's an assortment."

She pulled the pocket doors to the bedroom open. Soft sunlight glowed from the other side of the closed curtains. The dark wooden floors and dark blue walls gave the room a somber, tomb-like feel, and it mimicked the underground well enough that she felt a shiver. The room held a curtained bed large enough for five people, and piled on the blue-and-gold blankets were dresses. Dozens of dresses.

A rush of excitement raced from the top of her head to her toes and back again. She had never had so many clothing options!

Raven shut the pocket doors and went to examine those options.

Beside the dresses were undergarments of beige silk. That Zander had ordered her underthings filled her with hot, hot air that pushed against the inside of her face and her chest. She dropped the robe and quickly dressed in drawers and pulled a soft silk chemise over her arms. She grabbed the closest dress and pulled it over her head. Too big. The next was too small, the next too big, the next a strange style, but then she tried on a sage dress that fit perfectly. She laced up a corset of dark gold.

On the floor were three pairs of the same brown leather shoes—different sizes. She found the pair that fit best and returned to the sitting room. Zander no longer sat. Instead, water ran in the bathroom. Raven stood for a moment in the sitting room, then meandered to the large windows that looked over the garden. A high wall separated the Winchesters' grounds from the neighbors' equally sprawling grounds.

What must it have been like to grow up in a place like this? With fine clothes and servants? With more rooms than people? Without fighting for hand-me-downs and leftovers?

A knock landed on the main door, and she froze. She glanced at the bathroom door, but Zander gave no indication that he'd heard. The knock came again, louder. Raven opened the doors.

Two servants stood in the hall. A young woman held a tray of tea and cookies. The other was an older man with slicked-back white hair. The young woman bowed, the teapot and cups gently rattling, but the old man stood still as a statue. His nose crinkled as though he had smelled something awful.

"Master Baxter ordered tea *for two*," said the older servant, his voice matching his distasteful look. Raven hadn't missed the emphasis.

"Oh." Raven stepped out of the way.

The young woman walked the tray into the sitting room and placed it on the low table in front of the fireplace.

"Thank you."

The young woman bowed once again, but the old man didn't budge. They started back down the hallway, and Raven shut the doors. Her heart pounded; someone didn't want her here.

Raven poured a cup of tea into one of the two delicate china cups, added a cube of sugar, and took a sip. She added a second cube of sugar. They rarely had sugar for tea in Silver Glen. They had what the traders brought, which was never much. On her second sip, she decided that one sugar cube had been plenty. Despite the too-sweet tea, it warmed her throat and her insides like the bath had warmed her outside.

Halfway through her first cinnamon cookie, Zander walked out of the bathroom, wearing nothing but a towel around his middle.

She almost choked. The upper half of his bronze body was sculpted and lean. His damp dark hair hung to his shoulders. Water shimmered on his chest and taut stomach, pulling the sparse hair at a downward angle. Thin scars crisscrossed his skin with no discernable pattern; they must have been from his days in the Gray Elite. She wanted to ask him about it, but her throat refused to form words.

"What?" Zander cocked a brow. "Someone stole my robe. You'd rather I walk out naked?"

Her face burned, and she yanked her eyes off him and focused on her shoes.

"Where'd that come from?" His bare feet appeared in her view. His legs were sculpted and strong. He plucked a cookie from the plate.

"Your servants brought it when you were washing," she said.

He tensed. "What did they say?"

"That Baxter ordered tea."

Zander sat down beside her, eyes intent on her face. The towel came open over his thigh, and she fought to keep her eyes on his face. "What exactly did they say?" he asked.

She blinked. "Uh...that Master Baxter ordered tea for two, I think is what he said."

"He?"

She briefly described the servant who'd spoken and the servant who'd held the tray.

"Demetri," he spat. "What did you say?"

"I said thank you."

He nodded, eyes on the tray.

"Why does it matter?" she asked.

He turned his gaze back on her. He wore the same look that he wore when he aimed Birdie. Focused. Intent. Predatory.

Zander took her hand in his. "Raven, listen to me, this is important. While you're here, don't speak to anyone without me there."

She frowned. "I am capable of speaking—"

"I know you can," he said, his words quick and desperate. He squeezed her hand. "That's not what I'm talking about. People here are vultures. They will pick apart anything you say and use it against you. I know you won't mean anything by it, but there are people here who live to destroy other people. Please, Rae, don't talk to anyone without me."

To monitor her. To make sure she didn't say anything stupid.

She nodded. "Okay."

Zander sighed, stood, and took his cookie into the bedroom. Raven dared a glance at his retreating back, and what she saw stole her breath. On the right side of his lower back was a sprawling circular tattoo of steely gray; the whorls looked like the runes she had seen from the black market. She blinked, and he walked into the bedroom and out of sight.

The towel plopped on the floor, and she took a loud sip of her tea. She didn't need to think about him without a towel.

Why would Zander have a rune tattooed on his back?

Zander led her to the Orange Lounge, which got its name from the blood-orange wallpaper. Tall windows let in plenty of light and overlooked the front lawn. Baxter stood at the windows, his back to them. He had traded his Gray Elite uniform for a housecoat of deep purple. At the sound of the door, he turned and greeted them with a warm, practiced smile.

"It's been too long," said Baxter.

Zander shrugged. "That makes one of us."

Baxter's smile never faltered. If anything, he looked amused.

Lunch was served at a small table within the light of the windows, big enough for four people, set for three. Baxter and Zander sat across from each other, leaving Raven to sit between them. No servants lingered in the room. Though birds chirped pleasantly outside, Raven had a dreadful feeling of being trapped.

"Father isn't here," Baxter said. "He and Mother are on business in the east."

Zander's shoulders relaxed, but only slightly. "And you've sent word that I've arrived, no doubt."

"No. Not yet. I wanted to speak with you first." Baxter looked to Raven, then back at Zander. "You had us all worried when you disappeared. Father turned the house upside down, thinking you'd hidden somewhere, and Mother had the patrols scouring the city for weeks."

Raven swallowed a gulp of cider. *Disappeared.*

"I sent a letter," Zander said bitterly.

"A month later," Baxter said, a ghost of a smirk on his face. "Mother had started to face the grim reality that she might have to plan your funeral."

Zander chuckled.

"You think I joke?" Baxter glared at his brother, humor gone. "She cried for weeks. Barely ate. Father sent her to the hospital twice for observation, concerned the grief was too much."

Guilt replaced Zander's smirk, and he looked down at the expertly folded napkin binding his silverware.

Baxter continued, "When your letter arrived, Mother had gone with Aunt Meryl to write your obituary."

"I'm sure it was heartfelt," murmured Zander.

"Since Mother wrote it, I'm sure it was," Baxter said bitterly. "And I wouldn't know of its contents; no one got to read it. When your letter arrived, she had the obituary burned."

"I'll leave her an apology before I leave," Zander said, his tone tense.

Baxter frowned. "You're leaving? Again?"

Zander sighed. His eyes flickered to Raven, then to the window where Lenhala sparkled in the sunlight. "This isn't my home anymore, Baxter."

Baxter turned his gaze shamelessly onto Raven. His brows rose. "Oh. I see." He pursed his lips. "You didn't mention a girl in your letter."

"I hadn't met her yet," Zander said.

"Where are you from?" Baxter asked Raven, but before she could open her mouth, Zander said, "Small village north of here."

Baxter leaned back in his chair and pinned his brown eyes on Zander. "Still keeping secrets, are you?"

"Isn't that part of being a Winchester?"

Baxter laughed. "I suppose it is. Still, I know I can't stop you from leaving or force you to wait until our parents return. Tomorrow night is the Summer Solstice Ball. All I ask is that you attend. Prove to the world that our mother isn't mad for thinking her *favorite* son is alive."

Raven didn't miss the spiteful emphasis on "favorite." She glanced between the brothers, neither looking enthused about the other. She felt a pin of remorse for what Lena might be thinking of her right now. Did her family think her dead? Or had Mel told them the truth?

Zander's laugh sliced through her thoughts, bitter and humorless. "Don't try to guilt me into staying." His smile vanished, and he glared at his brother. "We both know Mother thought more highly of you. Better marks at school, better business sense, more friends."

Baxter shrugged. He didn't argue with any of those things. He turned his gaze again to Raven. "And think how it would be for her to attend the event of the year. It would give her something to remember."

With both brothers looking at her, she flushed. A certain maliciousness underlined Baxter's stare, a soured judgment for the girl he thought had stolen his brother.

"I'd rather be on my way as soon as possible," Zander said to Baxter.

Baxter's gaze lingered a heartbeat too long on Raven; then he nodded and looked away.

Raven released a slow, calming breath.

"I'll make you a deal, Brother," said Baxter. "Stay until the ball, and leave the morning after. I promise not to send word to our parents that you are here."

"You'd lie to Mother?" Zander raised a brow.

"Oh, no, if she asks, I will tell her that you were here but that you left again. I will tell her honestly that I promised you not to tell her," Baxter said, adjusting his collar. "I would never lie to my own mother."

Zander considered the offer. "You promise this?"

Baxter put a hand over his heart. "On my honor as your brother, I promise you, I will not send word of your presence to our parents."

A heartbeat passed. "Fine," Zander said. "I accept. We leave in two days."

Zander and Baxter held a long, silent stare. Raven shifted in her seat, and both sets of eyes turned to her. Baxter smiled, and Zander frowned; she had the distinct feeling that both brothers held back what they wanted to say. As they began to eat, the silence thickened with what had been left unsaid, and she suspected it had everything to do with Zander's sudden disappearance six months earlier—*that had left his family worried.*

He had not left with his parents' blessing or their knowledge, which made the weight of the little iron box in her pocket like a hundred stones.

Winchesters and secrets, she thought—just as Zander had said.

After lunch, Zander took Raven for a walk of the house. He walked her through the formal dining room, which had an oak table capable of holding forty guests, a number of sitting rooms with distinctly colorful wallpaper, the kitchens, and the room where his mother did her painting. Canvases in varying states of completion scattered the room—most were stunning.

Wouldn't it be nice to live a life where she could paint rather than work? Raven didn't voice those thoughts to Zander, who took in the wiles of his home with distaste.

He showed her the library, a room of thousands of books, and told her to pick a few out for herself. He meandered to the windows while she ran her fingers along the spines. So many books! She'd never seen so many at once! Zander helped her choose a few that were adventures, not dull history. Books in hand, they started back toward his room.

"What is the Summer Solstice Ball?" she asked softly. She didn't like the way her voice echoed in the empty hall.

"A ball they hold during the solstice."

She rolled her eyes. "Thank you, I'm glad you clarified that part of it. I would have never figured it out on my own."

He smirked. "That's what I'm here for." They reached his room, and once on the other side, his smile vanished. "It's just a party."

"Your brother said it was the event of the year."

He sighed. "That's because it's the summer party. But it's just another party. There's fireworks, drinking, dancing, and all the backstabbing chitchat you could want."

"Fireworks?"

"They're these things that have fuses like candles, and when lit, they fly into the sky and burst into colors with an ear-splitting bang."

"Oh," she said, trying to imagine such a thing. She sat down on the couch and stacked the books beside her. "And you would rather not go?"

"I would rather have the stomach flu," he said dryly. He plopped down onto the couch beside her.

"You would rather leave immediately," she said.

He half laughed. "I'd rather not have been dragged back here at all."

She fingered the edge of one of the leather-bound books. It didn't have the frayed edges and withering pages that hers had. Someone had read it but not many times. She had never held such a book, and a part of her didn't want to defile it by opening it. "You didn't tell your parents that you left," she whispered.

Zander released a heavy sigh. He leaned forward, elbows on his knees. "I know. I was hoping to avoid this, but I guess I can't anymore."

She reached into her dress pocket and closed her hand around the box. She had kept it on her person at all times, like Zander had said.

"It's not the best of stories," he said quietly.

"Tell me anyway," she said.

He gave her a weak smile, nerves and guilt showing through. "The truth is, I stole the box. I wasn't given the task of hiding it."

The box suddenly felt twice has heavy as it had before. *Stolen.* The thief had stolen it back. She scooted closer to Zander and placed her hand atop his. He wrapped his fingers around hers and gave her a sheepish smile.

"Do you hate me for lying?" he asked.

"No more than I did before," she said.

His smile stretched his lips, but it did not reach his eyes. "I grew up privileged. I grew up admiring my father. I grew up thinking the Gray Elite had done right in slaying King Reginald and his family and inserting their rule instead, but I thought all that because that's what I had been taught. I'd been raised to think highly of the Gray Elite and lowly of the dead king. But, as I grew up, I saw the Gray Elite rule in motion. They stole infants who showed signs of magic, enslaved those who disagreed, and I decided that I didn't like them.

"And then, when I was nine, I discovered my father, a Gray Elite, had been working in a secret order against the Gray Elite since before I was born. They protected magicians and sent them beyond the Gray Elite's grasp. They wanted to reinstate the kingdom to its former glory. I'd always thought the rumors of a resistance were a joke, but it was real, and I jumped at the chance to be a part of it, just as my brother had done before me. My father welcomed me into the order's ranks with open arms, and for the first time, he was proud of me."

"Resistance?" Raven whispered. It sounded like a story, something parents would tell their children to explain why bad things happened. It sounded like the stories of the Revenant, a story to explain disaster and the unknowns.

Zander nodded. "They call themselves the Order of the Hawk. The hawk was the symbol of the king of Rhynwier. They say it was the symbol of the god whose name the Gray Elite have worked so hard to erase from history."

"The Sisters?"

"No, before them," Zander said. "It's one of the things the Gray Elite doesn't want people to talk about or know." He pointed toward the books on her other side. "They've spent hundreds of years destroying evidence that a god existed before the Sisters. Give them another hundred years or so, and they will have destroyed the Sisters too."

Raven felt a pitting in her stomach. Though she did not claim to be devout, the idea that the Gray Elite could just erase such a thing chilled her bones.

Zander leaned back into the couch and squeezed Raven's hand. "I was so happy to be a part of the Hawks. I was so happy to be involved in something bigger than myself, something that I thought could change the world."

"But...what could the Hawks do against the Gray Elite?" she asked.

"They smuggle magicians out of the city." A shadow passed over his face. "The Gray Elite want nothing more than to rid the world of magic, to make sure that their machines are more powerful, and we make sure that magic stays alive. We—"

Raven gripped his hand. "You take children away?"

"To save their lives," Zander said, frowning. "I know it's not a perfect situation. Even as the Hawks save them, every day, children are taken by the Gray Elite. They're never seen again. They never say what happens to the children, but we all know."

She paled. He didn't have to say it. *Killed.*

"The Hawks work in secret all over the city and the countryside. Protecting magicians we find is one thing, but we also work against the Gray Elite rule, taking out troublesome automatons, disrupting their functions, taking out figureheads, and making sure the Regent knows that he doesn't have complete control."

"Taking out figureheads," she repeated. She dropped her voice. "You kill them?"

His eyes became hard. "Just like they have killed thousands of magicians. The people the Hawks take out are people who ordered those deaths. We are killing the killers before they can hurt anyone else."

She swallowed. Dark logic but logic nonetheless.

Zander held her hand between both of his. "This is why I didn't want to come back. The underbelly of the city is vicious, but the topside is just as bad."

"What happened?"

"Hmm?"

"You didn't finish your story," she said. "Why you left."

His smile vanished. "Oh." He cleared his throat. "I went to my father's office one night. I don't remember the reason I went, but I overheard him and a few officers talking. They knew a coup would result in Gracita declaring war, and thousands would be slaughtered because of it. The Gray Elite has an army on the ground and in the air, and the Hawks were a small band of rebels. They had found something that they had been looking for, something they could use that would guarantee a victory against the Gray Elite, and they were planning on using it."

Raven breathed, "What?"

Zander's eyes grew dark. "Altair's Augur," he whispered.

She blanched. "That's just a legend," she said, her voice barely a breath.

He shook his head. "I thought so too. But it's not. I've seen it. It's underground, under the city. It's been there the whole time."

She caught her breath in her throat. Altair's Augur was a doomsday device named after the ancient philosopher and engineer who'd supposedly built it. Legends said the augur produced a blinding white light that obliterated an enemy city in the blink of an eye. Hundreds of thousands of people, gone in a flash of light.

"It's folklore," she argued.

"It's history," Zander said. "It's another part of history that the Gray Elite want to erase. A few books about it remain, but they are kept in secret."

"By the Hawks?"

He nodded. "Another thing we do. Preserve the history before it's gone forever. Some say the augur was built by the old god, but no one knows." Zander leaned forward and rubbed his temples. "I couldn't believe it was real. I didn't want to. I couldn't believe my father would be involved in something so horrible, something that would kill so many people at once."

Raven couldn't either. Altair's Augur. Underneath her feet. The city felt substantially less sturdy.

"I stole a vital piece of the machine. It won't work without it." His eyes traveled to her pocket, where she held onto the box. "I ran for my life with it."

"And you ended up in Silver Glen," Raven finished, "on the edge of the world, where no one would think to look."

He nodded. "And that is where we have to go," he whispered. "Because that device cannot be used. By anyone."

She nodded. She understood, though she didn't want to believe it. To save people, to prevent unthinkable disaster, they would have to return to Silver Glen. It made sense, logically, although it left a terrible pitting in her stomach. "But, before that, your brother is right."

Zander frowned.

"You must allow me the privilege of attending the Summer Solstice Ball. If I'm going to live the rest of my life as kitchen help, I am going to enjoy what freedom I have left."

Zander laughed and brought her hand up to his lips. As he kissed her hand, a tingle zapped underneath and over her skin from her hand to her toes to her scalp like a shock. A pleasant shock.

"And, if you're going to the ball, you'll need something to wear," he said, leaning back and gazing up at the ceiling. "It's a fashion event. But, before that, we need to talk about our cover story."

"What do you have in mind?"

They decided to stick with the story that Zander had met her while traveling. They had gone to Oun on a journey through the countryside. She knew nothing of why he left or that he had been from Lenhala.

And, as Zander told her twice, they had to leave before his father returned. His father would know he took it, and his father would be furious enough to do anything to get it back.

Raven took one of the books and nestled into the cushioned seat below the large window in Zander's sitting room. She quickly lost herself in the story and didn't return to the real world until someone cleared their throat. Zander stood over her. He had pulled his dark hair back and wore simple trousers, a plain white silk shirt, and a clean vest. His black leather boots shined. He didn't wear his holsters; he looked thinner without his guns.

"Are you going somewhere?" she asked.

"I've got some people to see," he said quickly. She started to close her book, but he added, "Alone."

Her heart fluttered. Alone, without her.

"I won't be gone long, or at least, I hope not." He glanced nervously to the window.

"Why can't I go?" She would love to see more of Lenhala.

"Because..." He fought for words, huffed, and said, "Because I can move faster without you."

His words stung, and she leaned back against the seat's wooden wall. "Oh. It's that, then."

He let out a sigh. "I don't want the Hawks looking any closer at you than they need to. For all they know, you don't know anything about me or why I left or them. Do you still have it?"

She nodded, patting the box in her pocket.

"Good. Don't let it leave your person. Ever. I'm serious, Raven." He knelt down to look her in the eye. "Don't mention the Hawks to anyone. You think I'm Gray Elite; that's it. You're a simple girl from a simple town."

She nodded.

He squeezed her hand, then left. She waited until the doors closed, then slumped further into the pillows. A simple girl from a simple town. That's all she was. Too naïve to go with him to see anyone from the Order of the Hawk, too backwater to understand secrets, and too stupid to understand how his world worked.

She returned to her book with an attitude that had gone sour.

A knock sounded on the door, and Raven froze. Should she answer it? The knock came again, a quick two-toned knock. She shut her book and walked to the door. She straightened her shoulders, lifted her chin, and opened the door.

"Dresses, miss," said the servant on the other side.

Two servants brought in a rack of dresses—fine dresses, much finer than the ones she had tried on earlier. Dresses for the ball, she realized.

She said nothing as the servants pushed the rack into the bedroom or as they curtsied and left. She listened to their soft shoes in the hall; then she went to inspect the dresses for herself. They were lovely! Silk and velvet and shined buttons of gold and silver and pearl. She pulled a few from the rack.

They were all so revealing. All strappy shoulders or bare shoulders, low backs or no backs at all, with tight bodices and low necklines. She pulled out a dress of vivid royal purple. The shoulders and back were nothing but crisscrossing straps of gold velvet cord.

Raven glanced to the open door of the bedroom. With Zander not there to gawk or tease, she could try on as many as she liked! If he was hellbent on dragging her back to Silver Glen, she might as well pretend to be someone else for a while. Someone far more interesting and cultured than herself.

She unlaced her corset, pulled off her day dress and chemise—for where would a chemise go in these dresses? She didn't try on the purple one first; no, she went with a pink dress without shoulders. She opened his wardrobe to see herself in the mirror; the dress fit tight, hugging her chest and hips, while the skirt flared when she twirled.

She tried on a red dress with sheer panels for a torso, a bejeweled black dress, a sky-blue dress with no back and a barely-there bodice, and then a creamy yellow dress with a deep V that nearly reached her navel and left much of her breasts exposed. The sunlight-colored skirt twirled with her as she moved.

"That's not your color."

She stopped dead, losing her balance and careening into something solid and warm. She looked up to see Zander standing there, a smirk on his lips. Her face burned, and she pushed herself off his chest.

She cleared her throat. "I didn't hear you return."

"Good thing too, or I would have missed this." He motioned to all of her. He shamelessly glanced at the exposed skin between her breasts.

She flushed hotter and crossed her arms. "These are the dresses your servants brought up."

He scanned the rack, unimpressed. He fingered the skirt of a blue silk dress, his eyes elsewhere. Distracted.

"I like the purple one," she said. "I might wear it to the ball."

Zander blinked, then sought the purple dress from the rack. He fingered the straps, then let it flutter back into place. Unimpressed and unenthused.

Simple girl, simple town.

She swallowed, suddenly feeling foolish. He saw fine dresses all the time, on girls more attractive than her. Of course, he wouldn't think the dresses were special.

"Okay," was all he said. He went back into the sitting room and shut the bedroom door.

Raven stood there, staring at the back of the door. In a huff, she tore the yellow dress off and put her chemise and day dress back on. She busied herself with returning the gowns to the rack; she'd thrown them a bit haphazardly onto the bed.

She steadied herself, then returned to the sitting room. Zander was sitting, elbows on his knees, staring into the dark fireplace. He didn't so much as glance in her direction as she returned to her book, to her cushioned window seat. She found her place in the story and returned there. When she looked up again, Zander hadn't moved.

Where had he gone? Who had he seen? What had put him in such a strange mood? Then again, he had been in a strange mood since they'd met the Dwellers. Did it have something to do with the Gray Elite? The Hawks?

He's keeping secrets, said a mean little voice in her head. *Keeping secrets from you, from his brother, and from his father too. From everyone. He doesn't think you're smart enough to understand.*

A knock came to the door, and Zander stood with the fluid grace of a nobleman and trained soldier. A servant stood on the other side, his nose as high as any noble.

"Yes?" Zander asked as if he had been interrupted.

"Miss Ivaline Pemberton wishes to be received for dinner, sir," said the servant in a dry tone. "She is overjoyed to hear that Master Winchester has returned."

Zander sighed. "Fine. We'll receive her in the first-floor lounge."

"I will send word at once." The servant gave a slight bow and retreated into the hall.

Zander shut the door.

"A lady friend of yours?" Raven asked. *Miss* Pemberton.

"Of a sense," Zander said listlessly. "We went to the same school. Our fathers went to school together, joined the Gray Elite together, have had a weekly poker night since I can remember. So, yes, we know each other. I guess that makes us friends."

Miss Pemberton probably knew Zander better than Raven did, and the thought burned. Had he tried to kiss her too? She shoved that thought away. She had only known Zander for six months, and the people here had known him his entire life, eighteen years. It would be like Zander being jealous of Lena knowing Raven better. Nonsense.

Still, that bubble of bitterness and jealousy didn't recede. She returned her eyes to her book. "I suppose I will be dining in while you enjoy dinner with your lady friend," she said calmly.

"What? Oh. No, you can go." Zander sighed and stepped toward the bathroom. "Miss Pemberton isn't that bad." He stopped in the doorway. "She's a sickly girl, always on bedrest. She's spent the majority of her life indoors, away from people and stressful events. She rarely leaves her home. She's got a weak constitution."

"Ah," Raven said. "And your reappearance has spurred her to leave her home. She must think highly of you to attempt it."

Zander glanced at her over his shoulder, brows furrowed. She hadn't meant to snap at him like that, but she had. She wouldn't apologize for it. She turned her attention to her book, and a heartbeat later, the bathroom door closed.

For dinner, Zander donned a red housecoat and found Raven a simple shawl. Together, they walked to the first-floor lounge. Baxter had gone out for dinner, leaving them to dine with Miss Pemberton alone. Raven would be lying if she said she wasn't a bit relieved. Baxter would be one less person to lie to, to pretend for. A servant opened the lounge door for them, and Zander walked through first.

Miss Pemberton sat with her back to them, facing the window. A table had been set for three, the covered dishes ready to be served. Servants stood by to do just that. Miss Pemberton wore sky blue, and her blonde hair was done up in an elegant bun, secured with pearl-tipped pins. She sat straight, and a servant of hers—Raven assumed, for he wore different colors than the Winchester house servants—stood close by her.

At the sound of the door, her girlish, cultured voice rang out, "Is that dear Zander?"

Zander escorted Raven around the table to where the sickly Miss Pemberton could see them. A lady indeed, for she wore glittery dark kohl around her eyes and pale powder over her face and neck. Her eyes met Raven's, and a sweet, mildly bitter smile came across her lips.

"And this must be the darling girl who swept him off his feet," she said.

Raven started to speak, but Zander interrupted by pulling out her chair. She sat.

"Yes," Zander answered, his tone light. "I do apologize for leaving like I did. I didn't expect to be gone so long."

Miss Pemberton smiled. She cocked her head to the side and snapped, "Charles, leave us."

"Are you certain, miss?" drawled her servant.

"Yes, yes, I'll call if I feel uncertain," she said, waving a delicate, white-gloved hand toward him.

"As you wish, miss." Charles relocated to the hallway outside.

"Git is what he is," whispered Miss Pemberton in a tone that struck Raven. She pinned her eyes on Raven, and her lips quirked upward like she knew something Raven didn't.

Raven bristled. Miss Pemberton didn't relent her stare.

Zander leaned in closer, his humored voice in her ear, "Haven't figured it out yet?"

Miss Pemberton smiled at her—really smiled. Through the powder and kohl, Raven saw a face that she already knew. *Ivy.* Ivaline. Her mouth fell open.

Ivaline winked playfully.

Zander spoke to Ivaline, "I'm glad to see that you're doing well enough to pay me a visit. I do appreciate your company."

She's a sickly girl, spends a lot of her time indoors.

Raven felt struck; Ivaline spent a lot of time indoors so that Ivy could be a free girl out in the woods. But how had she gotten here so fast? There had to be a Hellcat tunnel that led into Lenhala.

Spies and scouts, Zander had called the Dwellers. All over the kingdom.

A servant served dinner, uncovering the dishes and pouring cider into cut crystal goblets. Zander and Ivy—*Ivaline*—spent much of it talking about people and places that Raven had never heard of, and she felt left out. She tried to pay attention to the names, but there were too many to keep track of.

"So tell me, Zander, how you met this darling of yours," Ivaline said with a coy smile at Raven.

Zander chuckled, and then he spun the fake tale of how he met Raven—for the listening ears at the door and to inform Ivaline of their cover. She soaked in the story, every word. At the mention of the Summer Solstice Ball, she let out a lady's gasp of surprise.

"You're attending the ball?" Ivaline clapped her hands together. "That is wonderful! I've planned to attend, but I've kept the option open in case my health takes a wrong turn. I am glad to know that you will be there, Raven. It will give me someone to talk to."

Raven nodded. She felt a small bubble of relief too. Ivy would be there, and she wouldn't be in a ball of total strangers.

"Do you know what you're wearing?" Ivaline asked casually, then she added in a drawling lady's simper, "I expect that you don't know many of the designers here in Lenhala. I wouldn't want you to be caught wearing something from last year or from one of the less tasteful designers."

She'd said it so convincingly, Raven felt a pitting of shame at not knowing those things. She reminded herself that Ivy sat across from her, not a simpering lady.

"Zander was kind enough to arrange a few gowns to be brought for me," Raven said as sweetly as she could, and Zander took in every word.

Because they were being listened to, and the charade of Ivaline needed to exist even behind closed doors, as well as whatever charade Zander was playing, Raven had, however much she hadn't agreed to it, been pulled into the charade.

"I must see them," Ivaline said. "After dinner. I refuse to allow my dear here to wander through the Summer Solstice Ball in anything less than perfect."

After dinner, Ivaline—and her attentive servant—followed Zander and Raven to his bedroom, to the dresses. Ivaline rummaged through the dresses one by one, whispering insults at each. Too bright, too low, too shimmery, wrong fabric, horrid color, too many straps, not enough coverage—the list went on through the entire rack.

"Where in Minerva's name did you get these, Zander?" Ivaline playfully struck him on the arm with her lace-and-pearl fan.

"I asked one of the servants. I gave them her size, and this is what I got."

Ivaline put a hand to her chest, gasping as though physically struck; her servant jerked a step toward her but, upon realizing the act had been an exaggerated response, returned to his passive pose.

"You relied on *the help* to find her something suitable to wear to the event of the summer?" Ivaline shook her head, her chin high. "That will not do." She snapped her fingers and said sharply, "Rora."

A mousy-haired servant girl stepped into the bedroom and gave a quick bow. She wore the colors of Pemberton House. "Yes, miss?"

"I need you to run down to Raffela's and ask for the Gold Star, the one that I liked. She'll know what I mean. Tell her it is a fashion emergency, and bring her and the dress here."

"Yes, miss." The servant vanished as quickly as she had appeared.

"Oh, that's not necessary—" Raven started.

"Nonsense," Ivaline said, waving away Raven's concern. "If you are to be seen with me, then you will be dressed in nothing less than the best. And I know the best." She put a hand over her heart. "Raffela is a dream with a dress. Just you wait and see."

They waited for Raffela in the downstairs lounge while drinking tea. Ivaline went on about the designers of the city, names that Raven would never remember, and their fashion choices and horrible dresses. Ivaline talked nearly nonstop, and it was hard for Raven to see Ivy behind all the glitter and glamour and chitchat.

Footsteps sounded in the corridor, and before a servant could move to answer the doors, they flew open. A tall, tan woman rushed inside, her flaming red hair a wave behind her. She wore a glittering blue scarf over her broad shoulders. The servant girl, Rora, carried a garment bag in her arms.

"I heard there was an emergency!" Raffela stopped in front of Ivaline, bent to one knee, and gently kissed her hand. "I am at your service."

They shooed out the servants and Zander, and the designer had no qualms about stripping Raven down to the bare nothings; Ivaline spoke constantly over the dresses that Zander had managed to find, and Raffela added small comments and agreements when helping Raven into a gown of blue and gold.

Compared to the others, the blue and gold dress looked a world better. With a few adjustments, it fit like a dream.

"That is much better," Ivaline said, nodding proudly.

Raffela kissed her fingertips and flourished them through the air. "Perfection."

Raven caught her reflection in the glass-front cabinet, and from the ghostly image she saw, the dress did look good. She did not get to see it fully, for Raffela stripped her, and she was left to dress herself in her day dress.

Raffela hung the gown in the bedroom and whisked the other dresses away to dispose of them properly, as she said, which Ivaline whispered meant she would sell them at a discount.

"Oh, the lighting is lovely for an evening stroll," Ivaline said longingly, her eyes looking out at the garden. "Come, Raven, walk through the garden with me."

She didn't have much of a choice, for Ivaline strung her arm through Raven's and guided her to the back door, then out into the glorious gardens of Winchester House. Zander stayed inside at Ivaline's behest, and she guided Raven toward the stone and iron gazebo surrounded by lavender shoots and tiny yellow flowers.

The twilight didn't last long, and the tiny yellow flowers started to glow—bioluminescence, Ivaline explained. A wonder of the city. Hundreds of bioluminescent flowers dotted the garden, yellows, purples, pinks, a rainbow of color. Not unlike the fungi in Silver Glen, Raven thought, though she didn't tell Ivy that. Still, the glowing flowers tugged on something in her chest, and for the first time in a while, she felt a little homesick.

"How has your stay been?" Ivaline asked softer, casually rather than simpering and dripping with fake politeness.

"Good," Raven said. "The capital's been more than I expected."

"You can speak freely," Ivaline said. "Just not very loud."

Raven released a sigh. "There's so much to keep track of, and I'm worried I'll say the wrong thing. Zander's got me on edge more than anything."

"He's terrified," Ivy said. Ivy, not Ivaline.

"His father?"

She nodded. "Zander made some hasty choices before he left, and I mean hasty as in not the best choices. There are a lot of people who are angry at him and confused, and his father is at the top of that list."

Raven nodded. Ivy knew more of Zander's past and disappearance than Raven did, but she didn't want the other girl to think her stupid on the matter, so she didn't ask for details. Nor did she know how much of Zander's past she knew regarding the Hawks or the iron box in her pocket.

"Everything is much more complicated than I imagined," Raven said.

Ivy chuckled. "Isn't it though? I wasn't kidding when I said I preferred the countryside over all this. Yes, it's sparkling and nice, and everything is just so dreamy, but it has a darker side. The price we pay for all this convenience and glamor is steep. Too steep for me."

The wind rustled through the trees in a haunting whisper.

Raven whispered, "Who are you?"

"That's a good question. I feel like two people sometimes." Ivy shifted and rested against Raven. "Did Zander tell you about the resistance?"

"Yes."

Ivy nodded. "I've spent most of my life in the resistance," she whispered. "My father is one of the officers spearheading it, along with Zander's father. I was a sickly child, and it was the perfect excuse for my parents to stay home more than others. As I grew up, the sickness went away, but it's still a good excuse for spending time away from the city or, as far as anyone here knows, locked away in a room at the house. I've spent more time with the Dwellers, and I come back here when I need to. Appearances, recon, that sort of thing." She gave Raven a sly smile. "Who'd ever suspect poor little Miss Pemberton of wrongdoing?"

"I surely wouldn't," Raven said. "The poor dear is pale as death."

"It's powder," Ivy whispered. "Works wonders."

The two girls sat in the gazebo until the sun finished setting, and Ivy's servant came to fetch her. Her mother had ordered her not to be out past a certain time, lest the cold of the night take her health in the wrong direction. Faking exhaustion, Ivy became Ivaline once again and allowed her servants to escort her to the waiting coach.

Raven returned to the house and to Zander's room, where he looked unenthused. He stood by the window, the perfect spot to have watched them from.

"What?" Raven asked, tossing the shawl over the back of the chair.

"What did you two talk about?" he asked.

"Just girl talk, nothing you'd be interested in."

He lifted a brow but didn't respond. Raven was to the bathroom door when he said, "Ivy's a good girl. But she can be reckless and a bit naïve at times."

"I like her." Raven shut the door. She didn't need Zander to tell her who she could be friends with. Ivy made her feel less alone in this strange world, and she needed someone like her.

Raven returned to her book; Zander paced. He remained on edge throughout the evening, barely speaking. He would halt his pacing now and again, and Raven would catch him staring out of the window, his eyes on something she couldn't see. What was he thinking about? His father? The Dwellers? The box in her pocket?

Her mind was still spinning. She could barely concentrate on her book. The box, the augur, Ivy and Ivaline. She had never had to take in so much information at once.

The sun had sunk in the sky, and the lights of Lenhala burned bright, hiding the stars from view. The lights of the airships dotted the sky instead. Even inside the house, she could hear the gentle rumble of the hundreds of engines.

The clock chimed ten, and not a moment after, a knock came to the door. Zander jumped to answer it first.

The servants had brought Raven toiletries and a pair of silk pajamas in a steel gray.

"Would the lady require a room of her own?" asked Demetri, the dreary old servant. Through his narrowed eyes, he glared at Raven with heavy and obvious disapproval.

"No," Zander said quickly. He closed the door in the servant's face. Raven started to speak, but Zander put a finger to his lips. He pointed to the door—Demetri hadn't yet walked away.

Several heartbeats passed. Still, Demetri stood. Waiting. Listening.

Raven slid off the window seat and took the pajamas from Zander. She ran her hand over the silk. "These are lovely," she said, not a lie. "And so soft!"

Demetri's boots started back down the hall, away from the door.

Raven looked to Zander, and her face warmed as she asked, "You wouldn't rather I sleep somewhere else?"

"No." He secured the deadbolt on the door and then started to unbutton his dress shirt.

Her face warmed, and her heart flipped; she turned her face away from him before he could notice.

"The servants would pester you, and I'd bet gold that Baxter would show up in the morning to see what information he could get out of you."

"Oh, I see," she said. It made sense.

She started toward the bathroom with her basket of girl-oriented toiletries. They had included a golden bottle of what looked like perfume.

From behind her, there came a swish of silk. Zander's shirt. Her thoughts drifted to the rune tattooed on his back. She wanted to ask him about it, but she held her tongue. Thinking about him without a shirt made her face burn.

"What's wrong?" Zander asked. "We've shared a smaller bed before."

She paused at the bathroom door and glanced into the open doors of the bedroom. True, his bed was twice the size of a normal bed, near triple the size of what any inn had had. Still, it was Zander's bed, his space, his house. She thought to the last night they'd spent at an inn; he had slept with his arm over her.

Zander crossed the room with silent footsteps. He still wore the silk shirt, but he had unbuttoned it, revealing the lean chest and stomach underneath. She tore her gaze from his chest and forced herself to meet his sapphire gaze. He wore an emotion she couldn't recognize, one she'd not seen on him but a few times.

"We're still pretending, Rae," he whispered. "Everyone here thinks I ran off with you. It would look strange if we slept in different rooms."

And everyone assumed the worst. Her face heated, and the word "whore" resounded in her mind. Her heart flip-flopped.

Pretending, she told herself.

"Raven?" He stepped closer.

She hugged the pajamas to her chest. "Of course."

She shut herself in the bathroom and took her time getting ready for bed. She left the toiletries on the counter and, wearing her silk pajamas, carried her dress back into the sitting room.

She held up the dress and started to ask, "Where—"

"Just throw it somewhere," Zander said from the bedroom, his voice tired. "The servants will pick it up when they fetch the laundry."

She blinked, confused. She glanced around the sitting room. Indeed, he had tossed his silk dress shirt into one of the armchairs, along with his pants and vest. Zander emerged from the bedroom in dark blue pajamas and took the dress from her arms. He then tossed it over one of the chairs.

"There," he said.

"Is that what the rich do with their dirty clothes?" She followed him into the bedroom. Without the sunlight to warm it up, the single candle beside the bed gave the room a very tomb-like feel. "Toss it aside like garbage for the lowly servants to deal with?"

"Yes," he said simply.

She crawled into the cushy bed, and Zander untied the bed-curtains. He pulled them closed on all but one side, his side, and then he blew out the candle. Bright moonlight—no, she realized—it wasn't moonlight streaming through the windows. It was city light and the glowing flowers.

Raven settled into her pillow and listened to Zander's soft footsteps. His weight pushed on the bed, and he crawled underneath the blankets beside her. He pulled the last curtain closed, shutting the space of his bed in near-total darkness. He settled into his pillow.

It had a very underground feel to it, and she didn't know if she liked it or not. While the dark mimicked the underground, it smelled too fresh, and the city was too loud.

"The servants don't come in my room that often because I don't want them to," he said quietly. "I can do things for myself." He inhaled and released a long sigh. "The city is nice, but I'd rather live outside it. I like the villages where everyone works, everyone pulls their weight, and everyone earns their supper, not like this, where it's a matter of how much money a person has or how powerful they are."

"This bed is nice, though," Raven said.

Zander laughed, a soft, tired sound. "Do you think they'll notice if we take it with us?"

"We could sleep outside instead, under the stars," she added.

"After we dance," he said, a near whisper.

She smiled; she couldn't help it. He hadn't forgotten about that. She hadn't either.

The morning came; Raven didn't have much time to herself. After breakfast, servants came in to help her get ready for the Summer Solstice Ball. They did her hair and makeup and helped her into the dress. A few hours after midday, Raven stepped out from behind the dressing screen and saw herself in the mirror. The blue and gold dress fit her splendidly, leaving her arms and back exposed, but showed little cleavage. According to Ivaline, cleavage was last year.

Her light brown hair had been done up with blue ribbons and gold beads that clicked as she moved. Her mother's locket rested on her chest. The servants had tried to remove it, but she refused.

The doors opened, footsteps entered, and then a low whistle sounded. Blushing, she turned, thinking it was Zander who had entered.

Baxter stood in the doorway. He wore his Gray Elite dress uniform, dark gray jacket, and pressed trousers with yellow stripes and white threading. It complimented his tall, lean frame—the frame he and his brother shared. Baxter had combed his dark hair back and parted it to the side, the Gray Elite style.

"You look stunning," Baxter said, giving her a charming smile.

"Thank you," she said, giving him a small curtsy. "You clean up well yourself."

He smiled. "'Clean up'? Is that a saying where you're from? It's cute."

She blushed. Simple girl, simple town. "Yes, it is."

She would rather not be thought of as cute. Children were cute. Small animals were cute. She, nearly a grown woman, was not cute.

Footsteps sounded in the hall—boots. Zander appeared behind Baxter, and at the sight of his brother, he scowled.

"What are you doing here?" Zander demanded. "Don't you have your own date to bother?"

Baxter chuckled. "Yes, and I was on my way out when—"

"Then you should continue on your way," Zander said.

Baxter closed his mouth and glared at his younger brother. "Very well," he said in mock-politeness. "I will see you both this evening." He turned on his heel and walked out.

Zander shooed the servants, leaving him and Raven alone. He hadn't dressed as Gray Elite. Instead, he wore a lovely suit of dark blue that fit his strong shoulders and lean waist. His velvet vest had buttons of gold. Someone must have told him her dress was blue and gold, for they looked as though they had planned it.

"You also look nice," Raven said absently.

"What? Oh, yeah." Zander glared at the doors, after his brother. He rolled his shoulders. "You look nice."

"You're not even looking!" Raven set her hands on her hips. Zander's sharp blue eyes met hers and then rolled down her body and back. She turned to the side to show him her exposed back.

"You look nice, Raven," he said. This time, his words were genuine.

She nodded. "That's better."

His eyes lingered on her a heartbeat longer, then moved to the window behind her.

"How are we getting to the ball?" she asked casually.

"By coach," he said simply. He took a deep breath, then released it. He came over to her, eyes serious and nervous. "Raven, you're about to walk into the lion's den. People are going to ask you questions, the same question over and over, trying to get information out of you."

"What kind of information?" She didn't know anything of worth.

"Anything they can turn into gossip, about me, about you, about anything," he said, almost pleading. "Don't answer anything directly."

She frowned, but before she could protest the absurdity of that command, he added, "Think how Ivaline speaks. She doesn't say anything that means anything. It's all mindless chitchat, pointless; around and around it goes. Talk like that."

"You want me to be stupid on purpose?"

"Not stupid," he said quickly. He set his hands on her bare shoulders and took a step closer. "It's a safety mechanism. Information is power. The less these people know about you, the better. Right now, our plan is to get out of here as soon as possible. Ivy's here, and that means we've got the Hellcat."

Zander had gotten that out of Ivy's words, her presence, and Raven hadn't thought of that. In that moment, she did feel stupid.

"Raven," he whispered, stepping closer. She could feel his breath on her lips. "We cannot let that box fall into anyone else's hands. We cannot afford to have anyone trying to find you or anything about you that might put us in danger tomorrow."

She nodded. "Okay."

"Where is it?" he whispered.

Her cheeks reddening, she lifted a hand to her bodice and pointed to where she had tucked the box—between her breasts.

He raised a brow.

"What? I don't have pockets in this thing," she whispered back, her cheeks getting hotter by the second.

His thumb touched her collarbone. He stood there a moment, eyes pleading into hers. She didn't know what else to say to him, and she didn't have the words—that same tingly feeling fluttered up through her ribs. Was he about to kiss her? She blinked, he began to lean in, and her heart jumped into her throat.

A knock sounded at the door, followed by a servant's drawl, "The coach is ready, Master Zander."

He cleared his throat, eyes looking anywhere that wasn't her. "Right, well, we best get this over with," he said, his voice a pitch higher than normal.

He offered her his arm; she took it, willing her heart to slow before it burst from her chest.

She could pretend to be ditzy and stupid for a night. A dark little voice in the back of her mind told her that she wouldn't be pretending. No one expected a simple girl from a simple town to be smart or cunning, and she didn't particularly feel either of those things.

Regardless, she refused to let any of that spoil this once-in-a-lifetime chance. Ivy would be there; Zander would be there; she would not be alone.

She took a deep breath, held her shoulders straight and her chin high, and walked with Zander to the garage. A well-dressed driver stood beside the readied ivory coach, and Zander helped Raven into the red leather seats. The golden cat automaton hissed to life, and the coach started out of the garage, down the winding lane, through the iron gates, and onto Lamp Light Way.

The entire city seemed to be getting ready for the ball, with suns painted on windows and storefronts and carts and stalls set up along the main streets, selling candies, candles, woodwork, clockwork, and all manner of things.

"I forgot to mention," Zander said, his voice drawling—for the ears of the driver. "This is a military event."

"So I should expect old men in suits with war stories?" She tried to imitate Ivaline's bored, polite tone, and when Zander didn't blink and the driver didn't even glance back, she suspected she had gotten it right.

Zander gave her a wry smile. "There are those too."

She tried to pick out what that meant; was there something else under his words that he wanted her to understand? A hidden meaning? Did it mean she should be careful when speaking to the military personnel? Or did it mean that people like Zander and Baxter would be there—sneaky and full of secrets? Ivaline's father was Gray Elite too, as was Zander's father; they were also part of the resistance. The Order of the Hawk.

She pieced together a meaning, unsure if it was the one Zander intended. There would be Gray Elite there who knew of the Hawks, those who were in the Hawks, and those who despised the Hawks. She would not know who was who without Zander or Ivy.

Raven, being the lovebird that she was, pulled Zander's arm a little closer to herself and gave him a warm smile, to let him know she had gotten his meaning. He gave her a warm smile in return, one that did not escape the driver's notice.

She could play a lady for a while, and she could play the game. Let them all think her simple and stupid. This time tomorrow, she and Zander would be far from Lenhala, and this ball would be a but a dream.

The Summer Solstice Ball was held at the old palace. It had once been the beating heart of the kingdom, the home of King Reginald; now, the Gray Elite used it as a play park for their social events. The Winchester coach trotted down the front drive, and Raven gasped at the grandeur. The palace was a masterpiece of ancient architecture. It rose three stories, all milky stone and pale marble. Each grand window held stained glass of gold and blue; each had an ironwork balcony. Dormers lined the roof, each arched with iron fashioned into the shape of a hawk in flight.

"It's beautiful," she whispered to Zander.

"It was even more beautiful before the Gray Elite moved in," he whispered back, low enough the driver couldn't hear. "See those platforms? Statues of the Sisters used to be there, but they tore them down."

Indeed, three stone platforms lay in the trimmed grass like river stones. In the center of the stones, a marvelous fountain spewed aquamarine water over a brassy automaton woman.

Their coach joined the procession to the front steps. One by one, the coaches paused, and their well-dressed occupants stepped out. Most of the men wore Gray Elite uniforms, and she spotted a few women who had opted for the uniform rather than a gown, although most of them wore gowns. The Winchester coach paused by the front steps, and a footman opened the door. He held his gloved hand out for Raven. She took it gently and stepped out, Zander on her heels.

They started up the sweeping stairs of white marble. Zander and Raven followed the example of the couple ahead of them and looped their arms together. Their coach moved on, and another took its place.

At the top of the stairs, a large set of dark wooden doors had been propped open, and three Gray Elite soldiers stood on duty on either side, faces impassive, and all armed with crossbows on their backs, a saber at one hip and a pistol on the other.

Raven whispered to Zander, "Why carry a crossbow and a pistol?"

He whispered back, "Crossbows are more ceremonial."

The soldiers paid little attention to the Gray Elite walking inside, but as Zander and Raven approached, every set of eyes followed him.

"It's good to see you back, Lieutenant," said the Gray Elite closest to the door. She nodded at Zander.

Zander nodded back as he guided Raven through the doors. They walked into a vestibule of amber walls and marble floors. An ironwork chandelier hung from the ceiling, lighting the room with a hundred burning glass globes. The ceiling had been painted in a dazzling display of copper and ivory—a scene of automatons and humans working together.

"Lieutenant?" Raven whispered.

Zander winked.

People lingered in the vestibule, talking and greeting; nearly every pair of eyes followed Zander. She didn't have to look. She felt them. She heard his name in whispers, curious and suspicious. He gave the whispers no mind, and she followed his example and held her chin high.

A lion's den, he'd called it.

And they were the fresh meat.

Zander guided her toward the other end of the vestibule, where golden curtains had been tied back from the doorway, and they walked into the ballroom.

Raven barely held in her gasp at the splendor before her. The copper and ivory of the vestibule continued into the ballroom. The floor had been shined to a near-perfect reflection; from the amber ceiling hung a dozen ironwork chandeliers; leaded glass made up an entire wall of arched windows, through which the sprawling gardens glowed in the afternoon light; and everywhere she looked, she saw carved amber, gleaming gold, and startling white.

Zander guided her along the mezzanine that stretched across the back of the ballroom, off which two wide staircases curved onto the ballroom floor. Two sets of dark wooden doors led off the mezzanine, but they were closed and corded off and guarded by Gray Elite.

Zander and Raven made it halfway across the mezzanine when a voice called out from behind them, "Zander?"

She felt him tense, but he turned to the speaker with a polite smile on his face.

A pleasant-faced young man strolled toward them. He wore the Gray Elite uniform with blue honors, and he had his blonde hair combed back in the formal style. A bored-looking girl with dark hair done up in a ruby comb hung off his arm. Her painted eyes ran over Raven, and in an instant, Raven knew she disliked her. Ivaline had pretended snobbishness, but this girl oozed it.

"It *is* you," said the young man. Relief and happiness warmed his face.

"Ezra," Zander said, neither relieved nor worried.

The two of them shook hands like old friends.

Ezra's golden brown eyes looked Raven over with friendly interest. "Is this the girl you ran off with?" His smile widened. "I can see why. She's lovely." The girl on his arm rolled her eyes and gave a small, quick sigh. Ezra's smile diminished as he looked at her. "Jasmine, I'll meet you in the ballroom," he said shortly.

Without a word, Jasmine slipped her arm out of his and glided down the steps to the dance floor. Ezra watched her go, frowning.

"I was secretly hoping she'd trip and fall," Ezra mused. He glanced at Zander. "Is that wrong of me?"

"You came to the ball with Jasmine Clemens?" Zander raised a brow at Ezra. "I thought you had better taste than that. Not to mention common sense."

Ezra shrugged. "I put off finding a date because I thought I'd be in Moorin, but here I am. And all the nice girls were taken." Ezra leaned against the brass railing. "But enough about me, what about you? Where have you been, Zander? And why haven't you introduced me to your new friend yet?"

"Where are my manners?" Zander put a hand to his heart, abashed. He chuckled. "Ezra, this is Raven Thane. Raven, this is Captain Ezra Deacon. He's a friend of mine."

Friend. Was Ezra also in the Hawks? She didn't ask. Instead, she gave him a warm smile and a curt bow of her head. "It's a pleasure to meet you, Captain."

"And she's polite," Ezra said with a smile. "You must tell me where you found her; I want a girl like her for myself."

The crowd thickened in the ballroom as more guests arrived. The chatter floated, the laughter lifted, and glasses chinked as toasts were made and cider and wine flowed freely. A servant passed by with flutes of cider, and Zander grabbed one for Raven. She sipped her cider as Zander told Ezra the cover story that they had created.

She paid partial attention; the ballroom was too stunning. Everywhere she looked, she saw something new. The dresses reflected in the floor, giving the impression that another party was happening below them. Ice sculptures dotted the tables. Her eyes found a graceful swan made of ice, and the long-ago dream came surging back to her. She'd dreamed that she and Zander had gone to a ball—and now they were at a ball. Maybe she had known all along that they would end up in the capital.

A band of humans played winds and strings, a gentle tune that swept more and more people onto the dance floor. The tall windows looked to the west; Raven imagined they would provide a stunning view of the sunset. Already, the afternoon sunlight shone off the amber and bathed the room in honey-gold. Come sunset, those colors would become molten.

"Ah, how well it is that her first time in Lenhala would be to the Summer Solstice," said Ezra, and Raven snapped her attention back to the two boys. Both were looking at her. Had she missed a cue? Had she already messed up the evening?

She gave Ezra a shy, embarrassed smile. Zander took the smallest of steps closer to her. "I'm sorry," she said, her voice tinny. "This place is beautifully distracting."

"You should see the Canterbury Theater," said Ezra. "It's a marvel in itself but not as bright."

"It's on my list of things to show her," Zander said. "But I'm in no hurry."

Ezra raised a brow, and this time, Raven got his meaning—he made it seem as though they were staying, to hide the fact that they were leaving so soon.

"Or the Balle Gardens," Ezra said. "They'll be blooming soon."

"Those too," Zander said, nodding. One song came to an end, and another began, and Zander glanced to the dance floor. "Oh, Jasmine is dancing with Benjamin Kilgore."

Ezra frowned but didn't look surprised. "That's to be expected. At least I won't have to dance with her. If I'm lucky, she'll find some poor soul to take her home instead of me."

Zander chuckled and guided Raven down the stairs toward the dance floor. Ezra quickly fell into conversation with a few other Gray Elite, all with blue honors. Captains.

Raven quickly discovered that her lack of knowledge about proper dancing didn't matter; many others missed steps and danced as they pleased. She and Zander danced in the sunlight, and it dazzled in his sapphire eyes and gave his dark hair a honey sheen.

All around her, the ball was a display of wealth. The ice sculptures didn't melt, automatons served cocktails and cider, dresses twirled with the dance, and chatter filled the air. It became another world. It had never occurred to her how many people watched her and Zander, how many people watched him, whispered about him, asked about him. She heard his name float by, heard talk of the rumors of where he'd gone, why, and how.

The song ended, and a slower song began. Zander pulled her closer.

Lovers, a voice in her head said.

They stood close enough to share breath. His hand rested on the bare skin of her back, and she set her hands on his shoulders. She found his eyes amid the golden room, two sapphires, and she found it hard to see anything else. They danced, and the rest of the room faded away. She heard no more whispering rumors of runaway lovers. She heard the music and the gentle thump-thump of Zander's heart underneath her palm.

The somber song ended sooner than she expected.

And just like that, Zander stepped away. He was leading her off the dance floor and toward where the drink flowed. He handed her a flute of sparkling cider.

Zander's eyes drifted over her shoulder, and she wanted to yank his attention back. At that moment, a voice said, "Ah, Zander, my boy."

A taller man with blond hair combed in the Gray Elite style approached. He wore many honors on his arm.

"Colonel Pemberton," Zander said at once. He extended his hand, and they shook.

Ivy's father, Raven realized. They had the same eyes.

"I'm glad to see you healthy and alive," said Colonel Pemberton. "I admit, I feared the worst when you vanished into thin air. How are you, my boy? Doing all right? Not gotten any of those nasty country diseases, have you? I hear there's a fever to the west that squeezes the life out of its victims in three moons."

Zander chuckled. "No, I haven't gotten any of those."

Colonel Pemberton glanced over Raven, and she had the impression that he already knew about her—then, she realized that if he, too, were in the Hawks, Ivy might have told him. However, she thought it best not to assume.

"This is Raven Thane," Zander said.

"It is a pleasure, Colonel Pemberton," she said, giving him a quick curtsy.

"Attractive *and* polite," Colonel Pemberton said. He chuckled. "Where did you find her? I should send my son there to find a girl too." He laughed, then dropped his voice back to a normal whisper. "Your mother was dreadfully worried about you, Zander. Your father too, although he held it in a bit better. I'm sure he's ripe with relief to know you're safe and sound. I know I am, and the news of your sudden reappearance has been the talk of the town."

Zander tensed. "I'm sure."

"Well, I must be off. People to see." Colonel Pemberton clapped Zander on the shoulder and then strode off into the crowd.

Zander held his face stoic as the next person demanded his attention, a man whose name Raven quickly forgot. She nodded and smiled when appropriate, but she unraveled Colonel Pemberton's words. She had felt the warning within them.

Your mother was dreadfully worried about you, Zander. Colonel Pemberton disapproved of how Zander's disappearance had put a toll on his mother. *Your father too, although he held it in a bit better. I'm sure he's ripe with relief to know you're safe and sound.* His father had been worried but not in the same way his mother had. He had known what Zander had taken. *I know I am, and the news of your sudden reappearance has been the talk of the town.* Everyone knew that Zander had returned, the Gray Elite and the Hawks—including his father.

His father knew.

That was why Zander had tensed. Because his father knew, and his father was surely on his way back from wherever he'd gone.

And they were running out of time to get out.

The ball went on with drinking, delicately arranged food, dancing, and endless chatter. Zander and Raven danced, and when they weren't dancing, Gray Elite surrounded them and peppered them with conversation and questions.

"Zander! Where have you been, boy?"

"Is this the girl you left us all for? My, she's a beauty."

"You're not wearing the uniform, Lieutenant. Is this a sign you've left us for good?"

"I'm glad you've returned. Your mother has been worried to death about you."

"I knew you were alive. You're too much of an ass to die like that."

The last one had Raven giggling. Zander frowned at her.

It was not just the officers who inquired about Zander. Their wives and dates eyed Raven with suspicion and interest.

Zander's disappearance had caused a stir among the aristocracy and the Gray Elite, and Raven understood why he had been hesitant to talk about it. Everyone seemed to know who he was the second they saw him, and everyone seemed eager to speak to him. They knew of his father. Many of them dropped his name, Brigadier General Winchester.

Raven didn't mind the sharp looks she received until she met the eye of a dark-haired girl in red who hung off the arm of a barrel-chested Gray Elite. The couple easily parted the crowd to Zander.

"Zander," said the girl in red. Her dress fit loosely. Strings at her shoulders held the dress together, letting the shimmery red silk flutter about her unrestrained chest. A braided leather belt hugged her hips, and the silk hung loosely to the floor. She fluttered her heavily lined eyes at Zander and then racked her gaze over Raven's frame. "So, this is the country girl who stole you from me."

Zander shrugged. "Nice to see you too."

Raven fought to keep her expression as masked as the other girl's. She'd *stolen* Zander from this girl? Raven glanced sideways at Zander, who didn't look the least bit bothered by this girl's presence or claim. Was she an ex-lover of his? The thought left a knot in her stomach.

The girl gave a warm, well-practiced laugh. "I can see why, though. She's a lovely little thing, and those eyes!" The girl's stare bore into Raven's, and she had the strange feeling of invasion. Her smile stretched. "Zander's always been a fool for a pair of brown eyes."

She fluttered her own brown eyes, as dark as her pupils.

"Raven, this is Marie Kenara," Zander said pleasantly, "a friend of mine. Marie, this is Raven Thane."

"And it is a pleasure to finally meet you," Marie said, extending her graceful hand. She wore a diamond ring on her middle finger and half a dozen silver bangles on each wrist.

"The pleasure is mine," Raven said as kindly as she could. They gently shook hands, and then the Gray Elite escorted Marie to the dance floor.

Raven didn't have the time to question him about his supposed ex-lover; another Gray Elite and her date appeared. Raven stood through several more introductions, none as exciting as Marie's, thank the Sisters.

Ivaline appeared in a fine dress of white and gray, making her look angelic against the gold around her. She had done her blonde hair up in an elegant twist, dotted her neck with diamonds and pearls, and walked on the arm of Ezra, who looked delighted by her presence. Ivaline's faithful servant walked not that far behind, one eye on his mistress at all times.

Ivaline spotted Raven and Zander and pushed her way toward them like she was the only person in the room, and by the awed stares as she glided by, others shared the notion.

"There you are," Ivaline said sweetly.

"I see you found yourself a date," Zander said, smirking.

Ivaline let out a lady's soft laugh. She patted Ezra's shoulder and batted her lashes at him. He blushed.

"I didn't bring a date," Ivaline said. "Can't make such promises to these young men with my health being the unpredictable beast that it is. And here, I walk through the doors and don't even make it to the ballroom before Ezra has found me and offered his arm for the night." Her eyes grazed over the dance floor. "And seeing as how his date has wandered off yet again"—she lowered her voice—"not surprising. If I had a token for every man in the room who's been with Jasmine Clemens, I'd have enough to open a new greenhouse in my name."

Ezra and Zander both chuckled; neither denied the claim. Raven looked between the two boys quickly, wondering if either of them had experienced Jasmine Clemens.

"And I see dear Marie has returned from her southern vacation," Ivaline said with mild distaste.

"Yes, she's been to see Raven and me," Zander said.

Ivaline glanced at Zander, and something unspoken passed between them. A heartbeat later, the glance had gone. Zander fell into a conversation with Ezra, and Ivaline snaked her arm from Ezra and stole Raven from Zander's. While the boys spoke of people she didn't know, Ivaline walked Raven around the dance floor and to the gardens on the other side of the ballroom.

Raven tried her best not to notice the stares that followed Ivaline as she walked—*glided*—through the room. They walked through the tall doors to the garden, and the chittering of the ball faded into the sound of a dozen fountains sprinkling water over automatons and stone. They walked toward the hedges and rosebushes and meandered through the shaded, evening-lit grounds. They passed countless couples hiding between topiaries and trees, underneath trellises, and in plain sight on wooden benches, hands and mouths in varying states of slow passion.

Ivaline led her around a towering rosebush and into an unoccupied gazebo designed for two people. The outer wall of the garden loomed on the other side of the hedge, gray stone and thick ironwork. They walked far enough that the sounds of the party dimmed; somewhere unseen, a fountain trickled and spewed. The sun had sunk enough to streak the sky in rich reds, oranges, and purples. The roses sweetened the air, and Raven felt the allure of such a romantic place.

"You didn't bring me all the way out here to frolic, did you?" Raven asked Ivaline playfully. "I must warn you in advance, I prefer men."

Ivaline gave a lady's chuckle and shot her a devious grin. "You prefer men, but that doesn't mean you won't give the other a try?" She raised a brow.

Raven's face burst into a fierce blush. Was she serious?

Ivaline sat on the gazebo's small wooden bench and patted the seat beside her. Raven sat, unsure of what it meant in Ivaline's eyes. Ivaline made her heart pound but not in the same way that Zander did.

"Whatever will people think?" Raven crooned.

Ivaline gave her a small wicked smile. She leaned in closer, slid her arms around Raven's shoulders, and whispered, "It's no small gossip that Ivaline prefers women, although Ivy does not."

Which was why men and women stared in awe as Ivaline walked past them. Another layer to her character, to her charade.

"Oh," Raven said, her voice a pitch higher.

"So no one will think twice when Ivaline steals Raven from Zander's arm for a few minutes of quiet fun," she said, winking. She leaned in, close enough that her breath puffed against Raven's lips. "How are you holding up?" she whispered.

If anyone caught them, they would think them locked at the lips, not whispering.

"We've danced most of the evening," Raven admitted; her breath bounced off Ivy's lips, tinted with cider. "Zander has done most of the talking, and anything that I've said has been simple and short."

"Good girl," Ivy whispered.

"I met your father."

"He's a great man. In truth, I couldn't have asked for a better father. He's both eager to see me independent and proud that I'm me." Ivy leaned in closer. "Did he mention that Zander's father is on the way back?"

"Yes," Raven said, glad that she had gleaned that much from his words.

"And, from what he said before we left, he is not in a good mood."

"I've gathered as much," Raven said, unsure of how much Ivy knew.

They fell silent, and as Ivy opened her mouth to speak, a scuffle came from somewhere behind them. Both girls whipped their heads to see, and to Raven's horror, half a dozen black-clad figures were inching toward the gazebo.

Ivy stood, a scream on her painted lips, but from the shadows, another black-clad figure approached. A gloved hand snaked around Ivy's mouth, and a dagger appeared at her throat a heartbeat before a black leather glove pressed against Raven's mouth, and something cool and sharp pressed against her throat.

"Look what we've found," whispered one of the black-clad figures. The speaker, like the rest, wore black from head to toe, leaving only his eyes visible. The speaker's blue eyes traveled the length of Raven and then did the same to Ivaline.

"That's Pemberton's brat," said one of the others. "We'd get a fortune for her."

Ivaline shuddered; her muffled whine seemed to agree with them. *Yes, my father will give you anything for my safe return.*

Raven remained still. The man holding his hand over her mouth and a dagger to her throat pressed his chest against her back, and she could feel how quickly his heart beat.

None of the men moved, and Raven had a terrible thought. Had they come looking for the box? She trembled, and the hand on her mouth flinched. Zander had told her to keep it on her person, and she had done just that; the small iron box currently rested between her breasts, held in place by the dress's built-in boning, softened with a velvet necktie she had found in his room.

The leader of the men looked between the two girls, thinking. Finally, he said, "We take the blonde. Leave the other as a message of what could happen to Miss Pemberton here."

Raven's heart sped, and Ivaline made a whine of protest.

The blade at her throat shifted, then began to press into her skin. Raven gave a muffled cry of protest—

And then the man's hand twitched, he let out a grunt of a sigh, and the dagger clattered to the gazebo's floor.

"Ralph?" asked the leader, blue eyes shifting over the thug.

The thug holding her let out a slow breath, a colorful curse, and then went limp. He tumbled down the gazebo's few steps and landed on his side. A bolt stuck out of his back—directly over his heart.

"I was wondering where you scampered off to," came a drawling voice.

Raven gasped.

Marie stepped out of the garden's shadows, a miniature crossbow aimed at the man holding a dagger to Ivaline's throat. "You're sneaking off with this little county scamp too."

"Get her!" hissed the leader.

The black-clad men dashed around the gazebo, and Marie shot one of them—but she couldn't reload her crossbow fast enough. They seized her arms and yanked the crossbow out of her hands; they smashed it against the stone wall.

Raven started forward, to do anything, but the thug holding Ivaline grunted. "No, no," he said, taunting by wiggling the dagger at Ivaline's throat. "Don't make no sudden moves, or you'll have a dead girl on your hands."

Raven balled her fists. If she bent for the dagger, he would kill Ivy.

The men surrounded Marie. They grabbed her arms and roughly yanked them behind her.

Blood pounded in Raven's ears. How had the night gone so wrong so fast? Where was Zander? Would he be worried when she and Ivy didn't come back? One scream, and the Gray Elite would come running, but they wouldn't get there fast enough to save Ivy or Marie.

And Raven was stuck. She could do nothing. She stared at the entrance to their secluded corner of the garden, willing Zander and Ezra to appear with a dozen armed Gray Elite behind them, but no one appeared. No one came rushing to their aid. Useless.

One of them struck Marie. Raven cringed at the sound his glove made when it collided with the skin of her cheek. The impact sent Marie careening to the side, held up by another man. She looked up at the man who had hit her, and then a wicked smile stretched her bloodred lips. And she laughed.

The leader spat an unsavory curse at her and pulled his fist back to hit her again. Marie's smile widened. The man let out a sudden gasp, stumbled backward, and let out a vicious howl of pain as he clutched his arm.

"Chief?" one of the men asked. He let go of Marie and ran to his boss's side.

With her free hand, Marie pulled the shoulder ties of her dress. The red silk loosened from one shoulder and then the other. It fluttered away from her torso and hung from the belt at her hips. As Raven had expected, she wore nothing underneath it. The sudden exposure of her breasts stumped the man holding her other arm, and she easily yanked it from his grip.

And then, in a blink of an eye, the men surrounding her let out a collective gasp of pain and collapsed to the ground.

Marie wore the face of a killer, determined and ruthless, and Raven sucked in her breath at the sight. She heard the man holding Ivy do the same. Marie's fiery dark eyes met Raven's, and a chill went down her spine.

Raven had seen that same look when Zander had taken on that Cage Bird. A predator.

"What...what are you?" gasped the man who held onto Ivaline.

"Come closer, and I'll tell you," she said sweetly. She ran her hand from her hip to her shoulder.

"Stay away," said the man, his voice shaking.

Marie took a step closer and wiggled her fingers at one of the men on the ground. He started to stand, his movement jerky and uncertain, unsettlingly puppet-like. The man stood. His eyes had gone entirely white—unconscious.

The man holding Ivy gasped.

"Run home, little boy," Marie said, her voice deadly. "Before I cleanse the earth of your presence."

He withdrew the dagger, shoved away from Ivaline, and scrambled toward the wall—he didn't make it. His fingertips grazed the stone of the wall, and then he went rigid. His arms snapped to his sides, and his legs stiffened. He took jerky steps back toward the gazebo. His eyes were wide with fear.

"I changed my mind," Marie said in her sweet, vicious tone. She sauntered toward the man, her hand extended toward him, her fingers moving slowly in his direction.

Marie walked past the gazebo, and Raven held in her gasp. There, on Marie's exposed back, was a sprawling rune tattoo. Just like Zander's. She walked to where the man stood, flinching and twitching and whining. With a wave of her hand, he collapsed on the ground. Marie set her heel on his chest. He begged, his words lost in his mumbling, and a second later, something snapped—the man gurgled and went limp.

Marie sauntered back to the gazebo, eyeing the other men.

"Are they..." Raven whispered.

"Dead," Marie confirmed, none too worried about it. "You all right?"

Ivaline put a hand to her unmarred throat. She nodded. "I've never been happier to have a stalker."

Marie gave her a wicked smile. She approached the gazebo and turned, pointing to her shoulder. "Help me tie this back."

Raven lifted the fallen back of the dress with shaky hands. Her knuckles grazed the tattoo, and to her surprise, the skin there was burning hot. Around the ink, the skin had reddened. Marie tied up the dress quickly and turned to fix Ivaline's hair.

"What did... What happened?" Raven gasped.

"An ambush," Ivy said. "Looks like the work of the Black Dogs."

Raven blinked.

"They're just a band of thugs," Marie explained. She finished with Ivaline and turned to Raven. She started to work on Raven's hair. "They're nothing to worry about. Sounded like they were looking to make a quick token by kidnapping a rich girl."

Raven stared at the ground, at the bodies. Dead. Without a wound. Without being touched.

"Magic," Raven breathed, her voice barely there.

Marie's hands paused on either side of Raven's head. Her dark eyes met Raven's, indifferent. "Does that bother you? Think before you answer. I just saved your ass. Oh, forgive me," Marie said, hand over her heart. "I forgot where we are. I meant, I saved you from these rapscallions and whatever nefarious deeds they might have committed, namely your murder."

Magic. Raven blinked, unable to believe it. "Thank you."

"We should get back to the party before someone wanders into this part of the garden," Ivaline whispered. "I'd rather not be here when these are discovered."

"I thought any press was good press?" Marie smirked.

"Being seen with a horde of dead bodies is not good press," Ivaline hissed.

The three girls left the secluded corner and, thankfully, didn't meet anyone on the garden path. They took the long way around the shrubbery, and when the brightly lit doors and windows of the ballroom came into view, Raven loosed a sigh of relief.

To the west, the sun had nearly set, shrouding the city in golds and purples. The color slowly leached from the sky, from the clouds, and from the city.

They stepped onto the main path to the doors, and Marie slipped her arm into Raven's.

"I'd appreciate if this night remained between the two of us," Marie said casually.

"I understand," Raven said. A magician, right in the center of the Gray Elite festivities. "You did me a great favor, and I will uphold your request."

"Such manners," Marie said, her grin wicked. "It's no wonder Zander snatched you up. I would have too."

Marie, Ivaline, and Raven returned to the ballroom, where the party continued as if nothing had happened. Marie vanished through the crowd, and Ivaline and Raven returned to where Ezra and Zander stood. They were speaking to a tall honey-eyed man who wore many honors on his sleeve. His silver-streaked blond hair had been combed aside. Ivaline took in a small hiss as they approached, but kept her face neutral and pleasant.

The honey-eyed Gray Elite spotted Ivaline and Raven, and his face broke into a wide smile. He smiled like Baxter, insincerely.

Ivaline made a show of handing Raven back to Zander, who held her a little closer than he had before.

"Thank you for keeping her entertained," Zander said to Ivaline, who took Ezra's offered arm.

Ivaline smirked. "It was no problem at all," she said sweetly. "But it wasn't in the way you're thinking of, naughty. Though, if you ever tire of him, Raven dear, feel free to seek me out."

"I will keep your offer in mind," Raven said, trying to mimic Ivaline's casual smile. Her heart still pounded from the garden, but she forced her face into bored neutrality.

With a small smile, Ivaline tugged Ezra to the dance floor.

"And this must be the girl you ran off with," said the Gray Elite, his smooth voice one used to giving commands.

"Yes." Zander cleared his throat. "This is Raven Thane. Raven, this is General Oliver Deacon. Ezra's father."

"It is a pleasure, General Deacon," Raven said with a short bow of her head.

General Deacon examined her through a clinical gaze, and she didn't like it. His eyes ran over her, head to toe. Assessing. She tried her best not to look like she felt it. To pretend that she had nothing to hide. To pretend that the little box was not nestled between her breasts. To pretend that she hadn't witnessed a magician slaughter a gang of thugs who had tried to kill her and Ivaline.

The talk with the general didn't last. Several others demanded the general's attention.

She met a few more Gray Elite, all of whom were delighted to see

Zander and interested in the girl who had stolen him away. They retold their story enough times that Raven was starting to believe it, although she knew it untrue. She focused on the story, on Zander—to keep her mind off Marie and her magic. Off the dead thugs.

The drink flowed freely, and the music sped up as the crowd grew restless, drunken, and chaotic. The dancing became hectic and ungraceful. Several men and a few women gave Raven lascivious glares and offers to dance, but she declined them all, and she held Zander's arm a little closer.

"I would like to go," she whispered.

He nodded and immediately set his sparkling cider on the closest table. They started through the crowd, and Raven cast her eyes for Ivaline or Marie, but she didn't see either of them. The dancing crowd consisted mostly of adults—drunken adults.

Halfway up the stairs, a bloodied scream echoed from the garden. The Gray Elite guards jumped from their positions, alert and ready, while the drunken crowd barely noticed. A woman came screaming into the ballroom from the garden and latched onto the arm of the first Gray Elite, her sobs fluting up as a strange instrument among the music. Though her blubbering was gibberish, Raven knew what had happened.

They had found the bodies.

Raven gripped Zander's arm and urged him up the stairs. He obliged without a word or question, and the two of them were in the vestibule and out the doors and climbing into the coach.

"Did I hear screaming?" asked the driver, brows together.

"Yes," Zander said politely, concerned as anyone could be. "I'm not sure what happened. Something in the garden."

The driver asked no more, and the coach pulled away as the chaos unfolded in the ballroom. Raven reclined against Zander as the coach pulled through the palace's gates and started through the city, calm by comparison, though many commoners had taken to partying in the streets.

"You should see the other districts," Zander said in her ear. "There are some bars and taverns that stay open all night, and people dance in the street until they pass out from the wine or from exhaustion. It's quite the sight."

The driver was listening; she saw his head twitch to the side every few moments to hear them better.

They *had* left the ball at a very convenient time, a little voice reminded her.

"Zander," Raven asked lowly, as to make it seem as though she did not want to be overheard, "what do you think happened? Why was that woman screaming?"

"I don't know. With all the drinking, Sisters only know what happened. She might have slipped something else into the party. A few years ago, someone slipped hallucinogen into the cider." He chuckled. "I wasn't yet old enough to attend, but stories were flying like bats in the night."

The rest of the ride went by in silence, save for the clacking of the automaton's paws on the stone street. She held onto Zander's hand, wary of black-clad figures lurking in the shadows, waiting for their chance to strike. Finally, the coach trotted through the gates to Winchester House. Every window was dark.

As they pulled into the garage, Raven stifled a yawn. She didn't know what time it was. She would need to sleep well if Zander wanted to flee that morning.

Zander led her into the house and into the quiet kitchen. He poured them each a glass of water. She drank it slowly. She could feel the terror of the attack under her skin, the panic, the odd sense of satisfaction when Marie had slaughtered those men.

They tried to hurt me and Ivy, she thought. *They were bad men. They deserved a worse fate than what they received. They deserved to be hanged, a warning to the others.*

"We should leave tonight," Zander whispered. He set his empty glass on the counter. He unbuttoned his silk shirt down to his vest. "Without telling anyone. They all think I'll be here tomorrow, and no one will think otherwise. I'll leave a note for my mother. This is too important."

"Tonight?" she asked, only half listening. Each time she blinked, she saw bodies.

Why did they have to leave that night? Why did they have to leave at all? Why not hide out in his room for a few days? Why not sleep until this strange feeling went away?

"We have a few hours," Zander said. "It will give us time to get things together."

Raven set her half-drunk glass of water on the counter and drifted to the backdoor to the gardens. The flowers were blooming with pinks, yellows, purples, and blues—beckoning. Without permission, she let herself into the garden. She wandered over the stone path, her feet not entirely feeling like her own, to the other side, where a marble fountain sparkled in the glowing flowers' light.

Her blue and gold dress reflected in the fractured fountain. She lifted the skirts and twirled, watching the colors shift. In the glowing flowers and radiant city light, her dress glowed.

"I'm glad to see you're enjoying yourself." Zander came to stand beside her. His reflection fractured as hers did. He had undone his vest and a few more shirt buttons, leaving several inches of his chest exposed.

In that moment, she made a choice. She did not want to tell Zander about the murders or magic. She didn't want to think about those things; she didn't want to acknowledge that they had happened, so she pretended that they had not.

And, just like that, they hadn't happened.

"I thought balls would be stuffy and stiff," she said, picking up the skirts of her gown and twirling slowly. "But everyone was dancing and smiling. I didn't think they would be so lively."

Zander smiled, a lovely sight in the glowing light, a lovely sight anytime. He took a step closer to her, his boots clicking on the stone. "And that was a tame party too, all things considered." His eyes wandered into the sparkling water. A shadow passed over his features, but when he looked back up at her, it had passed. "Some of the dinners I've been to have gotten out of hand to the point that guards were called in."

"Out of hand? How?"

He chuckled, eyes never leaving hers.

You've got his attention, all of it.

"People drink too much," he said with a shrug. "Then they think that being naked in public is acceptable or that punching someone is fine. Most of them end with someone being arrested." He laughed, and a shiver ran down her back. "Rich or poor, a drunk man is a drunk man in every city in the world."

The idea of Zander being at one of those parties, having fun without her, sent a dislike shooting through her bones.

"I was never a fan of them," he said, stepping closer. "They were more for adults. They would typically lock us kids in one of the wings of the house and then come back in the morning to make sure we hadn't died."

"What did you do all night?"

"We snuck out." He shrugged. "No one missed us, and we'd go wander the city, causing trouble, destroying public property, and the like."

"We?"

"Ezra, Marie, sometimes Ivaline, and a few others," he said. "Baxter was always the prude and sometimes the tattletale. Of course, when I got old enough to hit him, he stopped tattling."

"Of course." She could imagine Baxter being the prude.

She imagined them all being together, friends, having fun, and then thought of herself wandering the woods around Silver Glen, alone. Jealousy burned. It wasn't fair.

Zander stood a little closer, close enough that she could feel his breath. And then, he lifted his hand to her. "May I have this dance, my lady?"

"It would be my honor, good sir." She placed her hand into his. The heat from his hand surged and spread through her body. He set his other on the small of her back, just as he had done at the ball, but without the music, without the other people around them, it felt different. Did he stand closer?

They began a slow dance to the sound of the trickling fountain, to the night birds in the atrium, to the sound of their footsteps. Her heart beat like a drum. Could he hear it?

For a few moments, the city light became moonlight, and the night had gone smoothly—no magic, no murder, no secret conversations in the garden, no hidden messages.

Zander paused his dancing but did not step away. "Raven," he said, his voice a warm whisper against her cheekbone.

"Yes?"

He leaned closer. Her heart thudded so loudly, she knew he heard it. Blood rushed in her ears, her stomach clenched, and the world around her fell away; the mansion disappeared, and she stood in a different plane with Zander. He came closer still—would he kiss her?

She felt his breath on her lips. She closed her eyes, but she never felt his mouth. She blinked her eyes open to find Zander looking at her, sorrow in his eyes.

"Did I do something wrong?" she whispered.

"No," he said, barely a whisper. His hands twitched, and he let her go in a sudden movement that made her jump back; he moved like he'd been burned.

"Zander?"

"I'm sorry," he said as he turned from her. He started toward the house without a glance back at her. "We need to get going. We're running out of time."

She stood in the garden, dazed, and all her delight turned to ice. Shame. Guilt.

Simple girl, simple town.

A means to an end for Zander.

Raven deeply inhaled all the scents of the garden, the strange bittersweetness of the bioluminescent flowers, the flowering fruit trees, the musk of the fountain. She gave the garden one last look, knowing she would never see such a sight again, and followed Zander's path into the house. She found him waiting just inside, and he guided her up to his room.

They changed into traveling clothes and packed in silence, adding a few things that could be easily sold at any trading post.

"The easiest way to get to the Hellcat tunnel is underneath Pemberton House," he whispered as he stuffed a silver candlestick into his bag.

Raven nodded, folding a few extra shirts and soap into her bag. She adjusted her ebony dagger in her boot, felt for the iron box still tucked between her breasts—it felt safer there than in her pocket. Harder to pilfer. Between the silken bandeau and the short corset, the box was secured. She felt for the thief's wooden coin in her pocket.

She didn't know why she still had it. A keepsake of her adventure. A reminder that a wider world still existed.

One that she'd likely not see.

Zander donned his holsters and tucked Birdie into one side, his unnamed pistol in the other, and extra ammo in his pouch. The familiar sight of him and his guns settled something in her chest. She watched him tie back his dark hair. He had freshly saved the bottom half.

"Let's go," he whispered, tugging his pack onto his shoulders. He led the way into the dark, quiet hall. "We can get to the tunnels through the cellar. No one will see us that way."

Meaning she wouldn't see Lenhala again. She took a breath and accepted it and followed Zander's silent steps through the house. They made it to the first floor, and Zander stopped so abruptly that she ran into his back, smashing herself against his pack.

She sidestepped to spit a curse at him, but when she saw what had stopped him, her stomach fell into her knees.

A tall dark-haired man stood in the foyer. He wore fine traveling clothes and was handing his cloak and cane to a servant. The servant scurried away, and the man turned his sapphire eyes onto Zander. A cold smile stretched his thin lips.

"There he is," said the man, his tone not surprised or glad, but cold. Zander went rigid. "Hello, Father."

34

The air in the hall turned cold, the silence deadly. General Winchester and his son stared at one another with matching dislike, unease, and wariness. Raven swallowed; as often as she had infuriated her father, he had never looked at her like that.

Zander looked like his father, the same brown-black hair, bronze skin, and piercing sapphire eyes. They both stood tall and lean.

"Your mother is in the lounge," said General Winchester, his voice a drawl, airy and proper. "I suggest you show yourself to her before you flee." He motioned to the bag on Zander's shoulder.

Zander took a small step to the cellar door.

"I've stationed men down there," said General Winchester with annoyance. "You won't get out that way without my blessing. Unless you'd rather march down the street?" He unbuttoned the cuffs of his shirt and rolled his sleeves. "It would be foolish, considering what happened tonight at the ball."

Zander tensed. "Did I miss something?" he asked coolly. His tone so matched his father's that Raven felt a chill.

His father regarded him with mild interest. "It would seem that a few thugs crashed the Summer Solstice Ball," he drawled. "And wound up dead. No wounds. No injuries. Just dead."

Zander balled his fists.

"Strange murders." General Winchester undid the top button of his shirt. "And right under the Gray Elite's collective nose. Literally in their backyard." He smiled, but it did not show happiness. His smile teamed with cruelty. "They're saying the Hawks are to blame. Others say it's the Revenant's return."

"Are they?" Zander's words seethed.

"I should be asking you," said his father innocently. "I had just arrived back in the city when my people brought me the news. You were at the ball, were you not?"

Zander scoffed. "I wouldn't be so careless."

"These past six months might have softened your approach."

"They haven't," Zander whispered in a voice she hadn't heard before, deep and deadly—a threat.

"That is good to hear. Do see your mother, Zander. She's been in a tizzy since you left." His father walked down the corridor and vanished into his office—if Raven remembered the tour of the house correctly.

Zander stood still as stone. His eyes held a deadly glare, searing like fire. His fists were clenched, turning his knuckles white. Small sounds came from the first floor of the house, of people moving, as if until General Winchester had returned, the house had been sleeping.

"Zander?" Raven breathed.

He let out a long sigh, closed his eyes, and shifted the bag on his shoulder. He started toward the lounge on the other end of the hall. Toward his mother.

Raven hesitated on the stars. "Should I go upstairs?"

"No," he said at once. "Come with me."

They made it to the lounge, and Zander took a deep breath before letting himself inside.

A flaxen-haired woman sat on the chaise, her legs folded and her head tilted back. Her eyes were closed, and she held a hand against her forehead. She looked like a painting in her pale blue traveling dress, her hair slightly disheveled and feet bare. Her boots sat on the ground.

Raven saw the similarities between her and Zander, though Zander took after his father; Baxter took after their mother.

"Tea already? You have gotten fast," said Mrs. Winchester. "Best leave the sugar out, Margret, I don't think my stomach can handle it tonight. Not after the fish we ate. I'll be feeling ill for days, I'm afraid."

Zander set his pack on the floor and took a step closer. "Hello, Mother," he said flatly.

His mother's brown eyes shot open, and at once, they landed on Zander. She blinked once, twice, and then shot to her feet, disbelief turning into joy. She threw herself at Zander, wrapping her arms around his neck and pulling him as close as possible. A gasping sob left her throat.

"Oh, it's not a trick, is it? It's you! Not a ghost but my boy," she cried, kissing Zander's cheek and temple. She felt the shaved half of his head and frowned. "What is this strange hair you have? Is this one of those country things?" She pouted. "You always had such beautiful hair."

"I'm sorry," he said. "I thought my letter would get here a lot faster than it did."

Mrs. Winchester eyed her son a moment longer, taking it all in—the son she thought dead. Tears lined her eyes. She rested her hand on his cheek, and then her teary gaze settled on Raven. At once, the relief in her

168

eyes turned to distaste. She released her son and folded her hands in front of her, shoulders back, nose high—a lady. She regarded Raven like something dirty stuck to the underside of her boot.

"So, it's true?" asked Mrs. Winchester. She looked Raven up and down, taking in her trousers and simple corset—disapproving. "You left me for...this?" She motioned to Raven with a delicate, enraged flourish of her beige hand.

Raven flushed; no doubt, his mother thought the worst. Zander started to speak, but the door opened. General Winchester marched through. He shut the door swiftly behind him.

"Well? Where is it?" he demanded.

"It's hidden," Zander said flatly.

General Winchester frowned, rage burning in his eyes. Raven had the urge to reach for the box, but she held her arms at her sides.

"That is not what I asked." General Winchester glided into the room like a cat about to pounce. He stopped before his son. "Where is it?"

Zander didn't answer.

His father looked about to burst from rage. When he spoke, his voice barely contained it. "Do you know what happened the night you left?"

Zander didn't move. He didn't flinch. Mrs. Winchester looked between her husband and son, worry deep in her eyes. Raven felt as though she had invaded something she ought not to, and she wanted desperately to be back in his room, away from all this. To be with Ivy, who would explain it all to her and make it less horrible than it seemed.

"Because of you," said General Winchester, "because you failed, your brother also failed, and because both of you failed to eliminate your targets, the Hawks were discovered. They did not get to Princess Rosaria in time."

Zander paled.

"If she is still alive, she is no longer in Lenhala," General Winchester said, each word drenched in rage and guilt.

Raven bit her lip to keep from gasping. Princess Rosaria? No, she had died in the coup that killed the king and queen when the Gray Elite seized control. She couldn't be alive... If she was, it would be a lever against the Gray Elite rule.

Of course the Hawks would go after her.

But they hadn't succeeded. Because of Zander. And he looked nearly sick about it—he hadn't known.

General Winchester took in the ghastly look on his son's face with pride, and he continued, "If you had done your part, if you had done what I told you, if you had only listened, we wouldn't be in this mess. We would have had the Regent begging for mercy by now. We would have won. If you had stayed—"

"If I had been your puppet?" Zander exclaimed. "If I had done everything you wanted me to do for your cause? If you would have had your way, Father, the world would be in shambles."

General Winchester clenched his fists. A moment later, his fist collided with Zander's jaw. Zander fell backward into the bookcase, sending one of the glass baubles to the floor. It landed with a sickening crunch, sending the bauble into pieces.

"Joseph!" shrieked Mrs. Winchester.

Zander rubbed his jaw but didn't get up at once. His mother fell to the floor beside him, pulling his hand away to inspect the damage.

General Winchester's furious gaze flashed to Raven, and the box between her breasts suddenly weighed more than a sky city. She feared he might strike her next, but he held his fists at his sides.

"And this is the whore you ran away with?" General Winchester took in Raven's trousers and vest with distaste. "Everyone's told me about the beautiful girl my son brought back with him, the lovely girl from the country." He took a step closer to Raven, and though she wanted to run the other way, she held her ground. "Tell me, Raven, did my son tell you what he does for a living?"

Raven glanced at Zander. He still sat on the floor, his wide gaze pinned on her. Genuine fear shone in his eyes. His mother held onto his shoulders, holding him where he sat.

General Winchester pinched her chin and brought her gaze back to him.

"He didn't?" General Winchester's lips curled upward into a sneer of a smile. "He didn't tell you why he left? Why he fled in the middle of the night like a coward?" His smile turned merciless. His grip on her chin tightened. "I'll tell you. I'll tell you who my son really is."

"Father," Zander said, fearful warning on his tongue.

His mother gripped his shoulders, and General Winchester went on as if he hadn't heard a thing. "My son works for the Hawks, a group working to unseat the Gray Elite in this country and restore power back to the rightful ruler," he said calmly.

Raven remained silent; she knew that.

"But my son is a special part of the Hawks. Tell me, girl, have you heard of the Wraiths?"

170

She shook her head, a difficult task with his fingers pinching her chin.

He smiled; he took pleasure in her discomfort. "The Wraiths are assassins," he hissed. "Not all Wraiths are assassins, but the ones the Hawks have recruited are. My son was one of the best. I was so proud of him, I gave him the most important job of his life, to assassinate a single target, which would allow a domino effect that would allow the other Hawks to rescue Princess Rosaria from the Gray Elite stronghold. With her, we would be one step closer to victory over the Gray Elite. But my son decided to change those plans. He failed to kill his target. The chain reaction didn't happen, and the entire mission failed." General Winchester took a step closer to Raven, and because she did not want to feel his breath on her face, she stepped back.

"But I could have forgiven him for failing. We all fail from time to time, but then, I learned why my son failed. While most of the Hawks were in position, he snuck off, and he stole something very, very valuable to the Hawks. Something the Gray Elite would pay dearly for."

The box hidden between her breasts, the box only a hand away from where General Winchester gripped her chin.

"I'm only going to ask you once, Raven Thane." He lowered his voice to a whisper. "Where is it?"

She shook; she didn't have to pretend to be frightened. General Winchester took in her trembling, her teary eyes, and he released her chin.

"I-I don't know," she said, her voice wet.

One word resounded in her mind. *Assassin.* Zander, a killer, a murderer. He could shoot so well because he had had practice. He had the glare of a killer because he was one.

Raven blinked and stole her eyes away from General Winchester. She found Zander's eyes, full of fear and worry. His mother sat beside him, eyes fixed on her husband. Raven blinked, and then something hard collided with her cheek. She staggered back and tumbled to the floor. Someone shrieked, a scuffle—and Raven sat up.

She put a hand to her cheek where General Winchester had struck her; her hand trembled worse than her cheek throbbed.

It had been Mrs. Winchester who'd shrieked and Zander who had jumped to his feet, rage hot in his eyes. His mother held him back.

"Don't touch her!" Zander screamed, his fists balled. "She knew nothing of what I'd done!"

General Winchester yanked the pack off Raven's shoulders and began to rifle through it. Looking for the iron box. He ignored Zander's outburst and spoke with indifferent calmness. "I set up the world for you, boy. I had the plans set in motion to put this kingdom right side up again, and you threw it aside." He tossed the items from her bag onto the floor, the shirts, the soaps, the rations. "We had the power at our fingertips, the final solution, and you decided to take matters into your own hands."

Raven touched her lip; it had split. She tasted copper. Blood.

Not finding the box in her pack, he started to go through Zander's. If the pilfered goods bothered him, he didn't show it.

"Father," Zander started, exasperated.

His mother shifted her hand to his chest.

Not finding it in the other pack, General Winchester stood and kicked the bag aside. He glared at his son. "I set up the world for you, boy," he spat at Zander. "I arranged your marriage to Rosaria. You could have been a king. You could have been sitting on the throne of Rhynwier, had you followed your orders. A *king*. Yet you spat in my face. You threw it away. And for what?" His rage flared at Raven, and she shrank against the wall. "A country whore?"

Raven ruffled at the insult, but she did not want to garner any more of his attention.

General Winchester tucked his hands into his pocket. "My thief recognized you," he said to his son. "When we met to discuss payment for his retrieved item, he suddenly couldn't find it; then, he remembered meeting a young man who resembled me, frighteningly so, traveling with a young woman."

His thief. The thief who had stolen the box in the first place. The thief she had met on the stairs. The thief from Wayward Point. Raven felt her skin clam. Her heart raced, and the wooden coin pressed against her leg.

"He mentioned meeting the young woman on the stairs, the very night he had last seen the item in question." General Winchester returned his burning gaze onto Raven. Zander's eyes widened.

General Winchester took slow, casual steps to where Raven couched against the wall and then bent down to look her in the eye. He whispered, "Where is it?"

When she didn't answer, his palm met her cheek and sent her sprawling to the floor.

"Where is it?" he asked again, his voice venomous.

"She gave it to me," Zander said quickly, and his father stood, intent on his son. Zander swallowed; his entire throat moved. "I don't have it anymore."

General Winchester's frown turned into a scowl. He grabbed his son by the front of his shirt, yanking him out of his mother's grip. She jumped back, hands fisted in her skirt, face ashen.

"What did you do with it?" General Winchester spat, each word clipped.

Zander didn't answer, and his father's eyes widened with his assumed answer; in his fury, he threw his son to the floor.

"I knew it," General Winchester spat, furious. "I knew it! I suspected it that night. You've been spying for the Gray Elite. Guards!"

The door burst open, and five guards rushed inside, all armed and armored in dark blue leather and gray metal. Hawks. They grabbed Zander by the arms and hauled him to his feet, and in a few blinks, they had him cuffed and gagged.

"Joseph!" cried Mrs. Winchester. She grabbed for her husband's arm. "He's your son."

"He's no son of mine." General Winchester pulled his arm from his wife and marched after the Hawks.

Fear held Raven in place. The Hawks dragged Zander from the lounge, and only when she could no longer see him did her thoughts snap—she crawled to her feet and stumbled to the door. The Hawks were dragging Zander toward the stairs, and General Winchester walked behind them.

"Wait," she cried. She started to run after them, but two strong hands on her shoulders pulled her to a halt. Mrs. Winchester stood beside her, holding her back.

"No," said the older woman.

Tears gathered along Raven's eyes. "Where are they taking him?" she cried.

"Below. To the dungeons," said Mrs. Winchester, her voice low. She didn't look happy about it either.

Tears began to roll down her cheeks. Zander's sapphire eyes met hers a moment before they hauled him through the cellar door. The Hawks vanished down the stairs, and General Winchester slammed the heavy wooden door back into its frame.

The silence in the hall made her sobs that much more apparent.

Mrs. Winchester guided Raven back into the lounge and to the sofa in front of the window. The world felt blurred at the edges, unreal. A servant brought in tea for two, and Mrs. Winchester made Raven a cup of tea. She set the tea in Raven's hands and then made her own.

"What are they going to do to him?" Raven asked, her voice small.

"Drink," Mrs. Winchester said, her voice softer than it had been before. "It'll warm you up."

Raven lifted the dainty cup to her lips. The bitter tea entered her mouth, along with a strange sweet taste. Her first thought went to poison; she turned to question the older woman, but her words fell short. Lady Winchester was pouring a clear liquid from a golden flask into her own tea. She then took a drink.

"They call it moonwater," Mrs. Winchester explained. "It's popular in the south. This batch was infused with jasmine." She took a sip of her tea.

Raven drank her tea slowly. Indeed, she felt a sort of calm come over her. The warmth of the tea, the sugar, the jasmine moonwater.

"By the look on your face, you didn't know a thing," said Mrs. Winchester.

Raven shook her head. *Pretend.*

"I'm sorry it happened like that. Joseph was furious at Zander, and that anger has been fuming ever since. He's been trying to recover from that night's failure. It's been hard. We lost people that night, more than we should have."

"He's an assassin?" Raven asked, her voice small.

The older woman nodded grimly, eyes on her tea. "The Hawks operate in the shadows. We have to. That night, Zander was very close to exposing us."

Raven had questions bursting through her mind too quick to catch them all. The Hawks, the Wraiths, the mission that Zander hadn't completed. She settled on, "And...you are all right with your son being an assassin? A...Wraith?"

Mrs. Winchester gave a quiet, gentle laugh. She met Raven's eye. "Yes and no. No, because it is a dangerous, ruthless job. Terrible hours. High risk. Yes, because I am proud that my son is willing to do such a job in order to restore this kingdom to its former, rightful glory."

"You're a Hawk too?" Raven asked.

Mrs. Winchester nodded. "I took a bolt to the thigh," she said, placing a hand against her leg. "I haven't been able to walk the same since, and my career as a nimble scout and assassin ended."

"Assassin? You were a Wraith too?"

"No," Mrs. Winchester said. "I was an assassin, but I wasn't a Wraith." Raven opened her mouth, but Mrs. Winchester continued, "The Wraiths are...separate. Zander is one of the few who managed to gain entrance into their society of sorts. Don't ask me more about them. I don't know much more than that. It's a need-to-know type of society."

Raven blinked, trying to imagine the cultured woman before her as a ruthless assassin; but then she thought of Ivaline, of Marie. She swallowed a large gulp of tea. Zander had grown up among secrets, assassins, and rebels; and Raven had grown up in an underground mine. Simple girl, simple town.

"But enough about all this dreary business for tonight." Mrs. Winchester sighed through her nose. "I am exhausted, and you look like you've had a rough night as well. The ball, I take it?"

Raven had almost forgotten. She nodded.

"Tell me about it," Mrs. Winchester said, standing.

Mrs. Winchester escorted Raven upstairs. She walked with a limp, but had Raven not known it, she wouldn't have seen it. As they walked, Raven relived the splendor of the Summer Solstice Ball, minus the murders and magic.

"Did the Hawks murder those people?" Raven asked slyly, as if she knew she shouldn't ask.

Mrs. Winchester shrugged. "I can't say. The Gray Elite blame the Hawks for everything they can't readily explain. Any unsolved crime is blamed on the Hawks, to make them look like scoundrels and common street scum." She waved her hand between them. "Best not worry about it, dear. It could be something as simple as a fight gone wrong."

Raven nodded and hoped to the Sisters that guilt did not show on her face.

They paused in the third-floor corridor. "Which guest room are you staying in?" asked Mrs. Winchester.

Raven's cheeks got hot, and Mrs. Winchester frowned. "I've been staying in Zander's room," Raven admitted.

Mrs. Winchester's frown deepened. She let out a short sigh of disapproval. "Well, since Zander is occupied, I suppose it won't hurt for tonight. But tomorrow, I request that you relocate to another room.

Another bed." She started toward Zander's room. "I know this isn't the same as what you're used to, wherever you're from—" she paused to let Raven fill in the answer, and when she didn't, Mrs. Winchester continued "—but here, we stick to tradition. Men in one room, women in another. When you are married, you can do whatever you wish."

She opened the door to Zander's room and held it open, her motherly glare burning.

"Yes, ma'am." Raven took a sheepish step into the room, then turned. "I'm sorry for all the trouble we've caused. A part of me thinks that if I would have stayed home... I don't know. Then maybe none of this would have happened."

Mrs. Winchester cupped Raven's cheek, the cheek her husband had slapped. Twice. "It's not your fault," she said firmly; she meant it. "My son, for all his good qualities, has a few bad ones too. We all do. Best not dwell on what could have been, because it does nothing for the future." She stroked Raven's cheekbone, then released her. "Goodnight, Raven. I will see you in the morning."

Mrs. Winchester stepped into the hall and closed the door behind her. Raven let out a sigh, and then a sharp click resounded from within the door—her heart tightened. Heeled shoes retreated down the hallway, slightly uneven. Raven tried the door—locked. Mrs. Winchester had locked her inside. Trapped.

Raven sank onto the sofa. The Hawks had locked her in the house, and they had taken Zander to the dungeons. The *dungeons*. Doubtful he had a sofa to sit on or a bed to sleep in. But what could she do about it? What could she possibly do against the Hawks? They were armed and trained, and she was...she was a simple country girl with no training, no skills, no...anything. She slumped against the sofa and put a hand against the box General Winchester so desperately wanted.

So much worry over something so small.

Her heartbeat slowed, and all the exhaustion of the night came back to her. Too tired to wash, she went straight into the bedroom and changed into her silk pajamas. She tucked the little iron box underneath her pillow, kept her locket around her neck, and set her dagger on the pillow next to her—which would have been Zander's. After she had pulled the bed-curtains closed, she crawled under the blankets.

Even in the dark, the bed felt too large without Zander.

In a way, it felt like her room in Silver Glen. Dark. Secluded. Private.

She rolled onto her side; her locket moved against her skin. Rolling onto her back, Raven pulled her locket out of her pajamas. She ran her thumb over the gold, dull in the darkness. She had thought the engraved gold beautiful, but compared to the Winchester's finery, it held no worth. Like her.

She ran her finger along the seam of the locket.

Open it.

Raven pressed her fingernails into the seam, like she had done so many times, and tried to wedge the metal apart. She moved her nails closer together, closer to the locking mechanism, and then—

Click.

Her heart skipped at the sound. It opened. Fingers trembling, she opened the locket and—nothing. It was empty. No picture, no secret message from her mother, no well wishes for the daughter she had never known.

Her heart fell into her spine and stayed there.

As a child, she had imagined a secret message left from her mother that would lead her on an epic adventure like in her storybooks, to the stars, across the oceans, to the center of the world. All this time, the locket had been empty.

Raven pressed her finger into the locket's empty chambers. Her fingertip grazed something—grooves. An engraving in the metal.

She stumbled to free herself from the blankets and then tumbled through the bed-curtain. Raven half fell to the window and whisked back the curtains. Within the light of the garden, the engraving on the inside of the locket became visible.

A diamond within a circle.

The same image from the thief's wooden coin, the entrance to the Destiny Show in Wayward Point. A ticket to freedom. Raven blinked once, twice. Her hands shook; her mother had the Destiny Show emblem inside her locket?

A ticket to freedom.

What did it mean?

She closed the locket with a gentle snap and placed it beside her dagger. She didn't know what to think about the emblem, the locket, or the coin. She was too tired to think about anything tonight. She crawled back under the blankets and closed her hands around the iron box.

How could such a little thing cause so many problems? What was it?

A fine seam ran along the edges, as though the box had been perfectly designed to fit together. A box. Things went into boxes, so there must be something inside. The thing of great value, of immense stress and trouble. Whatever piece of the machine that Zander had stolen. A vital piece, he'd said.

Was it the Destiny Show emblem too?

Zander knew; he would have had to have known before he took it. A lever? A valve? The button that fired the machine? The password? The combination? Mrs. Winchester knew. General Winchester knew. Ivy might know too, as well as her father. Baxter too. Raven was the one left in the dark as to its purpose and function, as though they didn't trust her with the secret.

Because she was the simple girl.

Simple indeed yet smart enough to be holding the damn thing when everyone was looking for it.

The box grew warm under her touch.

Nothing she could do about any of her problems tonight. She released the box and tried to find sleep. Her exhaustion pulled her under quickly, but she slept terribly. Every little knock and creak woke her, fearful that the Hawks would burst into the room and tear it—and her—apart for the box.

Zander floated in and out of her dreams, beaten and tortured, bloodied and bruised. His father held the whip, asking over and over, "Where is it? Where is it? Where is it?"

Raven woke to blue-gray dawn light spilling through the narrow gaps in the bed-curtains. Sleep refused to return, and Raven pulled herself out of bed. She fastened her hand around the iron box and took it with her into the bathroom. She set it on the vanity, within her sight, and readied a bath for herself. She took her time soaking.

Clean and dried, she pulled Zander's silk robe around her and tucked the box into the pocket. She returned to the bedroom but stopped on the threshold.

The bed had been made. The curtains had been tied to the bedposts. Her boots had been straightened. Her dagger and locket had been set on the bedside table. Her traveling clothes had been taken. A blue dress had been delivered, along with a chemise and underthings and clean socks.

She hadn't even heard the door open. Someone had entered the room without her knowing it. Her skin crawled, and her stomach flipped.

Someone had gone through her things. Looking for the box in her pocket. Her hand tightened around the box; Zander had been right about keeping it on her person. It would seem that the Winchesters did not believe her innocence.

Raven dressed quickly, wrapped the box in velvet and tucked it between her breasts—secured by the lightweight corset. The hiding place had so far worked. Had it been in her pocket last night, General Winchester might have found it. This way, they would have to disrobe her to find it. That idea sent a wave of pinpricks down her spine and into her toes. She tucked her locket down the front of her dress, her dagger in her boot, and the wooden coin into her pocket.

The dress fit well enough. The blue-green material reminded her of a summer forest during a misty rain shower.

She tried the door handle—still locked. She returned to the couch. A heartbeat later, footsteps sounded in the hall.

"Is she awake?" came Mrs. Winchester's voice.

"Yes, ma'am," said a young servant girl.

Raven froze; a servant had been stationed outside the door. Listening.

The door unlocked, and Mrs. Winchester walked inside, followed by a servant carrying a silver tray. The servant set the tray on the table, tea for one and a letter.

"Thank you," Raven said.

"The letter is addressed to you," said Mrs. Winchester without kindness.

Raven blinked, then lifted the letter. Her name had been delicately written across the front. She turned it over; the wax seal had been broken. Mrs. Winchester had already read the letter. Raven pulled out the parchment.

A letter to her, requesting brunch, from Ivaline Pemberton.

A relief went through her bones, but she held herself steady, pretending that she did not care for the snobbish, sickly girl.

"It seems you've made an impression on the girl," Mrs. Winchester said bitterly. She knew who Ivy was.

"May I visit her?"

Mrs. Winchester's finely plucked brows rose. "I've arranged a coach for you," she said, her words clipped. "It will be ready shortly."

Raven nodded and asked quietly, "What about Zander?"

"The letter only mentions you," she snapped.

"Is he all right?" Raven asked, nearly pleading.

Mrs. Winchester met her eye—it looked as though the older woman had been crying. Raven thought of her dream. "He is fine." Mrs.

Winchester didn't sound convinced. "Drink your tea. I'll return to fetch you when the coach is ready."

Raven nodded.

Mrs. Winchester's eyes wandered quickly about the room. Her stare lingered a heartbeat too long on the bathroom door—the only room they hadn't been able to search. Raven brought her tea to her lips and pretended not to notice. Mrs. Winchester then left, locked the door behind her, and marched down the hall.

Mrs. Winchester escorted Raven to the garage where the lesser of the coaches waited. A servant climbed into the coach with her, a middle-aged woman with a sour expression. She beheld Raven like a misbehaving child who had missed a punishment. A spy, no doubt.

"This is Miss Geraldine," said Mrs. Winchester. "She will accompany you."

"A pleasure," Raven said, though she did not smile at the woman.

Miss Geraldine gave a curt nod of her head.

Neither of them spoke on the ride to Pemberton House.

The coach trotted down Lamp Light Way and to a beautiful house of white stone and black shutters. Pillars lined the front of it, and a veranda lined both the first story and the second story and went all the way around the house.

A Pemberton servant met them at the door and led Raven and her servant-spy to the second floor. The room was full of tall windows, all letting in copious amounts of sunlight. Plants dotted the floor: ferns, bamboo, and lemongrass. Ivaline sat at a small table designed for intimate company. She wore a housecoat, and her blonde hair was loose. Little makeup touched up her face, other than the pale powder.

"Ah, there she is," Ivaline said, her voice softer than it had been. Less vibrant. Sickly, she realized. Ivaline motioned toward Raven, then to the chair beside her. "Sit, dear, sit. Come join me."

Raven sat beside Ivaline, and the other girl let out a soft sigh. "I intended to come visit you, dear, but my health took a turn this morning. I wanted to see you again, so I had the audacity to request this meeting of you."

"It's no trouble," Raven said politely. The servants, both Ivaline's and Winchester's, were listening. "I would have walked across the city to have brunch with you."

Ivaline beamed.

Brunch was served, fruit and nutty cookies and tea, and Ivaline shooed the servants away, including Miss Geraldine. The spy-servant obeyed but with a deep frown on her face. The door to the lounge shut, and Ivaline let out a short sigh. She scooted closer to Raven and motioned for her to do the same.

"What in Minerva's name happened?' Ivy asked, her whisper worried and thin. She searched Raven's eyes for answers. "I get home last night and everything is fine, but when I wake up this morning, I hear Zander's been imprisoned?"

Raven swallowed. She didn't know how much Ivy knew, how much anyone knew, and she didn't want to be the one to say something she shouldn't. Her fear must have shown. Ivy put her hand over Raven's.

"They think him a traitor to the Hawks," Ivy whispered.

Raven nodded. "I don't know what to do," she admitted. She felt helpless.

"I'm not sure if there is anything you can do," Ivy said, staring at the ceiling. "The rumors are all over the place too. I've got Thalame running back and forth, trying to find out what's going on. The Gray Elite blame the Hawks for the murders, and the Hawks think they're being framed, and everyone is in a tizzy. It's bad press for everyone. The Hawks look like murderers, and the Gray Elite look like fools for letting it happen in their backyard." She sighed. "I admit, the alternative was worse."

"Thalame is here too?"

Ivy nodded. She pulled a white lace fan from her sleeve and began to fan herself.

"He's not really a Hawk, but he's a Wr—" She paused, and her eyes widened.

"He's a Wraith?" Raven whispered.

Ivy's lips parted. She searched Raven for a brief moment and then nodded. "You know about them?"

Raven paled and leaned forward. Thalame was a Wraith but not a Hawk. That explained why he and Zander were so friendly back at the Dwellers' camp. They knew each other. "Is this the part where you tell me you're one too?"

Ivy shook her head. "No, that's not a line of work for me. I don't have the attributes for it."

Raven sighed and leaned against Ivy, the better to whisper. "Mrs. Winchester explained it to me last night. When they took Zander away."

They ate, though Raven didn't have much of an appetite. Ivy didn't eat much either. She kept glancing toward the doors. Was she waiting for Thalame? Her father? For news? Raven found herself nervous waiting for *anything* to happen.

"I'm worried about Zander," Raven said. She thought back to her dream, of his father holding a bloodied whip, of Zander bleeding and panting. "Would his own father do that to him?" Raven asked, her voice thin. "Hurt him?"

"Hurt him? I wouldn't put it past old Winchester. The man might be a Hawk, but he's got the ruthlessness of a Gray Elite. Maybe two. I'd like to tell you that he'd never kill his own son, but...I saw him that night," Ivy said, her voice quiet, her lips thin. "When Zander fled. People died, and they blamed Winchester for it because it had been his plan. It was chaos in the Hawks. He was beyond furious."

Had that been the last she would see of Zander? Cuffed and gagged and dragged into a cellar? Her chest squeezed. The tea in her hands shook.

"I fancy a walk through the garden," Ivaline said, hand over her forehead. "It's too stuffy in here."

She rang a brass bell, and the doors opened. Servants cleared the table and helped her to stand. They followed behind as Ivaline walked arm-in-arm with Raven to the gardens. Ivaline walked slowly, feigning her sickliness, and the two girls meandered about. While not as extensive as the Winchester gardens, it housed all manner of apple trees and roses.

The wind rustled through the leaves, sounding like voices, like footsteps. Raven didn't know how far the servants would follow them into the garden, but the more she listened, the more the wind sounded like footsteps.

In her mind, she pictured black-clad figures running toward them.

Behind them came the sound of two feet, one person.

Why would only one servant follow them? Raven's gut flinched. Ivy didn't speak. Her eyes were elsewhere, on the trees, on the blue sky between them.

Had someone come looking for the box? Had Zander broken down and told them where it was? Raven paused to pretend to adjust her boot, but she pulled out her ebony handled dagger. Ivy blinked, brow furrowed.

The footsteps behind them didn't stop. They quickened.

Raven turned, dagger at the ready—and the stranger lunged.

In a heartbeat, she saw his face, saw his vile intention, the coldness and hatred in his eyes, and she plunged the dagger into his throat. She felt the blade slide through tissue and muscle and scrape bone.

Ivaline let out a shriek, and a dozen footsteps came running.

The stranger's eyes met Raven's. She had never seen him before. The body thumped onto the stones. And then the light in his eyes faded. Raven yanked her dagger free just as a dozen Pemberton House guards and servants rushed into the scene. Some guards carried pistols; others held swords. At the sight of the body on the ground at Raven's feet, no one moved.

Blood dripped from the blade in her hand. It puddled on the stones, splashed on her boot.

"What happened?" demanded one of the guards.

"He attacked!" Ivaline shrieked, hand over her heart. Tears pushed against her eyes. "Raven pushed him off and attacked him back."

She had killed him. His blood was still warm on her dagger, on her fingers.

Raven felt the world wobble under her feet. She couldn't take her eyes off the dead man, the human being whose life had gone from his eyes—because of her.

"Take them inside," said one of the guards.

Raven felt hands on her shoulders, guiding her. She heard Ivaline's gentle sobs. But her body felt ages away. She didn't feel the sun on her face, or the breeze; she felt the blood on her hands and iron box hidden in her bodice.

The Pemberton servants took Raven into a guest room and provided her with a fresh dress. She washed off the blood in the bathroom. Word had been sent to Mrs. Winchester regarding the attack, explaining Raven's prolonged visit. Gray Elite arrived shortly to investigate the attack. Raven watched them from the guest room window. They stood around the body, talking and gesturing to the stones.

It felt like a dream. An absurd dream. Surely, she would wake in her room in Silver Glen. None of this had ever happened; she hadn't gone with Zander, there was no thief, and she had not killed a man in a garden.

She wanted it to be a dream, but at the same time, she didn't.

She heard the voices outside her door; the Gray Elite wanted to talk to her. Raven held her gaze on the dead man. She couldn't look away. The guest room door opened and closed, and calm footsteps walked toward her.

"I hear you've had one hell of an afternoon."

It took a moment to place the friendly voice. She turned. Ezra Deacon stood at arm's length. Captain Ezra Deacon. His honey-brown eyes met her own, and he gave her a weary smile—one that spoke of his exhaustion, not of the commotion.

Ezra held out his hand, and she took it. He led her to the couch. She sat, and he knelt on the floor in front of her.

"What's going on?" she asked, her voice meek. "First, the bodies at the ball, and now, this..." She withheld the question she wanted answers to: was someone following her?

"I'd like to know too." Ezra ran a hand through his short blond hair. He let out a sigh. "We are looking into the man who attacked you and Ivaline. Don't you worry about that. We will take care of it."

Ivaline, he said—not Ivy. They were alone in the room. If he knew who Ivaline was, he would have used her real name. Unless he didn't think Raven knew.

"The guards told me what happened," Ezra said. "You took care of him before he could do you or Ivaline harm. Do you have any idea why he attacked you?"

Raven shook her head. She knew, of course, but she pretended not to. For all she knew, the man from the garden might have been oblivious to the iron box and the Hawks.

He gave her a kind smile, and the gentleness of it reminded her of Lena. At the thought of her half-sister, her heart squeezed. The gentleness of a smile like that went straight through the core. Ezra meant no harm.

"And here, we all thought you were a quiet girl from the country. You've got a wild side, don't you? You'd have to be a little wild in order to survive out there. No wonder Zander couldn't come home without you. I'd have trouble too."

He gave her a charming smile, and she found herself smiling back. "That's kind of you to say," she said.

"It's only the truth as I see it." His smile faltered. "I'm surprised Zander isn't here. Is he all right?"

She blinked. Did he know? "I assume so. I didn't get the chance to speak with him this morning. I slept in, and Ivaline's invitation came early." Changing the subject, she asked, "Is she all right? Ivaline?"

Ezra nodded. "It gave her quite the shock. She's taken to bedrest. The doctor is on her way, but her maid assures us that she will be all right in time."

Guilt slumped on her shoulders. Though she knew Ivy's sickness to be an act, the sight of her wide, fearful eyes in the garden stained the back of her mind.

Ezra took her hand in both of his, his warmth seeping into her skin, and he looked her in the eye when he said, "You saved her life today, Raven. And your own. That alone is commendable. Already, word is spreading of the wild woman who defended herself against the madman." His smile warmed his entire face. "You are a hero this day, nothing less."

"It doesn't feel like it," she admitted.

"What do you mean?"

"I killed a man," she whispered.

Ezra gripped her hand tighter.

"He's dead." She looked down at her hand, the one that had thrust the dagger through his throat. "I felt it, the blade hitting bone and muscle and ripping through them, I felt the impact, the blood..." She shuddered.

Ezra let go of her hand and wrapped her in an embrace. She abandoned all other feelings beside the comfort he offered, and she collapsed into his arms. She buried her head on his shoulder, and the dam broke. She cried onto his Gray Elite uniform. He held her all the while.

When the worst of the tears had subsided, he whispered, "It is no easy feat to take a life. A soldier will kill within his career. I have. It...gets easier, but it is never something I enjoy or look forward to. That man would have killed you, or worse, had you not acted. You did not kill an innocent man. He had a criminal record, and had he been taken into custody alive, he would have faced execution."

That small fact made her a little happy, but only a little.

A knock came to the door, and Ezra released Raven. "Enter," he said.

A Gray Elite marched inside. He saluted Ezra, saying, "Captain."

Ezra stood. "Report."

"General Deacon requests your presence, along with Miss Raven Thane."

At the sound of her name, she tensed.

Ezra helped her stand and nodded to the Gray Elite. "We're on our way."

The soldier departed.

"Why would he want to see me?" Raven asked.

"I can't say," Ezra said, shrugging. "But best not to keep him waiting."

Although Miss Geraldine did not look happy about it, she set out to return to Winchester House without Raven. Ezra promised the servant Raven's safe return and escorted her to a Gray Elite coach, a simple white coach with golden yellow trim. The horse was plain and steel, made for function, not fashion.

Ezra sat in the back with Raven, and the silent driver took them down Lamp Light Way, away from the residences and into the military side. Towering buildings of steel, brass, stone, and glass rose so high, it made Raven dizzy.

They stopped at a building near the edge of the city. Ezra walked her around the building to the city's edge. A stone wall bordered the city. On the other side, the hillside dropped into a steep angle. Too steep to safely build upon. Beyond it, Raven could see to the horizon. Rolling hills, forests, and a winding stream, dotted with villages.

It was a breathtaking sight.

Ezra didn't linger. He guided her into a towering building of gold-tinted steel. Inside, the decorations were simple and clean, almost clinical. The white walls and steel floors were polished to a shine. Even the sparse wood accents shone. Everything was square and straight-edged, and it felt like walking into a maze of boxes.

Ezra personally escorted her to General Deacon's office. His father's office, she realized. The office was a modest space of footstep-softening blue carpet and brassy furniture. The general stood with his back to them, facing the floor-to-ceiling window that looked out over the countryside. He held his hands behind his back and made no notion that he had heard the door open.

"General Deacon." Ezra stood with his heels together, like a captain addressing his general, not a son addressing his father. "I've arrived with Miss Raven Thane, as requested."

General Deacon said, "Thank you, Captain. You are dismissed. Please wait in the hall to escort Miss Thane home afterward."

Ezra didn't move at once. He glanced sideways at Raven, then at his father. "Sir," he said curtly. He stepped toward the door, and Raven wanted to grab him and make him stay, but held herself still. The door closed, leaving her alone with General Deacon.

"Sit," said the general.

She sat in the chair closest to her, a brassy three-legged chair with a leather cushion. General Deacon took in a deep breath, then turned to face her. He wore no humor on his clean-shaven face, no glint of amusement. He peered down at Raven like a criminal.

She wanted to sink down, but she did not want him to sense guilt. She held her shoulders straight, her back firm.

"Lenhala is organized," he said lowly. "The Gray Elite keep that organization, that order, and it keeps the city moving. These so-called Hawks want to destroy that order and return the kingdom to the profanity of magic that ruined it in the first place."

At the mention of the Hawks, her skin turned clammy. At the mention of magic, her hands trembled.

"The Hawks are nothing but murderers and thieves, a haven for criminals. That boy of yours did everyone a favor when he fled the city," General Deacon said. "He saved people, more than he got killed." He waited for her reaction, but when she didn't speak, he continued, "I know this may seem complicated and new to you, or Zander might have told you everything. I don't know. It doesn't matter." He sighed, and the lines around his eyes deepened. "Raven, do you know what he stole? What it does?"

There—the answer to the question she had asked since they had left Silver Glen. Dangled in front of her.

She swallowed; she knew it to be a piece of Altair's Augur, but she couldn't tell Deacon that. No, her best chance would be to play dumb, be the simple girl from the simple town.

188

Gently, she shook her head.

General Deacon sat and laced his fingers over the bare surface of his desk. Paperwork had been neatly arranged in folders.

"The Hawks had been threatening Regent Dunel with Altair's Augur for years," he said darkly.

Her stomach fell into her seat. Pretending, she gasped in surprise. "But...that's a legend. It's not real," she whispered.

"It is a real device," he said. "It existed long along, built by the first people to settle in Rhynwier. It was used only once and destroyed an entire city. Altair then dismantled it. The pieces were buried and hidden. It has taken a century, but those Hawks have managed to assemble it once more."

She leaned forward, elbows on her knees. Breathing became hard.

"But it is useless without the last piece," General Deacon said. His honey-brown eyes bore into hers. "The piece that Zander stole is known as the centrum of the device. It's the magical core that fuels the machine."

Raven's breath hitched. Not a lever or a combination, but the *magical* core. Something irreplaceable. The centrum of the device; its power.

Whoever had the centrum, controlled the augur.

The very heart tucked inside her bodice.

General Deacon leaned toward her. The light from the window extended the shadows on his face, and for a frightening moment, she saw not him, but a black-clad figure.

"And I want it," General Deacon said, each word a command. He extended his hand toward her.

Raven didn't move. She looked at his large hand, then at him, and feigned confusion. He wiggled his fingers for emphasis, and she said, "I don't have it."

He didn't look convinced. "My sources tell me that the thief the Hawks hired mysteriously lost it when he spent a night in the same town as you and Zander. At the same inn, if I'm not mistaken."

He knew that too? Sisters.

Panic heated her skin. She swallowed. Innocence was her only card. She said, "I-I don't know. Zander didn't tell me his plan."

"This is a serious matter, Raven," said General Deacon. "The centrum you hold has the power to destroy cities, *this* city, in a blink of an eye. The Hawks would do anything, sacrifice as many people as they need to get rid of the Gray Elite, to attack Gracita. They are ruthless."

"Is the Gray Elite any better?" she whispered. They were the ones stomping through the kingdom with their automatons, slaughtering anyone with magic, snatching infants from their cribs, and erasing gods.

General Deacon tilted his head at her words, his eyes glinting with something between humor and pity, and she wished she hadn't spoken. "I will not use the machine," he said slowly. "We will keep the centrum away from the Hawks, destroy it if we can, so that the augur cannot be used by anyone, regardless of intent. There is never a reason to kill so many innocent people, even in war."

She agreed with him, but she didn't want to give him the centrum. She didn't want to give it to General Winchester either. She wanted to run back to Silver Glen and hide it among the Sisters' ancient relics and pretend that it didn't exist.

She understood why Zander had fled. Why he had taken the box. Why he had been nervous about returning.

"Raven," General Deacon said, his voice fatherly but commanding.

"I don't think anyone should have that kind of power," she said.

"Then we agree," he said. "The Hawks are desperate, and in the hands of desperate people, poor decisions are made. The Gray Elite have no need for such a device. We have armies of automatons and human soldiers." He squared his shoulders and his chin. "We have already won the war."

Then, why does he want it so badly? He is just as desperate as they are. Use it against him. Desperate men are easy to fool.

"I-I don't have it," she lied quickly. Another word formed on her lips, but she hesitated.

He leaned forward, his face slack, eager, greedy.

"With me," she added.

"Where?" he demanded.

"Winchester House."

And just like that, the eagerness and greed in Deacon's face turned to something sinister. He stood, marched around the table with the quick, efficient steps of a soldier, and opened the door. At once, heels snapped together. With a few quick orders in jargon she didn't understand, half a dozen feet marched down the hallway.

Raven leaned forward on her knees; she didn't need to feign anxiety. It permeated her bones like disease.

Ezra appeared at her side, eyes worried. "Raven?"

He offered her his hand, and she took it. He guided her out of the office and down the hall, but she barely paid attention to where they were going; she worked to keep her shaky legs moving and not to collapse. Sisters, she had no plan! She'd only bought herself time to think of something better. The moment the Gray Elite arrived at Winchester House, they would know she had lied and come storming back.

Ezra led her down a hall that opened up to a wide balcony that faced the countryside. A fresh summer breeze grazed her cheeks. Gauzy curtains fluttered in the breeze. They walked to the ironwork railing. Down below, a grate spewed water that cascaded down the rocky hillside to a lake far, far, below. The height made her dizzy.

"Thought you could use some fresh air," Ezra said. "I know my father can be intimidating."

Raven fastened her hands on the railing and glanced over the edge. The iron felt cold in her grip. Beyond the wall, beyond the hillside, freedom spread to the horizon. Above, the roar and hum of airships came and went as they flew over the city.

"I didn't realize we were so close to the edge of the city," she said.

"This building is older." Ezra leaned onto the railing. His fingers drummed on the stone. Did his father make him nervous too? "This used to be a dormitory for Gray Elite recruits until a hazing went wrong." He pointed to the underside of the balcony, where the ironwork continued in a twisting, turning pattern. A relic from the old kingdom. "The recruits would have to climb over the ledge and climb down the ironwork to the window below."

Her stomach turned, but she asked anyway, "What happened?"

"One of the recruits slipped."

"Did he..."

"Oh, he died," Ezra said. "The fall shattered him. They never found his body. It's a long way down."

Footsteps sounded in the corridor. She turned, and her already queasy stomach flipped. General Deacon and a dozen Gray Elite blocked the hall, trapping her on the balcony. By the blank look on General Deacon's face, he knew she had lied.

"Anything?" General Deacon asked.

"I haven't asked," said Ezra.

Raven gaped at Ezra, and he refused to meet her eye. When he finally looked back at her, his honey-brown eyes weighed heavy with guilt.

"I'm sorry," he said to Raven.

His father likely made him do it. What a father.

"Where is it?" demanded General Deacon of her.

"I don't have it—" Raven started.

"Winchester House has already been searched," he spat.

Her breath caught in her throat—it hadn't been Mrs. Winchester in her room. It had been the general's people. And the general had seen right through her lie. Then...the servants at Winchester House were not trustworthy. Zander had been right to push them away.

Zander had known. He had known all along. And she hadn't listened.

"Step aside, Captain," commanded the general.

Ezra hesitated but did as his father said. He stepped to the side of the balcony. He looked nearly sick.

"Ready," said General Deacon, and at once, a dozen pistols were readied.

Ezra gasped but didn't move. His eyes flashed from Raven to his father.

"Aim." Hammers were pulled. General Deacon's hard eyes bore into hers. "Will I find it on your body?"

She took a step back. One bullet could kill a person. Twelve wouldn't give her a chance. She took another step back, and her tailbone hit the solid stone of the ledge, her lower back brushing the ironwork railing.

Ezra looked at her, pleading.

Over the ledge, certain death by falling. Before her, certain death by a firing squad.

The recruits would have to climb over the ledge and climb down the ironwork to the window below.

She sucked in her breath; Ezra had known, and he had given her a way out.

A plan formed. A stupid, desperate plan.

Sisters help her. She spun and climbed onto the stone ledge of the wall.

"What are you doing?" General Deacon roared.

She turned, her feet unsteady on the stone, the iron rail not leaving much room to stand. She looked General Deacon in the face and said, "If you shoot me, you'll never find it." She lifted an unsteady hand and knocked on the iron box inside her bodice. General Deacon's gaze fixed on the box, and his brows rose.

For a moment, no one moved.

And then, something crashed in the corridor behind them; something burst—steam and boiling water flooded the corridor. Screams sounded, an alarm rang, and chaos ensued. The ledge shook; Raven fell backward. In the panic, one of the guns fired. She clawed at the railing and, by some grace of the Sisters, found purchase on the ironwork. Her weight landed on her fingers, and she nearly let go; a yelp escaped her throat.

Ezra's voice shouted from above, "Don't look down!"

That was solid advice.

Raven focused not on the death below her, but on the window a few feet away. She started across the ironwork, pretending she climbed through the trees instead, letting her feet dangle only a small fall from the ground. The trick didn't work; her mind knew exactly how far it was to the ground—too far.

She inched her way toward the window, her fingers cramping, her arms shaking, her mind thinking of the distance she would fall if she let go or slipped. The window came within distance, and she lunged all her weight toward it. She careened through it and landed on tile, her breath ragged.

She made it.

She would have to give a proper offering to the Sisters if she made it back to Silver Glen.

She allowed herself a few moments for her breath to return and her body to stop shaking. As she pushed herself onto her hands and knees, a searing pain tore through her arm. Her sleeve had been torn, and blood soaked into her dress. The bullet had grazed her. The wound didn't look dire, and the blood had already started to clot.

She stumbled to her feet. She had landed in a bathroom, the men's bathroom, by the equipment. She pressed her ear against the painted metal door. Panic sounded on the other side but farther away. Footsteps thundered on the floor above her; men were shouting, an alarm like a thousand bells was ringing, and someone was shouting orders above it all.

It wouldn't be long before someone came looking for her here. She slowly opened the door, and seeing no one in the narrow hall, she slipped out of the bathroom. The hall looked empty; the offices held paperwork and personal effects but no Gray Elite. By the mess, it looked like they had evacuated. Raven had made it to the end of the hall when another explosion sounded from somewhere above her, followed by a renewed sense of panic.

Pipes within the walls creaked dangerously. It sounded as though the building would tumble down any moment. The rumbling, the alarm, the pain in her arm—her heart beat faster and faster.

She turned down another hall, looking for anything that would lead outside. What she would do once she got outside, she didn't know. She would think about that when she got there.

"Hey!"

Raven spun; her heart jumped into her throat. Standing in a doorway was Ivy.

"Come on, before someone sees you!" Ivy whispered loudly. She had changed her dress for close-fitting trousers, a black blouse, and a charcoal corset. A thick leather belt on her waist held a number of knives and tools.

Raven ran to Ivy and through the door she held open. It led through a utility room, and on the far side of the room was an iron grate door that led to a narrow stairwell. Iron stairs and bare stone walls went up and down, connecting all the utility rooms in the building. Ivy started down. Raven didn't question her friend's direction and followed a step behind her.

On the other side of the walls, water gurgled and slushed; pipes clanked with water pressure. The stairwell smelled musty and dank, like stone that never dried. Dim yellow lights illuminated the stairwell, and shadows gathered in every corner. The farther down they went, the louder the water, the stronger the stench. At last, they reached the bottom of the stairwell. Ivy led her through an old metal door and into a dark tunnel; the yellow lights continued but left a horrid distance between them, leaving much of the space in shadow. They had come out onto a stone walkway barely wide enough for two people. Beside it ran a sluice channel thick with water and debris. The sewers. The stench was worse, the dank accompanied by something that Raven did not want to think about.

The sluice gushed toward a speck of daylight—the pipe that fed the waterfall underneath the balcony.

Ivy walked the opposite way of the waterfall. She led Raven down the walkway and through a series of crisscrossing tunnels. The further they walked, the less intense and rapid the sluice. Smaller pipes fed the main sluice channel, rainwater and drains trickling and dripping. They walked, walked, walked, and though the bleeding had stopped, Raven's arm throbbed. She could barely move it.

Between the pain in her arm, the stench of waste and mildew, and the incessant panic, Raven felt nauseated and lightheaded. She followed Ivy's blonde hair—a beacon in the dark.

And they walked.

Above them, people chattered, a siren wailed, and the clanking of automaton animals and their coaches beat against the stone street. The sound came and went as they walked, as they passed underneath streets and cellars.

Still, they walked.

Finally, Ivy came to a halt. They entered a side passage, then a room, then through a secret door in the stone into another room—a cellar of barrels and baskets and sacks. Ivy paused, and unable to hold her weight any longer, Raven collapsed to her knees. The stone between her fingers shifted in and out of focus.

"That doesn't look good," said a male voice. Thalame knelt in front of her, his face doubled and hazy.

A hand fastened on her wounded arm. She gasped.

"Not the worst I've seen," he said. "Coulda been sewn up a while ago."

"What? Don't give me that face, you know I'm not good with first aid," said Ivy.

Thalame laughed; then he ripped the sleeve off Raven's arm. Something cold touched her wound, something that stung, but Thalame held her still. She squeezed her eyes shut. It stung beyond words—surely, he was sawing her arm off, to ward off infection, to be rid of the blasted thing.

"Hand me those, will ya?"

Something else touched her arm, something warm; then she felt nothing between her shoulder and her elbow. She rested her forehead against Thalame's shoulder while he wrapped her arm. He smelled of leather and sweat and smoke.

"There we are," he said. "That'll hold you together for a while."

Raven lifted her head from his shoulder, and Thalame's face came into focus. Ivy stood behind him, her face a bit green. For a moment, Raven wished she were still at the Dwellers' camp and none of this had happened, but she knew it had. She had lived it.

"Think it's safe to take this one upstairs?" Thalame asked.

Ivy shrugged. "About as safe as ever, I'd say."

Raven leaned on Thalame as Ivy led the way through the cellar and into the first floor of Pemberton House. They walked to a small lounge where Thalame carefully set Raven down in a chaise.

"You'll be all right in a few hours," he said.

Raven blinked. Ivy wasn't there. She tried to get up, but Thalame pushed her back down. "You're woozy right now, girl. That'll wear off in a bit too. Ivy's gone to fetch you something to eat to settle your nerves. Maybe something to drink too. Sisters know I could use something strong."

Raven lay back on the chaise with Thalame's hand on her shoulder, the warmth of his skin soaking into hers. She closed her eyes and let it soothe her. Her arm stopped hurting. Her panic eased. She settled into the chaise; she'd not been so relaxed.

"Here we go," Ivy said.

A clank jerked Raven out of her daze. Ivy had brought a tray of tea and cookies.

"You all right?" Ivy asked.

Raven blinked, but Ivy wasn't looking at her. Thalame was sitting beside Raven on the chaise, leaning forward onto his knees, pain twisting his features. He'd taken his shirt off. One hand clutched his shirt; the other clutched his side.

"Yeah, I'm all right," he said.

"You don't sound all right." Raven blinked; every heartbeat brought her further out of the sleepy daze.

Thalame met her gaze and smirked. Sweat lined his brow. "Nah, it's nothing."

She thought of Marie, of how she had pulled the straps of her dress before she used her magic, of the tattoo that had felt hot to the touch.

"Do you have a tattoo too?" Raven whispered.

Thalame met her gaze once again, but this time, he didn't look happy. Ivy dropped her empty teacup, shattering it against the tray.

"What does that mean?" Raven asked softer.

Thalame's eyes widened, suspicious and worried; his lips fell into a frown. He swallowed, and his whole throat bobbed. He stood slowly and then turned. There, against his dark beige skin, in the same spot as Zander and Marie, was a tattoo.

"It's the same," Raven whispered.

Thalame turned. The knuckles holding onto his shirt had gone white. "The same?"

"You saw Marie's tattoo," Ivy said, absently picking up the pieces of the broken cup.

Thalame looked between Ivy and Raven and then sat back down. "She knows?" he asked Ivy.

"She was in the garden when Marie took care of the Black Dogs," Ivy told him.

He turned his gaze back to Raven, less angry than he had been.

"You can use magic," Raven whispered, understanding slamming into her chest like a bullet. "That's what it means. You're a magician."

"It's not the tattoo that gives me magic," Thalame said. He felt his back, felt the tattoo, and then pulled his shirt back over his head. "The tattoo is what keeps the automatons from sensing it. When I do use my magic, the tattoo burns, which is why I removed my shirt. It's a rune that burns off the magic essence or whatever it is that the automatons can sense."

Raven's heart beat faster and faster. Marie's tattoo meant she had magic. Zander's tattoo meant *he* had magic. The world wobbled, and Thalame's hand once again met her shoulder. Slowly, the world righted itself.

"I can heal," Thalame said quietly. He motioned to Raven's arm. "Physical wounds, and I can calm the wounds that don't bleed." He had calmed her just then with just a touch of his hand.

"Thank you," she said.

Ivy handed Raven a cup of tea, and she reached for it with both hands—the pain in her arm had lessened. She barely felt it.

She glanced at Thalame as Ivy handed him a cup. He had healed it. With magic.

Just like that, something had broken between them, a wall that she hadn't realized existed until it had gone. She felt closer to them. She also felt the fragility of it. The forbidden nature of speaking of magic and those who could use it.

Raven took a sip of tea. "What power does Marie have?"

"She's a blood binder," Thalame said. "She can control the blood in another person's body, make them act like puppets or turn it against them. That's what she did to those guys in the garden. A sudden, effortless death."

Raven didn't ask for details. She opened her mouth, but Ivy spoke first, "Don't ask what Zander's powers are. Ask him yourself."

Thalame nodded. "It don't feel right to tell you his secrets."

Raven nodded and took a long sip of her tea. The other two joined her around the tray. They ate mostly in silence. Thalame didn't drink tea; he drank something dark red and sweet-smelling.

Pemberton House stood quiet. Above, she could hear the thumping of turbines, the roar of the engines, and the hissing of great airship engines. Still, a siren wailed somewhere.

"What is happening out there?" Raven asked.

"Oh, it's hell out there right now," Thalame said, stuffing half a cookie into his mouth. He chewed and swallowed, and then said, "I heard that a crazy woman killed a thief, got taken into General Deacon's office, and then tried to assassinate him. They say she had this whole elaborate plan to sabotage the water filtration system and plunge the whole building into chaos."

"What?" Raven gasped. "That's not what happened! He tried to kill me!"

"We know that," said Ivy. "Deacon doesn't like losing, and he lost against you. He's pinned you as a criminal."

"Publicly," Thalame added. "And because someone threw out the Winchester's name,"—he looked suspiciously at Raven—"Gray Elite forces have stormed the property."

Her heart squeezed.

"I doubt they'll find the Hawks' cave, but you never know," Ivy said, looking into her tea. "My father left to see what he could do."

She didn't care what happened to General Winchester or his wife after what they had done to her, but if something happened to Zander...she wouldn't be able to forgive herself.

"I'm sorry," Raven said.

"You didn't do anything," Ivy said kindly. "Deacon is behind it. He probably sent that thief to either kill you or provide a way for his Gray Elite to slip in and bring you to him." Ivy held her gaze but said no more.

"If it weren't for little Ivy here and her steam trap, you might have gotten shot," Thalame said, pointing over his shoulder at Ivy.

She shrugged. "Those old pipes are easy to clog, easy to burst." Ivy gave Raven a wink. "The plan now is to get you out of Lenhala. We'll take you back to the treehouse and figure the rest from there. The Hellcat isn't too far. We can—"

"What about Zander?" Raven asked.

Ivy and Thalame exchanged a dark look. A bubble expanded in Raven's chest, then suddenly deflated as she realized—they were planning on leaving Zander.

"Raven—" Ivy tried to reason.

"No!" Raven shouted. "I'm not leaving him!"

Thalame frowned. "Zander's in the dungeons. I'm not sure if I could even get in there."

"But we can't..." Raven felt tears and anger and frustration pulse behind her eyes. Zander, bloodied and beaten, resurfaced in her mind. "I can't leave him."

The silence that fell thickened uncomfortably. At last, Thalame spoke, his voice grim. "I'm guessing you got something of a plan?"

Raven hung her head. "No. I don't have anything." She glanced at her boot's empty buckles. "I don't even have my dagger anymore."

The Gray Elite had taken it as evidence.

Ivy chuckled. "About that." She pulled Raven's dagger from her side. "I cleaned it off for you."

Raven blinked several times. The ebony handle sparkled in the light. The steel shone like a reflection. Shaking, she accepted her dagger. "Ivy...thank you."

"Don't mention it," she said, waving her hand. "Seriously, don't. I don't do well with the sentimental stuff. Just ask Thalame."

He chuckled, and a blush came over his cheeks.

Raven slid her dagger into her boot, and admittedly, she felt more prepared than she had before.

"Well, considering we're all a little beat up from today, I suggest we all think of a plan tonight and discuss it tomorrow morning over a pot of coffee." Thalame stood. Raven started to argue, but he held up a hand. "You're still injured, and I'm magically exhausted. We wouldn't stand a chance. And I come up with my best ideas when I'm 'bout to fall asleep."

The servants in Pemberton House were scarce. The three of them walked up to the second floor without meeting anyone. With the unease between the Gray Elite and the Hawks, Ivy refused to sleep in her room. Too obvious, she said, if someone came to kill her in her sleep. Ivy, Raven, and Thalame took over one of the smaller guest rooms. Thalame stole away to wash in another bathroom while Raven and Ivy shared the guest room's overly large bathroom. Raven opted for a bath, while Ivy took the shower.

Raven took care to peel the box in her bodice off with her clothes. Raven glanced—Ivy did not have the magic-blocking tattoo on her back.

All three of them fit into the guest room's large bed; Ivy insisted on sleeping in the middle. Bed-curtains closed, clean and in a fresh nightgown, Raven felt a strange sense of relaxation, even as she clutched the little iron box in her nightgown's pocket. The even breathing of the other two eased her panic; she was glad that Ivy had suggested they sleep in the same room. The thought of sleeping in an unfamiliar bed, alone, in a city hunting her down, gave her an anxious, lonesome shiver.

In the morning, Raven, Ivy, and Thalame retreated into the library lounge with a tray of fruit, crackers, and cheese. Pemberton House was eerily quiet. Ivy's father hadn't yet returned, and though she denied it, worry paled her face, and she frequently glanced out of the windows at the drive.

"A lot of Gray Elite coaches on the road," Ivy said absently.

"They're looking for someone," Thalame said, black coffee raised to his lips. He looked at Raven.

They were looking for her, he meant. She pulled a grape from the bunch and tossed it into her mouth, trying her best not to look worried about her newfound status as a criminal.

They ate, and after his coffee, Thalame explained the layout of the Hawks' lair. He had been there a few times with Zander, though he had never joined the group officially. According to Thalame, a lot of the Hawks didn't like having so many Wraiths in their numbers.

"Makes 'em nervous," Thalame said, "to have so many magicians."

The Hawks had built their headquarters in the tunnels underneath the city, an ancient branch of dungeons from a civilization long gone, complete with narrow halls, dark stone, and cramped cells far enough below the ground that no one could hear the prisoners scream.

The idea of Zander being locked and screaming in such a place made her breakfast turn in her stomach.

Thalame went over entries and exits, where the guards would be standing, and the most likely place they would have taken Zander.

"But, since Zander is a Hawk, a Wraith, and a Winchester on top of all that," Thalame said, "I'm betting that he'd be taken to the upper level. It makes it easier on us to find him and easier to get him out. However, the only problem is that there's guards everywhere."

"Leave those to me," Ivy said.

Thalame gave her a wary glance but didn't object. "If we enter the tunnels under Pemberton House, we'll enter the dungeons from the south." He pointed to his hand-drawn map. "From there, Ivy draws the guards away, and Raven and I get Zander out. Then, we get out. We reconvene underneath Pemberton, and if something happens and our rendezvous point is compromised, we reconvene at Star Point."

"Where?" Raven asked.

"You'll be with one of us," Ivy said. "We'll know the way. It's another access to the tunnels that will take us home. The northwest tunnels."

To the Dwellers' treehouse.

Thalame stood and walked to the windows. "Now, there's a lot of Gray Elite out there. And they're looking for Raven," he said grimly. He turned and fixed his stare on Raven. "No matter what, don't go up top, or you're a dead girl. Understood?"

Raven nodded. She'd rather not be dead.

"The Gray Elite will be on high alert, but so will the Hawks," Ivy said. "After the raid on Winchester, the other members will be bracing for the worst."

"And, I've got a surprise for you." Thalame walked to the mahogany cabinet and removed a false bottom. He pulled out a bag, and from that bag, he pulled out a smoky black outfit padded with leather and steel plates. It had plenty of places to hold daggers and throwing knives. Short dark blue robes covered the shoulders, robes made for combat and movement.

Thalame handed the outfit to Raven, who took it in both hands. She ran her fingers over the fine material, soft and durable. The leather was supple, the steel lightweight and strong.

"It's Wraith wear," he said. "It will not only hide your identity, but will give you an advantage of stealth. Wraiths are respected within the Hawks, and if you stick with me, no one will think otherwise."

Raven nodded, though the idea of parading around the Hawks as a Wraith set a strange fire inside her ribs. Excitement and nervousness.

Thalame turned his back while Ivy helped Raven into the Wraith's outfit. It fit snugly, but she could move more in it than in anything else she had worn—she could move as though she wore nothing at all. The cloak hid everything but her eyes, and she felt strangely powerful with the anonymity. She slid her ebony dagger into her boot, and Thalame nodded. He made a few small adjustments to the belts and buckles.

"There," he said, a grim smile on his face. "Hold yourself proud. Real proud. It takes a special person to break into the ranks of the Wraiths. Not just any magician can do it. You're hellbent on protecting other magicians from the Gray Elite, or anyone else who thinks magic's evil or worth an execution, and preserving magic itself. Got all that?"

Act like Zander. He'd always held himself proud and steady.

Thalame changed into his Wraith wear, and he looked at home in the leathers and steel. She tried to picture Zander inside those leathers, but the image was blurry.

Before they left, Raven visited the bathroom. After taking care of business, she stood in front of the floor-to-ceiling mirror. She looked nothing like herself. She looked powerful, mean, and someone to be leery of, not at all like the naïve girl from Silver Glen.

She had tucked the box in her pocket; it had been the easier place while Ivy helped her dress. Now, she set it on the countertop and undid the buckles of her cuirass. She ran her fingers along the nearly imperceptible seams in the box.

Such a tiny thing. So much trouble.

She heaved a sigh. Zander's life depended on her.

No mistakes.

Ivy remained in the house as Raven and Thalame returned to the tunnels underneath. He led the way and occasionally gave her pointers on her walk, her posture, and her manner.

Their entrance into the lair of the Hawks lay underneath Winchester house, and as expected, two Hawks stood guard on either side of the ancient iron doors. They eyed Thalame and Raven as they approached but said nothing as they entered. They made their way through the narrow, dark halls. Chatter echoed from side rooms. Hawks panicked over the raid of Winchester House, worried of the panic in the Gray Elite.

"Who will be next?" asked a man to another, gesturing to a map laid over a long wooden table.

They passed several rooms that looked like offices, quarters, and a medical bay, but Raven walked with disinterest, like Thalame had quickly taught her. She wasn't here to gawk at the new setting, but to see an old friend whose name had caused quite the stir within the ranks. She was here for personal gain, to tease and scold, not to rescue.

Thalame led her through the hold and to the iron door to the dungeons. A single Hawk guarded it.

As Thalame and Raven approached, the Hawk held out his gloved hand. "This area is restricted."

"Restricted?" Thalame drawled, his voice dripping with an assassin's murderous honey. "I know who's behind that door."

The Hawk glanced between the two Wraiths before him, nervousness obvious.

"I came all this way to see what the fool's done for myself. He's a Wraith, and the Wraiths will deal with him as they see fit."

"The general will have the final say," said the Hawk, though he didn't sound convinced.

"Yes, yes, whatever makes the old man feel important," drawled Thalame. "Let us through, Hawk."

The Hawk hesitated, then stepped aside. Thalame opened the door to the dungeons, and Raven walked through without a glance at the guard—superiority, Thalame had instructed her.

The dungeon felt worse than she'd expected. The low ceilings, low lighting, and dreary, dank air felt oppressing and hopeless. She casually scanned the cells that lined the walls, the thick iron bars hiding a few prisoners, none of whom seemed intent on making eye contact with a Wraith. The walls, floors, and ceiling were cold gray stone blocks. Iron brackets held torches—few were lit. Enough to leave much of the space in darkness.

It felt like a place assassins would retreat to. Dark, menacing, and forbidding.

"Wraiths who work for the Hawks are assassins," Thalame whispered. "Those Wraiths are the last thing people see; if you see one, it means you're gonna die. It's given the Wraiths a nasty name in the city."

Just like the stories of the Revenant, she thought.

"Not all Wraiths are like us, though," he whispered with a wink.

They walked through the first level of the dungeon but did not find Zander. Thalame casually guided her down a stairwell and onto the second level. The cells contained more people; one man in a tattered Gray Elite uniform, his hair shaggy and tangled, eyed them as they passed, almost pleading.

Despicable that anyone could do this to their fellow human beings.

The more she found out about the Hawks, the more she didn't trust them any more than the Gray Elite.

Zander wasn't on the second level either. They started down the stairs to the third level, and Raven's anxiety rose with each step. If Thalame showed any sign of anxiety, he hid it well in his saunter.

They strolled through the third level, and at the far end, came to a guarded iron door. At the sight of the Wraiths, the guard outside straightened.

"We've come to see the high security prisoner," Thalame said with a lilt in his voice, a playful cruelty.

"He's not allowed visitors," said the Hawk.

Thalame chuckled. "Do we look like visitors?"

"The general said no visitors," said the Hawk. Thalame stepped closer, and the Hawk twitched.

"We are not visitors," said Thalame, his voice venomous—a warning. "Wraiths deal with Wraiths, and we are here to see what our friend has done to warrant such foul treatment."

The guard swallowed. "Make it quick."

Thalame gave the guard a smile—it lit up his eyes in a menacing glint. The guard turned the wheel on the door, unlocking the heavy deadbolts on either side, and the thick iron door opened. Thalame walked inside with Raven on his heels.

A single torch lit the space. Zander slumped against the far wall, his hands chained. Her breath lodged in her throat—he had been beaten. His clothes were torn and bloodied. A cut ran from his temple to his chin, barely missing his eye. His hair had come loose and hung in dirty clumps.

Zander lifted his head and chuckled—his voice was dry—at the two Wraiths. "Here to finish me off, then? Make it quick; I don't think I've got that much longer to wait."

At his voice, her chest heaved relief.

Thalame motioned for Raven to take the lead, and she sauntered to where Zander sat. He watched her every move, his eyes dulled and glassy, but murderous. He hadn't recognized them.

Raven bent down and brushed his dirty hair from his face. "Looks like someone's had a rough night," she crooned.

Zander's eyes narrowed. Thalame chuckled. Zander looked from one Wraith to the other, his thoughts sluggish. Raven, feeling the rush of the cruel playfulness, tapped her finger gently underneath his chin, drawing his attention back to her.

Each breath came ragged, and Zander's eyes locked onto hers. Searching. Then, his sapphire eyes widened. His breath tumbled from his lips, a ghost of her name.

"Took you long enough," Thalame said, appearing at Raven's side.

"What are you doing?" Zander whispered, unable to look away from Raven. Genuine fear shone in his eyes.

"Getting you out, mate," Thalame said.

Zander shook his head. "What? No, you both need to get out of here while you can."

"Not without you," Raven said, and Zander met her gaze. She meant it. She wouldn't leave Lenhala, or this dungeon, without Zander.

"How?"

Thalame checked his timepiece. "We've got about...three minutes."

"Before wha—"

The answer came in a distant *crack*. An explosion. A second explosion rattled the very walls of the dungeon.

"Oh, that was closer than I expected." Thalame blinked. He pulled out a key and thrust it into the cuffs binding Zander. "Which means our time is shorter than I anticipated. Move."

The chaos erupted as they had planned. Ivy's blast had triggered the Hawks to scramble, abandoning their posts in the dungeon in fear they were under attack. Thalame walked ahead, while Raven supported Zander's weight. They walked as fast as they could toward their exit, not the one they had planned on, but the closest exit to them.

They made it through the exit and into the tunnel below, and then they heard the *clash* of steel against steel, the *thwang* of crossbows firing, the thunderous *blast* of pistols—bolts and bullets hitting steel, leather, and flesh.

"I thought you said it was a distraction?" spat Zander.

"It was," Thalame said, looking in the direction of the fighting.

"Which means something went wrong." Raven's heart tumbled into her stomach. No mistakes. She steeled herself. "We keep moving."

Thalame obeyed, and they made their way down the tunnel. All the while, the stone rattled and rumbled, and a few loose stones clattered to the ground. The majority of the fight seemed to be happening above them. They came to a crossroads; footsteps were rushing from the left. Somewhere, a deep voice shouted orders.

Thalame reached the corner and held up his hand. Raven lingered a step behind as Thalame peeked ahead.

He spat a curse. "Gray Elite."

"What?" Zander and Raven gasped at the same time.

Raven continued, "Here?"

Thalame curled his fist and thrust it into the stone wall. "What was she thinking?" Thalame spat. "She's exposed us!"

Whatever Ivy had done, it had drawn the Gray Elite into the underground lair of the Hawks. The panic on Thalame and Zander's faces stirred her own. An invasion.

Thalame led the way through the tunnel, away from the Gray Elite, down a shadowed access, and into another tunnel, a little farther from the main horde of fighting. The sluice that ran down the center shook with all the commotion. With a thunderous crash from above, the ground shook, the ceiling cracked, and the walls rumbled. The rushing water crested and waved with the uneven shockwaves.

"Move!" Thalame shouted.

And then, an ear-splitting crack opened the ceiling; debris and pipes and water came thundering down, blackening the air, dousing the pitiful lights. Thalame shrieked, and Zander grabbed Raven's arm and yanked her the opposite way. They crashed onto the walkway. Thalame's shriek ended with a splash—he'd fallen into the gushing waterway.

"Thalame?" Raven called, but no answer came.

"The water's moving too fast," came Zander's gasp. "He's already gone."

Raven scrambled to the edge of the walkway and gazed into the trembling waters. "No, he can't be!"

"I didn't say he was dead," Zander spat. "I said the water's already moved him on. It'll take more than a cave-in and a river to kill him off; don't fret."

She didn't have time to worry about Thalame. Raven scrambled to her feet and helped Zander stand. He winced and clutched at his side. Raven moved to examine a possible wound, but he waved her hands away.

"It's nothing bad," he said. His face said otherwise. "A broken rib, probably. Happened yesterday."

She frowned but knew there wasn't anything to be done right now for him. They had to get out and away. They would fix him up at the Dwellers' treehouse or at Ivy's house. Whichever came first.

They started down another tunnel in the near dark. Raven kept her hand along the wall, the other around Zander. The fighting faded with every step, with every junction. The air still smelled like old wet stones, tinted with mildew. Zander said little, and she didn't have the heart to start a conversation.

They made it to the hatch that took them into Pemberton's cellar, and Zander struggled to climb the ladder. Raven stayed on his heels, ready to catch him if he stumbled. He hoisted himself through the hatch and into the cellar with a painful groan. She pulled herself up after him, grateful to leave the dank sewer tunnel behind.

A sudden burst of light blinded her, and the hatch slammed closed behind her.

"Well, now, look who it is," said the drawling voice of General Deacon.

Her eyes adjusted to the light. General Deacon stood on the far side of the cellar, his uniform scratched with patches of dirt and blood. Gray Elite surrounded the cellar. Each had a crossbow or pistol aimed at Raven and Zander.

The general wore a vicious, victorious smile. "Two rats have come out of the sewers."

Her first thought went to Ivy, to her father. They had searched her house too. Raven didn't have time to dwell on that—a poke in her back urged her forward, the tip of a bolt. Hands ripped the hood of her cloak away from her face. A Gray Elite pushed her toward the center of the cellar, and another grabbed Zander by the hair and threw him at General Deacon's feet. Zander winced but then schooled his face into neutrality.

"No!" Raven took a step forward, but an unharmonious series of clicks halted her—several more crossbows aimed at her. She froze.

General Deacon glanced between Raven and Zander, and he laughed. He nodded to his men, one of whom grabbed Zander by the hair and yanked him to his knees. Zander gave her a withering look.

Trapped.

"You still have it," General Deacon said—not a question. His eyes wandered to her chest, to where she had knocked against the little box. Raven swallowed, her face warming, despite it being the hiding place of the box.

Zander frowned at her; he knew where she'd hidden it.

General Deacon said simply, "Give it to me."

Raven didn't move.

"Unless you don't think this traitorous scum's life is worth it," said General Deacon.

She clenched her fists. The stupid box had caused all of this.

General Deacon whistled, and one of the Gray Elite withdrew a pistol from his side—*Birdie*. Raven's skin prickled at the sight of the familiar gun, and her rage bubbled at the sight of Birdie in a stranger's hand. The Gray Elite poised the barrel against Zander's temple.

She tried not to flinch. "If you kill him, then I'll never give it to you," she said, her voice wavering.

"Yes, but he'd be dead," said General Deacon, like he didn't care either way. His grin turned menacing as he eyeballed her frame. "And you would be too. Or, we can end this without violence. We can all walk away."

She swallowed, and he noticed. His grin grew wider. The Gray Elite pushed the barrel against Zander's skin, forcing him to turn his head.

She met Zander's sapphire stare; he held no fear in his eyes, only stark defiance.

Don't give it to them.

Her stomach felt like it might upheave her breakfast.

The soldier cocked Birdie. His finger settled onto the trigger. He started to apply the pressure.

"Don't," she breathed, her voice a whisper of itself. He pulled Birdie away from Zander's temple.

With shaking hands, Raven started to undo the buckles on the leather covering her chest.

"Raven," Zander warned. The Gray Elite holding his hair yanked; Zander winced.

"I have it," she said weakly.

She unbuckled the front of her cuirass and unbuttoned her undershirt just enough to retrieve the velvet-wrapped box from its hiding place, without showing them any more skin than she had to. Though the Gray Elite eyed her hungrily, General Deacon looked only at the box. She unwrapped the velvet and held the little iron box in her palm.

General Deacon stepped closer to her, and she closed her fingers around it. "Let him go," she demanded.

General Deacon nodded, and the Gray Elite pulled back Birdie. They released Zander. He stood on shaky legs, gave the man holding Birdie an evil stare, and started toward where Raven was standing.

"You stole Birdie," she said to the Gray Elite. She tightened her fingers around the box.

Zander blinked, then stared at the man.

"Give him the bloody gun," General Deacon growled, desperation leaking into his voice.

Desperate. Foolish.

Another Gray Elite aimed a crossbow at Zander, finger hovering over the trigger. The Gray Elite unloaded Birdie, minus the bullet in the chamber, and handed her to Zander. He immediately pulled his crossbow from his shoulders. He aimed at Raven.

"Try anything, and you're both dead," said General Deacon. "You have him, the gun; now, give it to me before I take it."

She loosened her fingers around the box, and General Deacon lifted it like a precious gem, unworthy of his human touch. A mad grin spread over his face.

"Kill them both?" asked the Gray Elite who aimed at Zander.

Raven tensed, and she felt Zander tense beside her. He had Birdie and a single bullet; she had a few daggers and throwing knives. She counted four bolts and three bullets aimed at her, and at least that many at Zander. They were outnumbered, and she didn't know if whatever magic Zander had been hiding would be able to protect them.

"No." All of the general's attention rested on the box. Enough that he started to walk away, toward the stairs. "Give them a few days to enjoy each other. They will all be dead soon enough."

The Gray Elite held their aim, walking steadily backward. Then, they were gone, up the stairs, through the door. Outside, the whirl of an engine started. Fierce hisses signaled the rising of an airship. The beating of a propeller rose into the sky, higher and higher, quieter with each passing heartbeat.

Beside her, Zander sat down on a barrel of whiskey. He ran a shaky hand through his dirty hair and set Birdie down on the barrel beside him.

Raven heaved a sigh of relief and collapsed to the floor. "Sisters, that was stressful."

Zander's eyes snapped to her. "What?" His voice turned cold. "Do you realize what you just gave them? What you've done?"

The sound of Gray Elite in the Pemberton house stirred her panic anew, and she jumped to her feet. "We need to get out of here before someone comes looking for us. I don't trust General Deacon for a second." She turned and started toward the hatch to the tunnels.

Zander growled. "You just signed the death warrant of thousands of people. Innocent people. What is wrong with you?"

His tone and his words stung, but she bent down to open the hatch. Pemberton House had been compromised, and she didn't want to linger. She climbed down into the empty tunnels. Zander climbed down after her. She jumped the last few rungs and set off at a brisk pace, eyes ahead of her. She heard the hatch close, Zander's uneven steps on the ladder, his boots on the ground. Then he stormed after her.

"Where are you going?" he demanded, his voice venomous.

"To Star Point," she said.

He let out a gasp.

"That was where we were to meet if Pemberton House was compromised. And, by the sounds, it is. Do you know the way there?"

"Yeah."

"Good, because I don't," she said.

He jogged to walk beside her.

"And we need to get out of here before they figure it out. I don't know how much time we've got, and unless you want them storming down here looking for the both of us, I suggest you hurry up. We have to get to the Hellcat before the time's up, or they're leaving us."

Zander sidestepped in front of her. He threw one arm out to halt her. He kept the other at his side. His blue gaze pierced her, even in the shadowy tunnel. His breath heaved. "What the hell are you talking about?"

"I'm talking about the very narrow window we have to get out of Lenhala," she said, ducking underneath his arm. "We can discuss the next step in the plan later." He started to object, and she spat, "And then you can tell me what powers you've been hiding under your shirt."

That shut him up.

Raven and Zander walked the rest of the way to Star Point in silence. It felt like hours, and then the sewer tunnels opened into a natural cave. One side opened to the late afternoon sky, the clouds beginning to glow with the western-tilted sun. They were in the hillside on the other side of Lenhala, far below the city. The sluice joined an underground river that ran out of the cavern's mouth and cascaded down the mountainside. A stone bridge crossed over the wide river, and on the other side, a tunnel vanished into the rock—that tunnel would take them to the Hellcat.

From the tunnel, she could make out the voices of Ivy and Thalame. Raven's heart leaped; he had made it. Ivy had too. Sisters, she couldn't wait to get on the Hellcat and leave all this behind. She could almost feel the wind whipping against her cheeks.

Raven started over the bridge. Zander caught up with her, grabbed her arm, and pulled her to a halt. He sidestepped in front of her.

"Okay, we're here, we're safe. What did you do?" he demanded.

She met his eyes. They were at the Hellcat; they had made it. She saw no point in hiding it further. She glanced to make sure the others hadn't come out to see them, and then she reached for the chain around her neck. She pulled the locket from her collar. Zander's eyes followed, enraged and curious.

She hesitated, then snapped her locket open.

Inside, a red stone the size of her little fingernail glowed. Its red-yellow light reflected in Zander's eyes, which widened considerably. Heat radiated off the stone, a nauseating heat, and she snapped the locket shut, trapping it inside.

"What"—Zander blinked—"is that?"

"It was inside the box," Raven whispered. She tucked the locket underneath her collar.

He gasped. "You *opened* it?"

When she had been studying the box in the bathroom in Pemberton House, she'd had the mad thought to open it. She had employed one of the thinner, sturdier daggers on her Wraith's wear.

"The centrum," Zander breathed. "The core of Altair's Augur. I thought it was a legend. I-I heard my father mention it, years ago, but I didn't understand it. This... He was talking about this. And you..." Zander gawked at her, disbelief overriding any rage he felt. Then he laughed, and his frown bloomed into the widest grin she had seen on him since they arrived in Lenhala. "You are something else."

He started to lean in, and this time, before anyone else interrupted, she leaned in to meet him. He pressed his lips against hers and slid his hand around her neck and into her braided hair. She tightened her hands on the front of his dirty shirt, pulling him closer. Heat radiated from her toes to her fingers, shaking its way along her spine. Time crawled to a stop, and all she knew was Zander.

They broke apart, but Zander didn't step away from her.

"How did you get it out?" His eyes wandered to where the locket hid under her leathers.

"I didn't touch it with my hands," Raven said. "I used my hairpins to get it out and my sleeve to touch it."

"What did it feel like? Anything?"

"Warm," she said. "I could feel its warmth through the fabric. I suspect that if I had touched it, my skin would have burned."

Even then, she felt a tingle through the metal of the locket. But she decided against telling him about it. He might want to touch the locket, to wear it, and the very idea of parting with the only keepsake of her mother made her furious.

"A magic burn," Zander said. "I've heard about them. They're the worst."

They stood for a moment longer, neither speaking, only looking at one another. Underneath them, the stream gushed against the rocks, pouring from the mouth of the cave, tumbling down the mountain. In the tunnel, Ivy's sparkling laugh broke the silence.

"Zander," Raven breathed, and he took the smallest of steps closer.

His eyes flickered to her lips.

"Unless you're going to kiss me again, we really should get going."

His arrogant smirk returned, and with it, all the warmth in her heart. He leaned forward and placed a quick kiss on her lips and then took a step backward to the tunnel. "Let's get going, then."

The Hellcat didn't provide time to talk. They hurtled along the dark passageway for what felt like hours, up, down, side, side; it was a maddening ride that blurred the edges of Raven's falling panic. By the time the Hellcat came to a screeching halt at the familiar platform at the Dweller's treehouse, Raven heaved a heavy sigh.

None of them talked while they exited the car. Thalame was limping, she noticed, and he leaned on Ivy. Zander walked beside Raven, and though he held his face mostly neutral, every few steps, he would grimace in pain. He caught her noticing and tried to give her a charmed smirk, but it fell short of his eyes.

It wasn't until they climbed up into the leafy treehouse that Thalame let out a chuckle. They went into one of the sitting rooms, and Thalame collapsed into a wicker chair with plenty of cushions. Ivy sat beside him. Above them, the starry sky blinked between the leaves. Candles and lanterns burned low for the night.

"Well, that was some getaway," Thalame said bitterly.

"Those explosions didn't go the way I thought," Ivy said quietly. All eyes turned to her. Guilt pulled her lips downward. Dust spotted her hair and clothes. "The Gray Elite were on my doorstep, and I had to act fast."

Raven felt a pin poke her heart. She gasped out, "Your father?"

Ivy glanced back at her with wary eyes—she didn't know.

"It's hard to say anything." Zander leaned back with a hand resting on his side. "The Gray Elite know where the Hawks go. They've found the tunnels. It won't be safe there anymore, and the Hawks will be scattered."

"What do we do now?" Raven whispered to Zander.

He met her gaze, shrugged carefully, and then held out his hand to her. She took it.

"I don't know," he said. "The Hawks won't be enthused to see us; neither will the Gray Elite."

"We'll be wanted people on both sides." Thalame grimaced. "The Wraiths might be indifferent, knowing them."

"How many of them are there?" Raven asked. How many magicians were hiding in the shadows?

Zander gazed back at her. The low glow of the candles warmed his bronze skin. He gave her a tired, mischievous grin. "I can't say for sure."

"They're scattered," Thalame added.

"They're an ancient order," Ivy supplied, a wonder on her face. "They go back thousands of years and got their name because they wielded magic as deadly as their blades."

"You make 'em sound a lot more romantic than they are." Thalame chuckled.

The room went silent. Crickets and cicadas chirped through the trees.

Zander squeezed Raven's hand. His sapphire eyes were lined with sleeplessness, and she spotted dried blood in his hair. If he was upset that she had found out about the Wraiths, he didn't show it.

"Shadows," Zander whispered.

Raven blinked.

"My power. Shadows." He pointed to the shadow underneath her chair. At his command, the shadow moved of its own accord, a puddle of blackness, shifting along the floor. It shifted into shadow animals, then it flashed back to its original position underneath her. Then, in his palm, a blue-black shadow appeared like animated water, flowing at his will. Deep blue flowed into deepest black and bruised blue. Then vanished.

"A hundred years ago, the Wraiths were the first ones the Gray Elite went after," said Thalame. "The Wraiths fought back too, and the Gray Elite quickly learned not to mess with 'em." He sighed through his nose and put a hand over his ribs. Healing. "Of course, it won't be all of us on the wanted posters. You two," he pointed at Zander and Raven, "caused the majority of the mess."

Zander glanced sideways at Raven, curious. His mischievous grin tilted upward. "What did you do?"

"A few things," Raven said.

His curiosity only grew.

With Ivy's help, Raven explained what had happened in the garden at the ball and all that had happened since then.

"You honestly jumped off the balcony?" Thalame's eyes glittered with amusement. "I thought Ivy was making that part up."

"Clever move," said Zander, smiling—though worry shone in his eyes. He squeezed her hand. "Don't ever do that again."

Their return caused a stir within the Dwellers, and the four of them were whisked away to the infirmary. Folded shades blocked their cots from each other, but it didn't block the sounds. Zander had broken two ribs and bruised a few others. Thalame had a few fractures in his left leg; he had been hurt worse, but he had healed himself as much as he could without burning his skin off.

A few cuts and bruises, but no one had gotten horribly hurt.

That she knew of.

With all the fighting, the steel and the bullets and the bolts, people would have died. Both Hawks and Gray Elite. But she calmed herself with knowing that her friends had survived relatively unscathed.

Within the next several hours, they washed up, ate, and listened to the news trickle in from the surrounding towns. Dweller scouts brought back all sorts of news.

According to the scouts, General Deacon had survived assassination, naming Raven Thane as his attacker and Zander Winchester as a spy. The Gray Elite followed suspected Hawks to the Winchester House, where they had taken General Winchester and Mrs. Winchester captive; both were unscathed. With each scout, Ivy's eyes brightened. With each scout that did not bring news of her father, her eyes dimmed a little more.

Raven listened halfheartedly after a while. An assassin, her? General Deacon claimed that she had attacked him—making it impossible for her to return to the city without a disguise. Neither could Zander. Not that she was eager to go back so soon. Or ever.

You did sneak into the Hawks' lair as an assassin.

"So the Hawks managed to keep Winchester out of it?" Thalame said.

"My father is crafty," said Zander, eyes narrowed at a spot on the floor. "He would throw his lackeys in front of him if it meant saving his own life and reputation. I'm sure he threw his rank around until he got his way."

Raven swallowed. That man had bargained his own son for a chance at the throne, for a chance of power.

The night wore on, and news trickled in slower. Hawks were arrested; Hawks were executed in the street—although not all were Hawks. Scapegoats. Regent Dunel had spoken in defense of the Gray Elite and their violent actions, claiming that the scourge of the Hawks needed to be cut out before it grew to devour the city.

More people dead because of her.

Raven leaned her head back. Stars twinkled between the crisscrossing branches that roofed the lounge. Between the leaves, a night breeze rushed in with the scents of summer, of blooming flowers, of dirt, of tree bark, and haze.

Finally, a scout she knew came into the lounge.

"Niall?" Thalame said at once, his tired eyes zoning on the tinker.

Niall nodded once. A small team followed him. "Good news," he said. "the plan went without a hitch."

"What plan?" Zander said, eyes narrowed.

Niall smiled, and a blush came over his cheeks. Thalame spoke for him and said, "The other secret plan we had. That while the Gray Elite were busy with us, we'd sneak into the Capitol Building."

Zander blinked, then grinned wide. "And this plan of yours went without a hitch?"

Niall nodded. "Not everything I touch blows up."

Thalame chuckled. "Well? What news?"

Niall folded his arms over his chest. His face became triumphant and grim. "She's alive. She's been taken to Moorin."

Moorin, the capital city of Gracita, the heart of the Gray Elite empire. A city said to be swarming in automatons and machines, built with metal and stone, because the Gracitans had never been able to wield magic.

The air in the room thickened at the news.

"It gets better," said Niall. "She's in the Tombs."

Zander spat a curse, Ivy paled, and Thalame let out a rough gasp. Raven was the only one unaffected by the news, and when she met Niall's gaze, she asked, "Who?"

"Princess Rosaria," answered Zander, his voice hoarse.

Her skin prickled at the name, and it tugged on the back of her mind. Something someone had said that she couldn't quite remember.

Zander's hands curl into fists. "It's my fault she's locked up there," he said quietly. "I'll break her out."

The resolve in his voice unsettled Raven. The fierceness in his eyes unnerved her. All for this princess.

"It will be hard," said Niall. "No one has ever broken out of the Tombs."

"Few leave at all," said Thalame. "Unless it's in a casket or an urn."

Words shriveled up on Raven's tongue. A voice in the back of her mind whispered, *Maybe the princess should leave it in an urn too.* She pushed the horrible thought away. She should not think such things, especially about people she had never met.

"It doesn't matter," Zander said, standing. "Rosaria would never allow something like the augur to be used, let alone exist. With her on our side, my father and the others would have to see reason. They couldn't refuse an order from her, or they would become traitors. We can't wait around for the Gray Elite to..." He hesitated and glanced at Raven.

They couldn't wait for them to realize they didn't have the complete centrum. She resisted the urge to reach for the locket and hold it, to feel the dangerous warmth that gently touched her breastbone. A caress.

"So, I take it the stories that you stole a piece of the augur are true," said Ivy, frowning.

Zander nodded. "That's why I left in the first place, to hide it, but it doesn't matter now. Deacon has it."

Ivy and Thalame exchanged a dark glance.

"You could have told us, you know," Ivy said, her voice low, bitter. "We would have understood."

Zander sighed and rubbed the back of his neck. "I couldn't risk anyone else getting involved. The fewer who knew, the better."

Ivy didn't approve, but she didn't argue. Raven understood what Ivy felt—it was exclusion, and Raven had felt it plenty.

"We need to move soon," Zander said, fist curled. "We need to move faster than the Hawks, than the Gray Elite. We have to be ready."

"Aye," said Thalame. "We'll be ready. Don't you worry about that. We'll start planning first thing tomorrow morning."

"Right after you two tell us the real story of what happened," Ivy said, standing. "No more secrets."

Zander nodded, though as they filed out of the room, he glanced at Raven.

They would not tell them about the centrum dangling around Raven's neck. It was too powerful a secret to share. Again, she resisted the urge to reach for her locket, to the centrum she concealed. She curled her fingers into her palms.

It's better that way, whispered the voice, clear as if someone spoke beside her.

She glanced at Zander beside her to see if he had heard it, but he hadn't. No one else had. They continued on as if nothing had happened. She followed their lead. She was too exhausted to dwell on strange voices she couldn't explain, or anything.

They reached the corridor where they would part, and Zander gave her hand a squeeze before he let go, and they departed.

Tomorrow, they would plan their rescue of the princess.

Tomorrow, they would tell Ivy, Thalame, and Niall what had happened since Zander fled the capital.

She collapsed into the cot beside Ivy's without washing or taking her boots off.

Tomorrow.

Acknowledgments

Writing a book is a task. It takes a ridiculous amount of brain power, time, and dedication. This book took all of those and a surprising amount of wine. I'd be lying if I said I did this all on my own. I had help and support at every turn; without that help and support, this book and its successors would not have reached completion.

Ryan and Laurel—thank you for your endless support at all hours of the day. I'm not sure what I'd do without you two. Ryan, thank you for all your help with coming up with names and for letting me know when my fantasy names are too much. Laurel, thank you for all that you've done, for taking my author headshots to turning my pitiful hand-drawn map into a beautiful piece of art.

Mom and Dad—thank you for being there at every turn. Never once was I told that writing was a waste of time, not a real job, or a fruitless endeavor. As an adult, I look back and see just how amazing my childhood was. Sure, you're not perfect; no one is. But as far as parents go, I could not have designed better parents.

The amazing team at Authors 4 Authors—I have endless gratitude for all of you. For pulling me out of the slush, for giving me this incredible chance, for giving Raven a chance—endless gratitude and heart emojis. I'm not sure where I would be without you, and I don't want to know. I am forever grateful to have become a part of the A4A family, and I'm looking forward to seeing where we go.

And lastly but in no way least, you, the reader—without you, I'm nothing. I read to escape. I read to do the impossible, to have larger-than-life adventures, to discover magic and dragons and anything imaginable. I write for those same reasons and to bring that sense of wonder and magic and adventure to others. Here is to you, and I hope my stories bring you joy.

About the Author

Beatrice B. Morgan lives in southern Illinois. When she isn't reading or writing, she is most likely playing a video game. She is a night owl, caffeine addict, yoga enthusiast, dog person, hopeless romantic, optimist, and shameless Ravenclaw.

Follow her online:

bbmorgan.com
Twitter: @BBMorgan_W
Facebook: @BBMorganBooks

Authors 4 Authors Publishing

A publishing company for authors, run by authors, blending the best of traditional and independent publishing

We specialize in speculative fiction: science fiction, fantasy, paranormal, and romance. Get lost in another world!

Check out our collection at https://books2read.com/rl/a4a
or visit Authors4AuthorsPublishing.com/books

For updates, scan the QR code or visit our website to join our semi-monthly newsletter!

Want more heart-pounding YA? We recommend:

FYR

by Lisa Borne Graves

At seventeen, Toury arrives in Fyr, where magic is power, a prince's love is deadly, and female autonomy is a dream. Formerly a loner and burden to her adoptive parents, she ruins her chances of a fresh start by offending an ogler who just happens to be the prince.

Alex, the Prince of Fyr, is no novice when it comes to pressure. He has to face his father's ailing health, the expectation to marry soon, and the hidden necromancers trying to take over the realm by exploiting his dark curse. At least there's hope in a cheeky savior, but Earth girls aren't so easy.

books2read.com/fyr